# UNIVERSITY DAILY

"All the News That Happened Today"

VOL. 7,708     SATURDAY, SEPTEMBER 22, 2017     $2.50

## University Student Murdered

*"This will not stand!"*

WASHINGTON— The art of making a believable fake newspaper front page has always come down to nailing the finer to craft the details perfectly. A lot of people think words thrown in, a haphazard way will suddenly come together to form a coherent whole.

"This is not the case," claims some champion of fake newspaper writing, Dr. Bartholomew Van Wrinkleman of Nagahand, North Carolina. He claims the secret to creating the best convincing entry of any publication is first to use a lot of unnecessarily emphatic and ridiculous verbiage. "I don't write this way because newspapers are written this way," said Van Wrinkleman, "but rather because it takes up more space on the page which is supposed to be filled with nonsense anyhow."

Van Wrinkleman went on to add that in addition to long words, it also is important to include a second version of the fake newspaper front page which leaves out all major headlines, titles, and images. The purpose of doing this is to provide an easy way for graphical designers or compositors to tailor the cover to their own needs.

The rest of this article is not going to be worth reading to the least. It is literally just fluff to fill the rest of the page.

Any reader who has wasted his or her time reading this far sure does write an overabundance of unnecessary paragraphs.

"I'm so close to the very bottom of the page now," said Van Wrinkleman. "And I will endeavor to give one final profound sound bite that effectively sums up the art of crafting a beautiful newspaper cover that isn't worth half its weight in news," Van Wrinkleman concluded. "I hope the detail put in to this single image will help future artists create far greater works of art than I have today."

# Byline
## *A Sohni Silver Mystery*

### KIMBERLY
### PAULSON

LOS ANGELES — The art of making a believable fake newspaper front page has always come down to nailing the finer to craft the details perfectly. A lot of people think words thrown in a haphazard way will suddenly come together to form a coherent whole.

"This is not the case," claims some champion of fake newspaper writing, Dr. Bartholomew Van Wrinkleman of Nagahand, North Carolina. He claims the secret to creating the best convincing entry of any publication is first to use a lot of unnecessarily emphatic and ridiculous verbiage. "I don't write this way because newspapers are written ten this way," said Van Wrinkleman, "but rather because it takes up more space on the page which is supposed to be filled with nonsense anyhow."

Van Wrinkleman went on to add that in addition to long words, it also is important to include a second version of the fake newspaper front page which leaves out all major headlines, titles, and images. The purpose of doing this is to provide an easy way for graphical designers or compositors to tailor the cover to their own needs.

The rest of this article is not going to be worth reading to the least. It is literally just fluff to fill the next page.

## Accused Taken Into Custody

NEW YORK, NY — The art of making a believable fake newspaper front page has always come down to nailing the finer to craft the details perfectly. A lot of people think words thrown in a haphazard way will suddenly come together to form a coherent whole.

"This is not the case," claims some champion of fake newspaper writing, Dr. Bartholomew Van Wrinkleman of Nagahand, North Carolina. He claims the secret to creating the best convincing entry of any publication is first to use a lot of unnecessarily emphatic and ridiculous verbiage. "I don't write this way because newspapers are written ten this way," said Van Wrinkleman, "but rather because it takes up more space on the page which is supposed to be filled with nonsense anyhow."

Van Wrinkleman went on to add that in addition to long words, it also is important to include a second version of the fake newspaper front page which leaves out all major headlines, titles, and images. The purpose of doing this is to provide an easy way for graphical designers or compositors to tailor the cover to their own needs.

The rest of this article is not going to be worth reading to the least. It is literally just fluff to fill the rest of the page.

Any reader who has wasted his or her time reading this far may also write an overabundance of unnecessary paragraphs. Continued on M

Venal
A CAYELLE IMPRINT

# Byline

*A Sohni Silver Mystery*

by Kimberly Paulson

Copyright © 2021 by Kimberly Paulson

For permission requests, contact the publisher below:

Cayélle Publishing/Venal Imprint
Lancaster, California USA
www.CayellePublishing.com

Orders by U.S. trade bookstores and wholesalers, please contact Freadom Distribution:
Freadom@Cayelle.com

Cover Art by Robin Ludwig Design, Inc.
Interior Design & Typesetting by Ampersand Book Interiors
Edited by Dr. Mekhala Spencer

ISBN: 978-1-952404-47-4 [paperback]
ISBN: 978-1-952404-46-7 [ebook]

Library of Congress Control Number 2020949848

A CAYELLE IMPRINT

This book is dedicated to my late mom, Joan Paulson.

Though she's been gone for a decade,

she still inspires me every day.

# ACKNOWLEDGEMENTS

I STARTED THIS BOOK WITH AN IDEA AND A DREAM, BUT SO many people along the way helped make it a reality. First and foremost, I thank my husband Jim and my children for their unflagging enthusiasm and support and for visiting me on the patio during those hours of edits. Their love makes me who I am and inspires me to be better.

I also owe a debt of gratitude to those who assisted me in my research for this book. It may take a village to raise a child, but it also requires one to write a book. The Honorable Elizabeth Pollard Hines was incredibly generous with her time and her introductions. Her contributions to this book were enormous. Washtenaw County Public Defender Delphia Simpson answered my questions and inspired me with her passion. Her excitement over the fact that the public defender in this book is "the good guy" made me determined to do right by Sohni Silver.Delphia also loaned me her investigator, Joel Herman, whose information and insider tour were invaluable. The Honorable Cylenthia LaToye Miller provided a judge's insight that helped inform my characters and plot. Eric Gutenberg, from the office of the Washtenaw County Prosecuting Attorney, was a good sport and fielded my questions with patience. He emphasized that the professional ethics in his office were very high, and I have no doubt that is the case. This book's portrayal of a not-so-ethical member of that prosecutorial office is entirely fictional. Last, but certainly not least, my former colleague Jim Carty educated me about automotive journalism.

With the assistance of all these amazing people, you would think my book would be entirely factually accurate, but I'm sure it isn't. In some cases, I took authorial liberties; in others, I just plain got it wrong. I take full responsibility for any inaccuracies.

I also must extend a big thank you to editor Allister Thompson. His spot-on assessment and recommendations were worth their weight in gold, and without them this book probably would have never seen the light of day.

Finally, I must acknowledge my late friend Simran Nanda, a kind, intelligent soul who was gone way too soon. She served as my inspiration for Sohni Silver.

# PROLOGUE

## ANN ARBOR, MICHIGAN

THE MEDICAL EXAMINER WAS PACKING UP WHEN DETECTIVE Jake Clarke arrived at Hill Street, but the crime scene team was still hard at work. The high-power portable light illuminated the young male victim who lay on his stomach in a large pool of his own blood. Yellow crime scene tape surrounded the perimeter.

The medical examiner, Dr. Julia Vandenberg, stopped by to talk to Jake.

"Pretty simple, as far as I can tell," she said. "Kid was stabbed in the back. Likely hit an artery. He bled out right here. Probably dropped right away. It's dark and there's blood everywhere, so it's hard for me to say if there are any other wounds. But I'll know more once we get him back to the morgue."

"OK. Thanks, Julia."

Jake had been asleep when the call came in. A dead young man, stabbed on a street lined with student housing just off the University of Michigan campus. His wallet was missing, but there was a good chance he was a student. The crime scene had already been properly preserved, and the evidence was being dutifully collected. He scanned the area, but there was little to see. No weapon, no wallet, no bag, no obvious evidence.

"Hey, Detective," one of the officers called. "I found his cell phone."

Jake donned gloves and carefully extracted an older model Apple iPhone from the front pocket of the victim's pants. It was still powered on, and because it had been compressed between the sidewalk and the victim's pelvis, it had avoided much of the pooled blood. Jake brought the screen to life, but discovered, as he usually did, that the phone was locked. Without the victim's password, he couldn't quickly access the information on the phone that could help him identify its owner.

"Bag it," he said to the officer.

He would examine it more thoroughly when they got it back to the station.

"Hold on," the officer said. "There's one more thing. I also found this in his pocket." He handed Jake a ticket stub.

The ticket had been redeemed at the University of Michigan hockey game that night. It would be a big help in establishing a timeline, and it might also help identify the victim. Jake could use the athletic department's records to identify who had purchased the ticket. He scribbled details from the ticket stub in his notepad, and returned the stub to the officer to include with the other evidence. His immediate goal was to figure out who this guy was, and notify his family. He had already sent officers to canvas door to door and check dumpsters and garbage cans in the area, and the crime scene team appeared to be wrapping up.

Jake headed towards his car. It was only one in the morning, but his day had officially begun.

That's when he saw the girl. Well, she was a young woman, really. She sat on the ground, legs crossed, next to an apartment building about fifty yards away, watching the action of the crime scene. She was wearing pajamas. As Jake approached her, she was crying.

"Can I help you?" he whispered.

She gasped. "Oh, Jesus you scared me! Are you a cop?"

"I'm a detective with the Ann Arbor Police Department. Do you know something about what happened over there?" gesturing to the crime scene.

"I don't know."

"What do you mean?"

"I was waiting for my boyfriend, Curt, but he never showed up. I assumed he just went home after the game instead of coming by here, but he didn't answer my calls or texts. I thought he was mad, so I just went to bed. But then I woke and saw all of this. Is someone dead?"

"Yes."

"Oh, God! Is it Curt?"

"Actually, we don't know who it is. What does Curt look like?"

"He's about five-ten. Has brown hair, in need of a cut. Probably about one hundred seventy pounds, medium build."

Her description matched the victim, but the details were general.

"Any distinguishing features?"

"Oh, yeah. He has a tattoo on his right arm. It says, *The Truth is Out There*, with an alien-like creature."

Jake took down the details in his notepad, then extended his hand to her.

"I'm Detective Clarke."

They shook hands.

"And you are?"

"Oh, I'm Kelly Burgess. I live here, just upstairs. Apartment 203."

"Miss Burgess, why don't you return to your apartment? I'll come by and let you know when we know more. We'll also have some questions for you."

"OK, but please let me know if it's Curt."

"I will."

Jake watched Kelly until she was inside, then returned to the scene. A morgue employee was loading the victim into the transport vehicle.

"Hold on a second," Jake called.

He jogged to the van, where the driver held open the rear door, and threw on a pair of gloves.

"I need to see his right arm." Jake unzipped the body bag and pushed up the victim's right sleeve.

There it was ... the tattoo. Just like Kelly had described.

The victim was no longer a John Doe. His name was Curt.

# CHAPTER 1

JAKE CLARKE SAT AT A TABLE WITH HIS BACK TO THE CAMERA.
To those who didn't know the detective, he seemed intimi-
dating. He stood at least six-foot-three, with a bald-shaved head
and deep-toned skin. Though in his forties, he was in excellent
shape, with broad shoulders and a narrow waist. His pressed
burgundy dress shirt and sharp-creased gray slacks made the
gun on his hip seem unnecessary, he could easily use his physical presence to compel accused criminals to cooperate. But
he didn't work that way. He was a by-the-book kind of cop.
He treated everyone with respect, and the lilt of his lingering
Jamaican accent had a soothing quality that put people at ease.

The interview he conducted was a perfect example.

The other man at the table, and in full view of the camera,
was homeless, as evident by his appearance and odor. But Jake
treated Henry Martinez with dignity. He'd brought Henry a
snack and a drink, and removed his handcuffs for the interview. A small but sturdy-looking Hispanic man in tattered

clothes, with days' worth of stubble, Henry had seemed scared and angry when he arrived. But Jake's personality had put him at ease.

Jake had asked the officers to bring Henry to the station for questioning as a potential witness in the murder of Curt Redmond. Local residents saw him sleeping in the area the night Curt was murdered. But an altercation with the man ensued when they retrieved him from the soup kitchen, and Henry arrived in handcuffs instead, which was not a situation conducive to asking for the man's cooperation. Officer Townsend insisted that Henry had tried to attack him and his partner, but Jake took his explanation with a grain of salt. Townsend was too aggressive for Jake's liking, and had been rougher than necessary with Henry. Regardless, Jake judged that the man with him in the interrogation room posed no apparent threat.

"So, you're probably wondering why you're here, huh?" Jake said.

"Yeah, I sure am." Henry's demeanor, though more relaxed, still showed wariness.

"I asked my colleagues to bring you here so I could talk to you about last Thursday night. I'm sorry about what happened at the soup kitchen. They were just supposed to give you a ride to meet with me. But in retrospect, perhaps dropping two cops on you wasn't the smartest move."

Henry nodded.

"The reason I wanted to speak with you was because I understand that you often sleep at the corner of Hill and

Packard, by the Cottage Inn, and that you were sleeping there on Thursday night?"

Henry thought for a moment. "Yeah, I think I was there Thursday night."

"Do you recall what time you got there?"

"Probably about nine-thirtyish. But I can't say for sure. I don't have a watch or a cell phone, so I don't always know what time it is."

"That's fair. We'll go with nine-thirtyish. Were you alone when you got there?"

"Yeah."

"What did you do once you arrived?"

"I'm sure I just settled in and went to sleep. I really just consider it a resting place. There's no other reason to go there. Well, except that sometimes at the end of the night, the employees give away leftover pizza."

"Man ... maybe I should start hanging out there."

"No kidding. That's some good pizza."

"Yeah, I love the Cottage Inn. Did they give out pizza Thursday night?"

"You know, I was asleep early that night. So, if they did, I missed it."

"Too bad. What time do you think you fell asleep?"

"Pretty much as soon as I got there. I worked a day's labor that morning, and I had an AA meeting that evening, so I was beat by the time nine-thirty rolled around. I'm sure I was out like a light no later than ten."

"AA meeting, huh? How long have you been sober?"

"Twenty months."

"Congratulations! Good for you."

"Thanks."

"So, you believe you were asleep by ten. Did you wake up at any point during the night?"

"Oh, geez, I don't remember. It's not unusual for things to wake me up when I'm sleeping outside. Dogs are the worst. But I can't remember that night specifically."

"OK, I have to ask. Dogs?"

Henry chuckled. "Yeah, they have to sniff everything. Ever had a cold, wet nose put on you when you're sleeping?

"Actually, I have. My childhood dog, Elmo—named after the saint, not the Muppet—used to do that to me all the time."

Both men laughed.

"Hey, I've got a photo I want you to look at." Jake slid a recent picture of Curt across the table. "Does he look familiar to you?"

"No. Sorry."

"Is it possible you saw him that night? Please look closely.

Henry studied the photo. "Not that I remember."

"Do you remember seeing anyone else in the area?"

"I'm sure there were people around, but I don't remember anyone in particular."

"How about anyone who looked out of place or seemed to be loitering, waiting for someone?"

"I wish I could help you, but I really don't pay attention. As long as I feel I'm safe, I just go to sleep. I find it better not to make eye contact with people."

"What about other nights you've slept in that spot, prior to Thursday? Remember anything or anyone out of place, unusual?"

Henry paused. "Are you gonna tell me why you're asking me these questions?"

"Have you heard about the college student who was murdered? It's been all over the news."

"I think I did hear something about that. But I don't know the details. Is that what this is about?"

Jake nodded.

"Why do you think I have information about it?"

"He was murdered on Hill Street, only about a block away from where you were sleeping that night?"

"Holy shit! I didn't know that."

"He was likely killed between ten thirty and eleven twenty. He probably walked right past you just before it happened."

"Is that the guy in the picture you showed me?"

"It is."

"Damn. He looks like a kid."

"He was only twenty. A junior at U of M."

"Oh, wait a minute," Henry said. "That must have been the night I heard all the emergency vehicles. They woke me up. They were so close and so loud that I actually got up and moved to another street. Even with their sirens off, those trucks made a ton of noise. And there were doors slamming, and people were shouting. There was no way I was gonna go back to sleep there."

"So, you fell asleep before the emergency vehicles arrived, and didn't wake up until they got there?"

"Yep."

"This is important. When you woke up, then got up and left the area, what did you see? Tell me anything and everything."

"I remember seeing one cop car already there. And then another pulled up while I was walking away. There was a fire department rescue truck. A bunch of people in uniforms were starting to gather."

"What about non-uniformed people? Did you see anyone walking or running away from the scene? Was anyone standing around, observing? Any cars parked nearby."

"I remember, as I was leaving my sleeping area, I startled a young woman who was carrying a pizza out of Cottage Inn. She got into a car with a guy behind the wheel, and they took off. And I remember a man coming out of the Subway across the street. I remember the woman because I scared her and felt bad about it. The guy I remember, because a sub sounded so good and I was jealous. Other than that, I don't remember anyone else."

"Any vehicles?"

"Nothing that stands out. I feel kind of stupid that this all took place right under my nose and I didn't know anything about it. I wish I could help."

Henry became panicked. "You're not thinking I did this, right? That's not why you brought me here, is it?"

"I'll be honest with you. We can't rule out anyone at this time. But to answer your question, that isn't why I brought you here. I was hoping you might have seen or heard something."

Henry seemed appeased. "Unfortunately, I didn't."

Though the questioning lasted about twenty minutes, Henry was unable to provide any useful information. To some, his story may have sounded hard to believe. But Jake was familiar with the ability of many homeless people, able to sleep in public places by tuning out everything around them. It seemed credible to him that a man like Henry, who was accustomed to sleeping through the background noises of public areas, could sleep through what was probably a quick and quiet murder, and then only wake at the sound of the emergency crews. Unfortunate, because he was in a perfect position to see the perpetrator, but Jake didn't get the impression he was lying. Henry also had no prior arrests in Michigan, according to the state's database.

Jake was about to let him leave, and had informed Henry that they weren't going to bring charges for the incident at the soup kitchen, when there was a knock at the door. Jake stepped into the hall, where Officer Townsend waited to speak with him.

"You're not going to believe this, Jake. We did a custodial search of that dirty old bag of his, and we found something. You need to come see for yourself."

Jake sensed his day was about to become more complicated. The search had probably turned up drugs, stolen credit cards, or something of the sort that would require more time and more paperwork, and ultimately pull him away from his top priority, which was solving Curt Redmond's murder. But what the other cop had for him was nothing so mundane, and frankly, beyond his wildest imagination.

"Check this out!" Townsend pointed to a leather billfold. "This is the victim's wallet. It still has his ID in it." He gestured to what looked like a rolled flannel shirt. "But this is the coup de grace."

Jake leaned closer to the shirt for better examination. Then he noticed the knife, which had been obscured by the shirt.

What it couldn't hide, though, was the blood. Dried blood covered the entire blade and the inside of the shirt.

"You've got to be kidding me!" he said. "To be clear, you found these inside his duffel bag? Just like this?"

"Sure did," Townsend said.

"Make sure you document everything perfectly, by the book. Bag it all and send it to the lab. And don't touch a damn thing."

"I'm on it."

Jake returned to the interrogation room, where Henry was waiting. Only minutes before, he had deemed Henry unthreatening and found him earnest. His ability to read people was usually better. Boy, had he been wrong.

"I'm afraid circumstances have changed, Mr. Martinez. We just found what you left in your bag."

He stared at Henry, but the man's demeanor didn't change. He looked curious.

"At this point, I need to read you your Miranda rights." Jake recited the familiar warning, studying Henry. "Do you understand these rights?"

Henry looked shell-shocked. "Yes."

"OK. Please sign this form to confirm that you were informed of your rights, and that you understand them. Are you able to read and write?"

"Yeah, of course." Henry signed the form and slid it across the table.

"Now we need to get serious. What do you have to say about what was in your bag?"

"I don't know what you're talking about. I have a shirt, a towel, some change, a couple candy bars, and I think some old sunglasses in there. Maybe a couple other things."

"Henry, you can drop the act now. We found Curt Redmond's wallet in your bag. And the bloody knife. We know you killed him."

The color drained from Henry's face. "No, I-I didn't kill nobody! I don't have no wallet or knife. What are you trying to do, set me up?"

"Why'd you do it, Henry? Were you drinking? Lost control?" Jake kept his voice leveled. Henry had started to trust him, so he thought it best to continue with a non-hostile approach.

"No!" Henry shouted, becoming more frantic with each question.

"Did you black out, Henry? You're not the first alcoholic to fall hard off the wagon."

"No! I wasn't drinking."

"Maybe you honestly don't remember doing it. Maybe you found the wallet later, and couldn't remember where it came from. But you knew you did something, didn't you? Something bad."

Henry crossed his arms across his chest and said nothing.

"There's no point denying it, Henry. We have all the proof we need.

"No, dammit! You're setting me up. I want a lawyer, now."

Jake maintained his composure, but silently cursed. He did not expect this man to invoke his right to a lawyer. At least, not so quickly. Now all questioning had to end. But at least he could hold him on a charge of resisting and obstructing, based on the incident at the soup kitchen. Henry would likely be unable to make bond, so he would remain in detention while Jake and his colleagues processed the evidence and completed their investigation.

He replaced the handcuffs on Henry's wrists and escorted him out of the room, where officers were waiting to drive him to the jail.

Jake returned to his desk with a smile. He had his guy. The case didn't exactly come together the way he'd expected, but all that mattered was that he got him. The community was safer without Henry Martinez on the street.

# CHAPTER 2

SOHNI SILVER ENDED HER PHONE CALL AND HURRIED TO HER boss's office, where the other attorneys in the Washtenaw County Public Defender's Office were assembling. She squeezed into the full room, her colleagues nodding greetings as she entered. Some held their gaze on her longer than necessary.

Sohni meant *beautiful* in her native India, and Sohni Silver lived up to her name. Though, you'd never convince her of that. With large brown eyes fringed by dark, upswept lashes, and full pink lips, her face had an angelic quality that made it difficult to look away. To those who knew her, though, it was her intelligence and compassion that made her stand out. In her five years at the public defender's office, she had proven herself to be not only a skilled attorney, but also an effective advocate for her clients, speaking for those whose voices wouldn't be nearly as loud without her.

Helen Sorenson, the County Public Defender, closed her office door and turned to face the group. On the surface, she seemed a dowdy woman, with straw-like salt and pepper hair hanging down, straight to her shoulders, and a freckled face without a trace of makeup. But the people in that room knew better, as did anyone who'd made the mistake of tangling with her. Their boss was fiercely intelligent, as tough as any man, and passionate as hell about making the world a better place. Her energy inspired them all.

"I just got a call from a reporter," she said, "and I'm sure it will be the first of many. Apparently, the police have made an arrest in the murder of the U of M student. The information hasn't been made public yet, but a reporter got a tip and arrived at the police station in time to see the officers arrive with the suspect. When the police wouldn't give the reporter any information, he then called me to ask about the status of legal proceedings against the man. According to the reporter, the man in custody appeared *unkempt* and *bedraggled*—his words, not mine—so he assumed he'd be requiring the services of our office since we represent those defendants who cannot afford attorneys. Of course, I explained that our office doesn't get involved in the representation of an indigent defendant until the court signs an order appointing us, and that such an order typically does not get entered until the arraignment. He finally figured out that I didn't have any useful information to offer him, and hung up."

The crowd's interest was piqued. The murder of Curt Redmond only four days ago had shocked the community. Though Ann Arbor's population was greater than one hundred thousand, murders were uncommon in the city. Such a brazen and inexplicable killing, especially of a university student, had created unease among residents, and the arrest in the case was welcomed news.

"I figured if I was already receiving calls about this case," Helen said, "when we haven't even received it yet, it was worth a phone call to the prosecutor. He was playing it close to the vest, but he confirmed that a man was arrested this morning, who is believed to—quote—have a connection with the murder of Curtis Redmond. At this time, though, he's only been charged with resisting and obstructing, which occurred when the police tried to bring him in for questioning. But Phil suggested that his office expects to amend the complaint soon to include additional charges."

"Do you think they've got the killer?" someone in the crowd said.

"I suspect they do," Helen replied. "It sounds like the prosecutor's office is all over this."

"So, what's the problem?"

"The problem is that this arrest and prosecution is going to cause a shitstorm. The man they arrested is not a gang banger or a career criminal. He's a simple homeless man who has, until now, flown under the radar. In fact, he's a well-known face around campus streets and local soup kitchens, and apparently well-liked. You know how much attention this case has already received. You can imagine what's going to happen when the press gets hold of this. I'm concerned that the homeless will be vilified, that the university or city council will bend to the pressure of students and their parents. It could truly change the landscape for the homeless in Ann Arbor. This case has farther-reaching implications than just this one man."

Ann Arbor had a large homeless population. Many came from other cities, even other states, to take advantage of the city's generous benefits and welcoming environment. For the most part, the university students and Ann Arbor residents lived in harmony with the homeless. If that harmony was disturbed, and distrust sowed, the city's environment could drastically change.

"When will he be arraigned?" said another attorney.

"Tomorrow, on the resisting and obstructing. There seems to be little doubt that he'll be appointed counsel. Most likely, he and all the baggage that comes with him will be ours. We obviously don't yet know what judge he'll be assigned to, and in turn, which one of our attorneys. But I wanted to give you a heads up, in case you're contacted by the press. There may also be press in, or outside the courthouse. I know you already know this, but it needs repeating. Do not, under any circumstances, speak to the press about a specific case. Direct all inquiries to me. And be wary of making comments to friends and family, or having conversations in public places. People will want to talk about this case. Limit conversations and dissemination of information to this office and the courtroom only. Understood?"

There were nods throughout the room.

"Also, we have an added responsibility with this case. How the public perceives this defendant may make a difference for all the homeless people in the city, and the treatment of them by others. No matter how the prosecution, the press, or anyone else wishes to depict this case, it is about one person, and one person only. Any questions?"

The assembled attorneys looked at one another, but no one spoke.

"OK, then. Get back to work. We'll know more tomorrow."

The meeting adjourned, and attorneys streamed out of Helen's office like ants, minds racing, and stomachs growling. Sohni retrieved her tuna sandwich from the refrigerator in the break room and nibbled at it while she responded to her emails. She was, perhaps, not what one would picture as a typical public defender, and her journey to the job she loved had included drama.

She grew up privileged. First, in India. Then, in the US. Her father's oncology practice brought the family to Ann Arbor when she was eleven. During her childhood, her world consisted of little more than school and family, largely due to her old-fashioned Hindu parents' strict cultural and religious values. Though attending the University of Michigan kept her close to home and allowed her parents to keep watchful eyes on her, Sohni found herself growing more distant from them and what she began to perceive as their obsolete belief system. Like a caterpillar emerging from its cocoon, Sohni burst from her protective bubble of adolescence and morphed into a well-rounded, free-thinking young woman. Her parents found it difficult to reign in her burgeoning independence and her newly developing views and interests, which clashed with those of her parents and were the source of many family arguments.

Sohni's parents were apoplectic when she accepted employment with the public defender's office instead of taking a position with one of the numerous corporate firms that had pursued her during her final year at the University of Michigan Law School. But her current employment had provided her with unbeatable experience. During her five years with the public defender's office, she had gained more hands-on trial experience than she would have in ten years at a big firm. Her job also provided her with a special kind of satisfaction that came from helping people who truly needed her assistance.

But cultural differences are not easily bridged, and it seemed that her parents would never fully understand, or accept, the choice she made or the person she'd become. Being emotionally distant from her parents, though, was not an entirely bad thing. She had endured more than enough years of their control and criticism, and space from them was exactly what she needed. She preferred to do her battling in the courtroom.

With her emails cleared, Sohni opened a partially completed trial brief due the next day, in what had turned into a particularly contentious case. She thrived working in the trenches, sweating over the minutiae to ensure her clients had received the full benefits of every right to which they were entitled. She had no interest in the spotlight, so she took guilty comfort in knowing that, as the most junior attorney in the felony division, a high-profile murder case like the one the office was about to receive would undoubtedly be assigned to one of the more senior attorneys, even if it landed in her assigned courtroom. She was more than happy to sit this one out.

Sohni checked the time on her cell phone. She needed to be in court, so she tossed the files into her briefcase and exited onto Huron Street. On the short walk to the Washtenaw

County Trial Court, where she was scheduled to argue pre-trial motions, she soaked up the weak, fall sun and chugged from her cardboard cup of joe.

Her client, a nineteen-year-old drug dealer from a broken home, would be transported to the courthouse from his jail cell, where he remained on a $10,000 bond—10 percent of which no one in his family could afford. Not that any of them gave a damn about him, anyway. Sometimes Sohni felt that she and her colleagues were the only ones who cared about what happened to the accused criminals assigned to them.

Her compassion made her a persuasive client advocate. But the very attribute that motivated her to go the extra mile, sometimes worked against her. On more than one occasion, her big heart had led her to become personally involved—too anguished over circumstances beyond her control. Though she had no children, Sohni was especially taken in by her young clients, like Anthony, the client she would fight for today. Even more than an attorney, those clients needed a mentor, a parental figure to change their lives for the better. But her role, though important, was limited to that of legal advocate. When the case was over, so was her involvement in their lives. That is, until their next arrest.

Another reason it was best that she would not be assigned to the Curtis Redmond case. The weight of an entire homeless community on her shoulders was more than she could bear.

# CHAPTER 3

THE LAST TEN DAYS HAD PASSED IN A DIZZYING BLUR FOR Sohni. The day after the impromptu staff meeting in Helen's office, her boss had called her back in.

"Henry Martinez was arraigned today," Helen said, "and as expected, requested an appointed attorney. We have no conflict, so we'll be representing him on the resisting and obstructing, and whatever else comes later."

"OK?" Sohni said.

"Yes, I know you don't usually handle cases in the Fifteenth, but today I'm making an exception."

Sohni's eyes grew wide. "You want me to represent Henry Martinez?"

"I do."

"But shouldn't a more senior attorney be assigned to such a high-profile case?"

"Perhaps. But after attending his arraignment this morning, I knew you were the right choice."

"Is this because the senior attorneys are tied up with other matters?"

"In part. But with public sentiment turning against Mr. Martinez, who is already part of a vulnerable population, I feel that he needs not only a good attorney, but a strong advocate. Mr. Martinez needs a champion. And that's what you do best."

Sohni was honored, but also nervous. She knew that by representing this defendant, she would have cameras shoved in her face, and be hounded by calls from reporters. She might even receive hate mail or threats. The community's outrage against Curt Redmond's killer was new to her.

She had barely had time to file an appearance before Henry's second arraignment on the murder charge. By charging *open murder*, the prosecution did not have to designate the degree of the crime, such as first or second, thereby leaving it to be determined at trial. With so little information and no time to confer with her new client, Sohni went in blind. She entered a not-guilty plea, and argued again for a reasonable bond that she knew would not be forthcoming. Since then, the prosecution had sent over a lot of the information relating to his charges. With Henry's probable cause conference imminent, she'd planned to devote much of the following day to reviewing what the prosecution had produced, and finally spending quality time with her client.

But now it was the middle of the night, and she couldn't sleep. Her mind raced with the tasks that lay before her. Weighing most heavily on her mind, though, was the media coverage of Henry's arrest. After his arraignment, the newspapers featured fearmongering headlines, followed by sparse articles that revealed only a few details about the man himself, and did little else than regurgitate the details of the murder already published several times over. Sohni dreaded what each day's coverage would bring. And like Helen, she worried about the repercussions Henry's arrest, and the public vilification could have for Ann Arbor's homeless population.

Finally, after drifting in and out of sleep for six hours, Sohni decided she might as well get up and go to work. The digital display next to her bed read 4:45 a.m. As she started to step out of bed, she felt an arm around her waist, pulling her back in. She had apparently woken Matt.

He was the straw that had broken her parents' back.

Matt Silver was a political science professor twelve years her senior and, to her parents' horror, Jewish. Though she had scarcely dated over the years because of her parents' disdain for casual affairs of the heart, they assumed that upon completing her schooling, she would marry. Specifically, they expected her to wed an Indian man from a good family, most likely one they had selected. But instead, she fell in love with Matt.

When they got engaged, her parents did not take it well. Far from the young, traditional Indian man they had envisioned for their daughter, Matt was a liberal, New York Jew, more than a decade older. Their engagement caused yet another rift between her and her parents. But despite their pressure, which included threats to disown her, she refused to be forced to choose between her parents and the man she loved.

Sohni and Matt married three months after she graduated from law school. Her parents didn't attend the wedding.

While they didn't disown their daughter—which wasn't an effective threat as far as Sohni was concerned—they never failed to make their feelings known about her husband, both to his face and behind his back. She never understood what they expected to accomplish with their hostility, as it only drove their daughter even further away. But then again, she'd accepted a long time ago that she'd never understand anything about their behavior.

"Where … you … going?" Matt said, in a groggy voice.

She smiled at the adorable, bleary-eyed man lying next to her.

"You're so cute when you're half-asleep."

He gave a lopsided smile and, with his eyes closed, he pulled her closer. Sohni took in the smell of him and the warmth of his body, and realized, at this moment, there was no place she'd rather be. And this early in the morning, no other place she needed to be. She scooted her body up against his and pulled the covers back over them. In two minutes, she was asleep.

Sohni awoke to the smell of coffee wafting in from the kitchen. After opening her heavy-lidded eyes, she saw that Matt's side of the bed was now occupied by a large orange cat. "Whiskers, what did you do with my husband?" she whispered.

Whiskers stretched his large body even further across Matt's side of the bed, asserting his claim over that prime piece of real estate. Sohni smiled and gave his head a quick stroke. Then she checked the clock, 8:06 a.m.

"Shit."

She shoved her feet into her slippers and bounded down the stairs toward the kitchen.

"Matthew Silver!" she shouted. "Why did you let me sleep so late?"

He met her in the kitchen doorway, wearing his favorite tattered robe, and a guilty smile. "I knew you didn't sleep much last night. I figured you needed your rest."

He leaned over and kissed her forehead … one of his paternal-like habits that she found annoying.

Sohni ignored him and made a beeline for the kitchen table, looking for the morning's newspapers. She found the *Michigan Courier* open to the business section, flipping through it until she found what she was searching for. One headline read, *Protestors Urge City to Reexamine Vagrancy Laws After Student's Murder.* The article, which discussed a small but vocal group of protestors, was discouraging. The reporter quoted a local conservative activist who claimed that "this plague of homeless people on the streets of Ann Arbor has gone on too long" and that "it takes something like the cold-blooded murder of an innocent child to make the university sit up and pay attention to the safety of its students."

Sohni groaned. While she felt horrible about Curt Redmond's senseless death, them referring to a twenty-year-old man, walking to visit his girlfriend after having a couple of beers, as an innocent child, was beyond absurd.

The activist, a woman from the outskirts of Ann Arbor, named Gina Malone, was circulating petitions to city residents, calling for the strengthening of Ann Arbor's laws against vagrancy. In other words, getting the homeless off the streets.

Ms. Malone was not a stranger to Ann Arbor politics. She was a loud conservative voice in a liberal city, and this was not her first rodeo.

Sohni understood the sentiment. People were justifiably rattled. But the manner in which the woman chose to express her convictions was always ugly.

Another article reported that the university had been bombarded with phone calls from anxious parents and students, and they were holding a public meeting tonight to address their concerns. Sohni trusted that the school would handle the matter responsibly and disseminate only facts, not rumors. But at the same time, the danger of parents withdrawing current students, or refusing to allow their children to attend in the future was real, and posed a legitimate threat to the school.

Matt brought her back to the present.

"Hey, hon, if you're already running late, you'd better stop reading the newspaper and get yourself dressed."

She checked the digital clock on the stove. "Ah! You are right, Professor." She gave him a quick kiss and ran up the stairs.

At work, Sohni turned to her priority task, reviewing the file sent over by the prosecution in the Martinez case. She and Peter Crawford, one of the office's investigators, spread out the papers on a conference table and began examining each page. Peter, a criminal justice student, was one of the non-attorneys that the lawyers relied upon to conduct interviews, track down information, and perform non-legal work on behalf of their clients. He had a knack for identifying parts of a case that needed more investigation, and finding information that others had missed, which was precisely why Sohni asked him to join her.

"It's thin, isn't it?" Peter said, referring to the size of the file.

"I thought the same thing," Sohni replied. "But look at this. The lab reports and the ME's examination are completed. They must have been expedited."

"This case must have the attention of important people."

"Appears that way, doesn't it? It's gotten a great deal of attention in the press. The victim was a twenty-year-old U of M student. It's sad."

"Yeah, no kidding. I feel for his parents."

"I know. I can't imagine. He was killed while walking to his girlfriend's apartment after a hockey game. He was found face down in the middle of the sidewalk on Hill Street, in a pool of his own blood. Geesh, did you see these crime scene photos, Peter? Have you ever seen that much blood?"

"Thank goodness, no."

"The 911 call was made at 11:21 p.m., by a graduate student, Jordan Belzer, he'd been studying with a friend in a nearby apartment. He was on his way home when he stepped in the victim's blood, before he noticed the body, slumped only six feet ahead of him, on the sidewalk."

"Oh, God! That's a bad day."

Sohni chuckled, despite the gruesome photos. "Belzer was cleared as a suspect, and had nothing useful to report."

Sohni and Peter flipped to the report prepared by the responding officers.

"The tentative cause of death was hardly a mystery," Sohni said. "The victim had obviously been stabbed in the back with a sharp instrument. Based on their observations of the wound and the massive amount of blood at the scene, they concluded that it likely pierced a major artery. But we'll have to look to the medical examiner's report for confirmation."

"It's unusual to see someone stabbed cleanly in the back like that, in connection with a robbery," Peter said.

"Yeah. Even weirder, the investigators found no sign of a struggle at the scene. The cops figure he was attacked from behind without warning. That sounds more like an intentional killing."

"True. But the victim's wallet was missing."

"But his cell phone wasn't. It was still in the front pocket of his jeans."

"Yeah, but wouldn't a man's wallet ... usually kept in a back pocket ... be a more likely target. Certainly easier to pickpocket."

"You're right. But if all he was doing was picking his pocket, then why stab him? Especially if the victim didn't even try to fight back."

Peter gestured to an evidence report. "Looks like they collected a lot of trace evidence at the scene."

"Yep. But look at this list. It's mostly stuff found on the sidewalk and grass. That's a heavily traveled public area. These items could have come from anyone. Did the evidence get tested?"

"Yes. But as you suspected, none of it seems to have any probative value. They sent some hairs, a piece of fingernail, and a few unidentified substances for further testing, but those results aren't in yet."

"I'm not holding my breath," Sohni said. They're looking for a needle in a haystack. Anything interesting in the ME's report?"

Peter picked out the medical examiner's report from the papers strewn before him.

"Cause of death was exsanguination by a stab wound to the back, which severed an artery. Just like the officers initially believed, he'd bled to death."

"Any conclusions about the weapon that was used?"

"The ME suspects a knife with an estimated six-inch blade, and an approximately one-inch-wide hilt, left a bruising pattern around the outside of the wound. An examination of the wound also led to the conclusion that the knife's blade was straightedged, not serrated or curved."

"Tox' screen?"

"It shows a small amount of alcohol in his system, but no drugs. Makes sense. He'd been out that night."

Sohni nodded. "Right. Probably had a beer or two."

"Oh, this is interesting," Peter said. "The ME found some recent abrasions on the knuckles of the victim's right hand, as well as a recent bruise along his jawline, most likely caused by blunt force trauma, and occurring close to the time of death."

Sohni's interest was piqued. Injuries of that type suggested that the victim was in a fight, throwing and taking punches.

"But crime scene investigators said there was no sign of a struggle at the scene," she said. "When did this fight take place? Do you see anything in the police records?"

Peter perused a number of documents, but only shrugged.

"Nothing here," he said.

"Any other injuries noted?"

"Nope."

"We need to look into whether the victim was a boxer or did martial arts. Something that would account for his injuries. Please add that to your to-do list. Let's also see if his name shows up in any police reports involving an assault, or if any of his friends remember one."

Sohni flipped to the next page of the ME's report, which displayed the outlines of a nude male, shown from both the front and the rear. On the rear view, a small red slash was drawn across the back of the figure, intended to represent the victim's stab wound. While there was nothing surprising about the location, shape, or size of the wound, what was interesting to Sohni was the medical examiner's analysis of the angle at which the knife entered Curt Redmond's back.

"Peter, look at this. The victim was seventy inches tall, five-ten. Yet according to the ME, the trajectory of the knife suggests that the assailant was at least as tall as him, likely even taller."

Sohni had only briefly met her client, but she remembered him being no taller than her.

"How tall is our client?" she said.

"According to his arrest report, he's five-six."

Sohni smiled and shook her head. "He's not even the right height. What evidence did the ME collect from the victim's person?"

"Some hairs on his clothing, not yet identified. Nothing obvious under his fingernails, but DNA swabs were done anyway. Some DNA swabs were taken of the area of his face that was bruised, his scraped knuckles, and his palms. Waiting on results."

"What witness interviews do we have?"

Peter pulled out a small stack of papers.

"There aren't many here," he said. "Three interviews were conducted the same night he died. The first was with Jordan Belzer, the guy who found the body. The second was a student named Zach Bender, the victim's roommate, and the last person to see the victim alive. Then we have the victim's girlfriend, Kelly Burgess, whose apartment he was headed to at the time of the murder."

"What did his roommate have to say?" Sohni said.

"He and the victim were both juniors and had been roommates since their freshman year, when they were randomly assigned to share a room at West Quad. They lived there for two years. During this school year, they shared a room at the Delta Phi fraternity house. They were close friends. Looks like the two of them attended the U of M versus Michigan State hockey game together that night. They walked a short way together, then split up, he estimates around ten thirty, with the victim heading to his girlfriend's apartment on Hill Street, and Zach continuing on to their fraternity house alone.

He said the victim was in U of M's journalism program, grew up in Ferndale, where his parents still live, and was dating a girl named Kelly. Victim has no enemies, and the roommate doesn't know anyone who would want to hurt him, et cetera."

"And his girlfriend?"

"Miss Burgess is also a student, but only a sophomore. Lives in an apartment on Hill Street, where she had been waiting for Curt to arrive after the game. Wow, he was killed only about a hundred feet from her apartment building. She said when Curt didn't show up, she texted and called him, but he didn't respond, so she thought he was blowing her off. She finally just went to bed a little after eleven. Said she had been fighting a cold and was really tired. She woke up when she heard the emergency vehicles, ran outside, and talked to a detective who returned to her apartment to confirm that the victim was her boyfriend. Says victim is not involved in drugs, gangs, or anything dangerous. Also has no idea who'd want to hurt him."

"Any other statements?"

"Looks like they took formal statements from a couple of students they spoke with during the neighborhood canvas. That's how the police became aware of Henry Martinez. The witnesses noted seeing Henry sleeping at the end of the block that evening. That's all they saw, though ... just a man sleeping. They worked with a sketch artist who produced this." Peter held up a sketch and passed it to Sohni. "By asking around at local soup kitchens and shelters, the police were able to identify the man as Henry Martinez."

"That's it?"

"That's it."

"There aren't any witnesses who saw the attack or remembered seeing the victim or the assailant? Or anyone who heard something that night?"

"Not as far as I can tell."

"So, all they had was a homeless man sleeping in the area? How in the world did they make an arrest?"

"Ah, this is how." Peter slid a piece of paper across the table.

"Oh, shit!"

"Yes. Oh, shit, indeed. Fruits of a custodial search."

"I've heard rumors of the so-called bloody knife in this case, but I wrote them off as urban legend. I never imagined it really existed. And he'd been carrying it around with his snack food for days."

"No kidding. This stuff only happens in movies."

"You know, I've represented plenty of guilty clients, but this disturbs me. I question the mental state of a man who could go about his life for several days while knowing he is in possession of a blood-coated murder weapon."

Peter pulled up a police photo of the knife on his laptop, and turned the screen toward Sohni.

"Wow, that's some knife!" she said.

Peter read from an evidence report. "It's been identified as a Buck fixed blade knife with a cocobolo handle and a polished brass butt."

Even in the low-resolution photo, its brass bottom shone, and the finish of the cocobolo wood held a lustrous sheen. It looked new.

Peter continued. "The report states that a knife like that is primarily used for hunting, or possibly collecting."

"I'm assuming its blade matches the ME's assessment of the wound?"

"Yep."

"Where would a homeless man have gotten a knife like that?"

Peter shuffled papers. "It looks like the police went back several years, looking for reports of a stolen knife that matched this description, but they didn't find anything. The type of the blood found on the knife was B positive, same as the victim's. The DNA test isn't in yet, though, so we don't know for sure if it's a match."

"Any fingerprints?"

"None. Interestingly, the knife had been wiped clean."

"That *is* interesting. Why would a killer go to the trouble of getting rid of incriminating fingerprints, yet hold on to the murder weapon? What do we know about the wallet?"

Peter pulled up a police photo of the victim's billfold.

"As far as the police could tell, nothing was missing. His wallet still contained thirteen dollars in cash, his Michigan driver's license, a Capital One Visa card, a Huntington Bank debit card, his student ID, and a Jet's Pizza punch card."

"Any fingerprints?"

"Nope. Also wiped clean."

"Do we know if any of the victim's cards were used?"

Peter found the relevant report and set it on the table in front of them.

"Doesn't look like it," he said. "The last time any of his cards were used, was prior to his death. Including his student ID."

Sohni frowned. "Let me get this straight. Our client supposedly follows the victim down the block, stabs him in the back for the purpose of stealing his wallet. He then never uses anything from the wallet, including the cash. Am I missing something, Peter?"

"If you are, then I am, too."

Sohni pulled the laptop toward her and opened a video file. "Let's watch the interrogation."

The screen came to life with grainy footage of a small interrogation room. Detective Clarke, dapper as ever, sat at a table with Henry Martinez. They chatted about Henry's whereabouts on the night in question, and whether he witnessed anything.

"He comes off well," Sohni said. "He's consistent and fairly articulate. Seems sincere."

The first part of the interrogation lasted about twenty minutes. Then the interview took a sudden turn. Jake left briefly, but when he returned, the entire tone of the interview changed. Officers had discovered the knife and the wallet, and Henry Martinez's status had just changed from person of interest to murder suspect.

"Man, I wish I could have been a fly on the wall when the officers searched that bag," Peter said. "Must have been quite a moment."

"No kidding."

They watched the remainder of the videotaped interview, observing the procedures and techniques used by the detective. Not surprisingly, Sohni could identify no misconduct during the interview. She'd always known Jake to be a straight shooter. Though Jake's conduct provided little of interest, Henry's demeanor was intriguing.

"Was it just me," Sohni said, "or did Henry seem just as sincerely shocked as the police by the discovery of the knife and wallet?"

"I agree. He seemed honestly confused."

"Did the lab test Henry's clothing?"

Peter searched for the relevant document.

"Yes. Other than the flannel shirt in which the weapon was wrapped, it found no blood on any of them, including on the soles of his shoes."

"How does that make any sense? When a knife punctures a major artery, blood is going to gush from the body. You saw the blood in the photos. This was only a six-inch knife. It would have been virtually impossible for the person holding that knife to avoid coming in contact with at least some of the blood, even if it was only splattered on his shoes."

"He could have been wearing the flannel shirt at the time. That had blood on it. Or he could have changed clothes."

Sohni pulled up the photos of Henry's clothing items.

"Look at the blood on the flannel shirt. It's only in a limited area, consistent with being wrapped around the bloody knife. I don't see blood anywhere else, and the police records don't suggest there was any. Plus, how many outfits can a homeless man living out of a rucksack have?"

"Not to mention," Peter said, "he'd have to find some place to change and clean himself up. Probably a public bathroom. Surely someone would have noticed a homeless man changing out of bloody clothes."

"You would think so. Did police check dumpsters, public bathrooms in the area?"

"They did, but they didn't find anything connected to the case. No bloody clothes or shoes, no gloves. No witnesses."

"Any security cameras?"

"The police claim they couldn't find any that would show the relevant area. That block is residential and mostly student rentals."

"Damn! Just one camera could make such a difference. Peter, please do a double-check on that. Also, see if any of the nearby residents have some cell phone video footage we don't know about. They may not even realize it."

"Sure thing." Peter scribbled on his legal pad.

"Did they search the victim's room, or anywhere else at the frat house?"

"Doesn't look like it.

"What about his parents' house?"

"Nope."

"What the hell? Someone's murdered, and you don't search his home? What about his cell phone?"

"Police took it. But I don't see that any forensics were done on it. No records of call logs, text messages, or Internet activity."

"That's odd, too. It's pretty standard to scour cell phone activity in a murder case, especially since several days passed between the murder and the arrest. We must be missing some items. Probably just an oversight. I'll send a message to Pauline and let her know to send the rest over."

"Pauline? Pauline Fitzgerald is the prosecutor on this case?"

"Unfortunately, yes."

They both laughed.

"Well, good luck with that!" Peter collected his laptop and his to-do list, and left Sohni alone with a pile of papers and her thoughts.

Sohni sent off an email to First Assistant Prosecutor Pauline Fitzgerald, inquiring about the missing information. Her message also served another purpose. It made a formal request that she be given access to the victim's cell phone so she could send it for her own forensic testing.

For now, though, she powered down her laptop and collected the papers back into the file. Armed with the prose-cutor's preliminary production, Sohni had another person to see … Henry Martinez.

# CHAPTER 4

SOHNI BUZZED AT THE R4 DOOR, WHERE ATTORNEYS ENTER the jail to meet with their clients. She identified herself, and from within the building the door lock was released, allowing her down the long, narrow lobby.

A bland jail-like room, if ever there was one. A row of attached gray plastic chairs lined a wall up to an off-white cinderblock wall. Five doors on another provided meeting rooms between inmates and visitors who can't enter the jail. Those rooms contained transparent dividers between the inmates and their visitors, which allowed eye contact but made verbal communication only accessible via phone handsets.

After bypassing the rooms, Sohni approached a thick Plexiglas window, where she presented her county ID and completed a professional visit form to identify both herself and the inmate. Finally, she signed the log book, and slid her phone and keys through the slot, where they would remain until she returned. The officers knew her well, but protocols were protocols.

The officer at the window radioed the central command office. The giant steel door opened, and she stepped inside. The second door opened after the first was shut. In that moment before the second door opened, when she was ensconced in the cocoon of steel, she fancied herself in a spaceship airlock from some Hollywood movie. The illusion was quickly dispelled though, by the flurry of activity inside, as the second door slid back. She was greeted by an officer who confirmed which inmate she was there to see, and directed her to a meeting room to await the arrival of her client.

Her first meeting with Henry, if you could call it that, consisted of a quick explanation of the newly added open murder charge, a discussion of his not-guilty plea, and a promise that she would return soon for a more comprehensive dialogue. Despite having appeared on his behalf at his second arraignment, she knew little about him or what he had to offer to his defense. She looked forward to the opportunity to finally make that personal connection with him.

As the officer entered the conference room, with her client in tow, Sohni stood and found herself eye to eye with Henry, confirming his height was indeed around five-foot-six. His weathered face spoke to years of working outdoors, and the hard set of his jaw suggested a toughness that came from a difficult life. His large brown eyes, though, were shockingly clear and warm, and seemed mismatched with the rest of his face.

Sohni smiled and gestured for him to have a seat in one of the gray plastic chairs set around the small square table. The officer closed the door behind him, giving the attorney and client privacy. Numerous windows in the meeting room allowed staff to monitor them to ensure the attorneys' safety and that no inappropriate transactions took place. An emergency button on the wall provided extra security for a visitor who found herself in an unsafe situation. Sohni had only used it once, during an unpleasant encounter with a mentally ill client that she would've rather forgotten.

Once that door closed, Henry started talking.

"Ma'am, I didn't do it! I don't know how none of that stuff got in my bag. I didn't kill nobody. They won't listen to me." He spoke with a southern drawl, to which Sohni was unaccustomed.

She placed a hand on his arm. "That's what I'm here to talk to you about today. And I will listen. But let's start at the beginning."

He nodded.

Sohni pulled out her legal pad and pen from her briefcase, and began the process of getting to know him.

His name was Henry Enrique Martinez, born in Texas to two undocumented Mexican immigrants, fifty-two years prior. His father was still alive, still undocumented, and living in New Mexico. Henry had lived in Texas for forty-two years, during which time he married and divorced, and held a variety of jobs in the construction industry. Four years ago, after losing his marriage, his job, and his money—apparently, due to an alcohol problem—he moved to Toledo, Ohio.

"Why Toledo?" Sohni said.

"My sister Angie lives there. She let me stay in her spare room for a while."

"Why'd you leave?"

"It was doomed from the start. She had two teenagers, so the four of us were living in a small house. It was pretty cramped in there. We were all on top of each other."

"You decided to move out?"

"Actually, Angie kicked me out. I was still drinking a lot back then. When I drank too much, I acted ... erratic. I guess that would be a good word."

"Erratic, how?"

"Belligerent, hot-tempered. Felt I was being disrespected by anyone who dared to question me. It wasn't a good look. And it was too much for Angie and the kids. She told me I wasn't welcome back at her house until I got some help."

"So, did you?"

"Not right away. I had to hit rock bottom first. Wandered, slept on the streets, panhandled.

"How long ago was that?"

"About three years. After the first few months of living like that, I managed to buy a bus ticket to Ann Arbor. Been here ever since."

"Are you still drinking?"

"No! I've been sober twenty months now."

"That's awesome! How did you do it?"

"I got lucky. Found a program at a local church, for people like me. *People in transition* they call us." He chuckled. "I think they mean bums. Anyway, they gave me structure, counseling, and lots of spiritual guidance. And I stopped drinking for the first time since I was a teenager. I still go to the AA meetings twice a week, and church services every Sunday."

"How does it feel?"

"I have to admit, it feels real good. I feel more in control of my life than I used to."

"But you're still living on the streets?"

"Yeah. Being sober ain't enough to get yourself an apartment and a job."

"Have you worked at all?"

"Best I seem to be able to do are some cash jobs, like handing out fliers, some construction day jobs. I ain't got a car to drive to jobs and most *real* jobs want you to have an address. Plus, my resumé don't look very good. I have three years of no work at all. And before that, I either worked cash jobs off the books, or got fired for showing up drunk. Who the hell is gonna hire me?"

Henry's story was nothing new to Sohni, who was well-aware of the cycle of poverty her clients were often caught up in. Drinking, drugs, or mental illness contributed greatly to the homeless population. Resources were scarce to help people who couldn't afford costly rehab clinics or psychiatric medication. Instead of helping these needy individuals, society relegated them to the streets, or the jails.

"I had to get sober first. Otherwise, I'd just get kicked out. But it's probably about time to start applying." His tone became bitter. "What's the point now, though? I'm stuck in here for who knows how long."

"Let's talk about that. Did you know the young man who was killed? His name was Curtis Redmond. He went by Curt." She slid across a photo of Curt from her file. "Look familiar?"

Henry shook his head. "Nope. The cops showed me the same picture. I don't remember ever seeing him."

"He would've walked by that Cottage Inn where you sleep pretty regularly. His girlfriend lived on that block."

"A lot of college students come and go. I really don't pay attention. Unless I'm asking for money, I find that avoiding eye contact is the best thing."

"You told the police that between ten thirty and eleven twenty that night, during the time Curt was killed, you were sleeping at that location. Is that accurate?"

"Yep."

"OK, walk me through your actions that evening. Where you went, who you saw, what you did."

"I ate dinner at the soup kitchen, the same one where they arrested me. I went to an AA meeting at the church. Some of us hung around afterward and just shot the breeze with the pastor. It was a nice night, not too cold, so I went downtown to the plaza where people like me hang out. Someone had a boom box playing some hip hop, so I stayed for a while, listening. Around nine, I got pretty tired, so I went to that spot by the Cottage Inn, settled in, and fell asleep."

Sohni scribbled down the information as her client recounted his activities of that night.

"Did you see or hear anything unusual that night. Take a moment and really think about it. Anything or anyone that seemed different or out of place?"

"That's all I've been thinking of. I don't remember nothing unusual. It was a quiet night. If there'd been yelling or shooting, I'm pretty sure I would've heard it. But I don't remember hearing nothing."

"Do you have any recollection of the people who may have walked by you that night?"

"No. Like I said, I just mind my own business. Unless they approach me or seem threatening, I just ignore people."

"Do you recall any vehicles parked nearby? Maybe one that seemed to stop and wait and then drive off suddenly?"

"No, nothing. It was an ordinary night."

"Henry, when the police searched your bag, they found a bloody knife and the victim's wallet wrapped in a flannel shirt. As far as I can tell, those items are the only link between you and the murder. How did they get into your bag?"

The man sighed and slumped in his chair. "I don't know. But I sure as hell didn't put them there."

"Did the flannel shirt belong to you?"

"Yeah. I kept it for colder nights. It was insulated, really warm, almost like a jacket. But that week, the nights had been warm for October, and I hadn't needed it in a while. I have a big ol' beach towel I use like a blanket on cool nights, so I only add the flannel if it's cold. I don't remember the last time I used it. It had to be at least a week before that night that I even took it out of my bag."

"Was the bag ever out of your sight between the time of Curt's death and the time you were arrested the next day? Did you let someone else use it or watch it for you?"

"No. Everything I own is in that bag. I never let it out of my sight. Even when I was sleeping, I always kept the straps over my arm so no one could steal it."

"Show me. Think back to that night when you were sleeping. Show me the position you were sleeping in, and where the bag would have been."

Remaining seated, Henry reenacted how he settled on the ground, lying on his side, with his back facing the restaurant. Sohni handed him her leather bag for him to use in place of his duffel bag, and he flung the straps over the crook of his elbow as he would have that night. She noticed that despite the straps secured to his arm, the bag itself was flung out a foot in front of him. She pushed her notepad across the table and directed him to sketch the scene, including the position of the building, the roads, the sidewalks, and of course, himself. She studied the ably drawn picture, noting that he lay facing Hill Street, the street on which the murder took place. His position put him less than a block east of the crime scene. His bag, flung in front of him as it was, rested close to the sidewalk that ran along Hill. Curt Redmond was believed to be walking west on Hill Street, and if her client was where he claimed to be, Curt most likely passed him only a minute or two before the attack.

Henry's depiction of the scene reinforced the idea that someone else could have attacked Curt from behind, then turned and fled the scene eastward, thereby passing close by the sleeping homeless man and his bag, which would have presented the perfect disposal place for the only evidence of the crime, because it not only hid the evidence, but also implicated the homeless man for the offense. Then again, the admitted facts also supported the prosecution's theory that Henry followed the victim, attacked him, and then returned to his spot near Cottage Inn, where he hid the knife and wallet in his bag. Without an alternative suspect, or at least an alternative motive for the crime, a jury would most likely believe the prosecution's version of events.

Strikingly, though, every detail of her client's recitation of events matched his previous statement. Though Sohni read any statements her clients had previously provided to the police, she still asked the same questions again to see if she got the same answers. A client whose story changed, or who suddenly forgot or remembered details, made her wary and caused her to question his credibility. So far, Henry's credibility was rock solid. He also appeared to be lucid and mentally stable, just as he did in the interrogation video.

Sohni pondered the strangeness of the case she had been assigned. It was not unusual for the prosecution and defendant to offer different versions of an offense, and usually the truth was somewhere in between. But there was no middle ground here. Either Henry Martinez was a cold-blooded killer, or he was an innocent man. Both alternatives made her shudder.

She stood and extended her hand to Henry, who grasped it. Instead of a handshake, though, his thick, calloused hand squeezed hers with desperation. For the first time since he'd entered the room, his defenses fell and his eyes seemed to plead with her, just as his voice did.

"Please help me Missus. Silver. I didn't kill no one. I'm not an angel, but I'm not a murderer."

Sohni felt his hand tremble, noticed the sweat on his brow, and heard the sincerity in his voice. She believed him.

# CHAPTER 5

SOHNI SLAMMED HER BRIEFCASE ON HER DESK. THE WEATHER had turned, with the unseasonably warm fall giving way to bitter temperatures. Her nose was red, and her hands numb from her walk to the office, but red-hot anger raged inside her.

Pauline Fitzgerald, not the most pleasant member of the Washtenaw County Prosecuting Attorney's office, on a good day, had just hit a new low in Sohni's book. At Henry's probable cause conference, only an hour prior, Pauline informed her that the prosecution was unwilling to make a plea offer, and wouldn't budge on bond, which the judge denied at the prosecution's request. The prosecutor cited public pressure to zealously prosecute the infamous *college student killer* as her justification, but Sohni knew better.

Washtenaw County voters would be electing a new county prosecuting attorney next year. Pauline's boss, Phil Jenner, had announced—earlier in the year—his impending retirement. As the most senior first assistant prosecutor, and certainly the most ambitious, Pauline was tapped to be his replacement. Her campaign had already begun, and she'd been appealing to many of Jenner's supporters to make her his successor. Her refusal to offer a plea to Henry had less to do with public pressure on the prosecutor's office, and more to do with Pauline's posturing as a tough-on-crime defender of the people. Image was all-important in her quest to lead the Washtenaw County Prosecutor's office. Or so she believed.

But it wasn't Pauline's hard line on a plea agreement that so riled Sohni. It was her unreasonable position on discovery.

"You never responded to my request to examine the victim's phone," she told Pauline.

"Oh, your request is denied.

"What do you mean, *denied*? Examination of a murder victim's cell phone is routine. What is your basis for not turning it over?"

"Your client doesn't own a phone. There couldn't be any communication between the two of them. Whatever is on Mr. Redmond's phone is irrelevant."

"You know damn well I'm not looking for communications between my client and the victim. I'm looking for all other communications. For some reason, neither the police nor your office has performed any investigation into the victim's electronic devices. That's unheard of in a murder investigation today. If you're not going to examine his cell phone, then I am."

"I guess a judge will have to decide that."

"You're damn right!" Sohni turned and stormed away before she said, or did, something foolish.

Though Pauline was the most difficult of the prosecutors Sohni worked with, Phil Jenner ensured that his assistant prosecutors operated fairly, courteously, and within the bounds of the law. Pauline's refusal to allow routine discovery requests were out of character, even for her, and it made Sohni furious. But it also made her curious. First, the police had not performed customary searches of the victim's computer and phone. And then the prosecutor wouldn't allow the defense to conduct its own search. There was something unusual about this case, and Sohni feared she was the only one who didn't know what it was.

She would prepare a motion to compel, and force the prosecution to explain its senseless position to the judge. Most likely the court would order Pauline to give the defense access to at least some of the electronic devices. In the meantime, though, with no plea deal forthcoming, and a hardline on discovery, she had no choice but to do her own investigation. And for that, she needed to check in with Peter. She dialed his number.

Two minutes later, Peter stopped by her desk.

"So whatcha got?" she said.

He plopped an expandable legal folder on her desk, pulled a chair next to Sohni's and sat down.

"First, I found no relevant video footage. The cops were correct that none of the store's security cameras showed the area where Henry was sleeping, or the sidewalk between there and where the victim was stabbed. I checked apartment buildings and houses in the area, but saw nothing that looked like a camera facing in the right direction. I called landlords for all the places along that strip, and they confirmed."

"Dammit!"

"Second, I re-canvassed all the homes and businesses in the area, and either talked to people or left my card. I've found no one who saw or heard anything. I asked everyone to check for photos or video footage they may have taken that night, just in case they caught something they didn't know about. I haven't heard anything back."

"It's amazing that nobody saw anything. How does that happen in today's world?"

"Third, I visited the places Henry claimed he went to that night and spoke to the people there. Those who remembered seeing him confirmed his timeline. I've got their contact information. Interestingly, every single one of them expressed utter shock at Henry's arrest. They all stated that Henry was typically calm and easy going. Not particularly social, but friendly when around other people, and that he seemed dedicated to his sobriety. None had ever seen Henry behave in a violent manner, and they had never seen him with a knife or any other kind of weapon. Not one of them recognized the weapon found in Henry's bag when shown pictures."

"That's great. Did you check his criminal record?"

"I did. He's got no history in Michigan."

"Wonderful. I learned that he's originally from Texas, and spent a short time in Ohio before coming to Ann Arbor. Can you check in both those states as well? Henry made a comment that he wasn't an *angel*, so I don't want any surprises."

"Sure."

"Did you get a chance to talk to Curt's fraternity brothers?"

"I did. It was kind of odd, actually. The guys didn't know much about Curt, and didn't seem all that affected by his death. The way they talked about him made him sound more like a boarder than a member of the fraternity. Curt's roommate, Zach, on the other hand, was popular. He was more social than Curt. But they told me that the only close friend Zach had was Curt, and there were times when the two of them would be holed up in their room for entire days. They said that Zach and Curt were like brothers."

"I definitely need to talk to Zach. I want to interview him in the room he shared with Curt, if possible. I confirmed that the police did not search his room, and did not take or inspect any of his electronic devices. Truly stunning. Maybe I can at least get a look at what's in there ... unless his family has already cleared it out."

"It's worth a try."

"Oh, any info on whether Curt was into boxing, or something to explain his injury?"

"His housemates seemed doubtful. They said he wasn't interested in sports or athletic activities. They said he was much more likely to be marching in a civil rights demonstration than sparring in a gym."

"OK. Maybe Zach will know more."

"I took some pictures of the spot where Curt was found, and where Henry was sleeping. They're on the thumb drive in the folder. I also took a video as I headed down the sidewalk from the Cottage Inn, to where Curt was found. I tried to pan around and pick up as much detail as possible, just in case you might notice something I didn't. It's also on the drive."

"Awesome!"

"Finally, I put together a profile on the victim based on information I got from other sources. Curt Redmond was the only child of a working-class couple, Frank, and Cathy Redmond. His father works as an auto mechanic for a Jaguar dealership. His mother for a dry cleaner. Neither Curt nor his parents have a criminal record—at least, not in Michigan — or any seeming notoriety."

"Did he have a social media presence?"

"He did. He's got Twitter, Instagram, and Snapchat accounts. Even LinkedIn. They confirm that he was very much into social causes—civil rights, LGBTQ, Medicare for all, Black Lives Matter, et cetera. He seemed very serious for a twenty-year-old. At that age, I was all about girls and partying."

Sohni laughed. "Peter, that was only five years ago."

"I guess you're right. Oh, one more thing that will be worth looking into. During my internet search, I came across several articles on a website called The Truth Zone, that Curt had apparently written. The Truth Zone is an online-only investigative journalism site that posts articles by journalism students. A summary is in the folder. I figured you'd want to go online and check it out for yourself."

"You know me well."

"Who knows. Maybe he pissed off someone with one of his articles."

"Thanks so much, Peter. You've given me a lot to go through."

"No problem. Let me know if you need anything else."

As Peter left, Sohni turned to her keyboard and navigated to www.thetruthzone.com. The homepage touted The Truth Zone as a forum for quality, investigative journalism by aspiring journalists, where only well-investigated and balanced reporting would be published. The site was simple, and surprisingly tasteful, lacking in sensationalism and obnoxious headlines.

From the contacts page, she found the name and phone number for the editor-in-chief, Tracy Zorn, and scribbled them on her legal pad. Sohni was surprised, the site operated out of a brick-and-mortar office right there in Ann Arbor. She added Ms. Zorn to the list of people she needed to speak with, and would read through Curt's articles later, when she had more time. Right now, she had a motion to write. Sohni would get access to Curt's cell phone, come hell or high water.

By the time Sohni received confirmation that her motion had been accepted by the court's electronic filing system, it was nearly 7:00 p.m. Though many tasks still remained, she decided they could wait, and called it a day. She packed up her briefcase, tossing in the file Peter gave her, so she could review it after dinner, zipped up her coat and headed to the parking lot.

As Sohni started her car, she heard a text alert from her phone. She didn't have to look to know it was Matt wondering why she hadn't yet made it home. Earlier that day, she'd told him that she hoped to be home for dinner by six thirty. But her day got long, and work piled up, as it often did, and six thirty came and went. He knew the nature of her work, so he knew that estimations of dinner times were aspirational at best. He also knew that she always texted him once she got to her car so he could plan dinner. Regardless, he worried. Sometimes too much.

Granted, his attitude wasn't entirely unjustified. Between the nature of her work, and her track record of self-destructive behavior, she offered a lot to be worried about. But she was a healthy grown woman, and demanded to be treated as such. Still, he couldn't help himself.

Sohni texted, as she always did, *Leaving now.* On the way out of downtown Ann Arbor, she noticed a mass of people assembled in a public square, bundled in scarves, hats, and gloves. Despite the bitter temperature, at least a hundred participants carried signs and chanted. One poster board read, HOMLESSNESS IS NOT A CRIME! Another, scrawled in bright green, read, HOMES, NOT JAILS!

The press could write all it wanted about the vocal minority who wanted to force the homeless off the streets. This was the Ann Arbor she knew and loved. She was grateful for the protestor's support, hoped that the powers that be saw their demonstration, and recognized it represented the real heart of the city.

Her two favorite men greeted her at the door. Matt, with a bear hug, and Whiskers with a winding rub around her ankles. A delicious aroma wafted from the kitchen.

"Mmm. Do I smell shrimp?" she said.

"You do. They're sautéing in a light white wine and lemon sauce."

"I didn't even realize I was hungry. But now I'm starving. How long until it's ready, Chef?"

"About five minutes. Just enough time for you to change into something more comfortable." Matt waggled his eyebrows.

Sohni smiled and rolled her eyes. "You are incorrigible, Mr. Silver."

She slapped him on his butt and jogged up the stairs to their bedroom, an orange tomcat following close.

Matt loved to cook, which worked out perfectly because she still had an unsteady relationship with food. Anorexia had threatened her well-being during high school. The unrealistic expectations of her parents, and the resulting feeling that she could never measure up, led her to control the one thing she could ... her eating. A smart and clever girl, she hid her illness from her parents. But her younger sister was no fool. Manju idolized Sohni and didn't miss a thing. Though she said nothing at first, Manju slipped candy bars into her sister's lunch bags, scooped out more ice cream than she could possibly eat herself while the two watched movies, and brought along two bottles of high-calorie sports drinks whenever they exercised together. To Manju's credit, she never told their parents. Their reaction probably would have driven Sohni deeper into her illness.

When Sohni finally entered college and moved out of her parents' house, Manju told her, in no uncertain terms, that she was going to make an appointment with the school's mental health counseling office. Manju handed her the phone number and made it clear that she would not stop nagging until Sohni started counseling. Manju's threats were never idle, so Sohni called, and she was happy she did. Her counseling sessions were freeing, allowing her to unburden herself of the unrelenting stress and self-doubt that she realized had been weighing upon her throughout childhood. Slowly, she began engaging with the new world around her, and as her confidence grew, the grip of anorexia lessened. Though it took time, she was eventually able to stop counting every calorie, and stopped examining her body on a daily basis.

Manju, whose natural full figure contrasted with Sohni's petite build, would strip down in front of a mirror, side by side with Sohni, to help Sohni realize how thin she was. At first, the brazen move by Manju made her uncomfortable, nudity was frowned upon in her home. But Manju wouldn't stop, and soon Sohni came to realize that she had little to fear from food.

Though she had overcome her eating disorder during those first few years of college, old habits die hard. She still consumed food in small bites, and would stop eating as soon as she felt full. The important thing was that she gave her body all the nourishment it needed. Didn't matter how she got there. But as a result, she was not well-suited to prepare family meals. Fortunately, Matt willingly took up the mantle, shopping for the freshest foods and trying out new recipes as often as he could. He loved to see her enjoy his cooking.

Sohni came back downstairs, clad in athletic pants and a Michigan sweatshirt, her hair loose around her shoulders. Given the choice, she would have spent twenty-four hours a day in those warm, comfortable clothes. Just the feel of them made her happy.

She took her seat at the kitchen table, where a plate of Matt's steaming culinary creation awaited. She cut the food into small pieces and began delicately eating one at a time. Sometimes she caught Matt watching her while she ate. He claimed he was fascinated by her tiny-bite technique, but she knew the truth. He was assuring himself that she was, in fact, eating. He was aware of how difficult her struggle with anorexia had been, and though he wouldn't admit it, his overprotective nature required vigilance over her food consumption. But the newspaper had arrived that morning, so they had more important endeavors that evening.

"Juliette Low's organization, Matt said. "Abbreviation, three letters."

"The Girl Scouts. Probably GSA."

"Perfect. Next one is Field of Dreams state. Four letters. I thought that was Kansas, or Nebraska, or one of those states with a lot of corn."

Sohni chuckled. "Sorry, city boy, but all corn-growing states are not interchangeable."

Matt laughed, too. "Will you stop mocking me, and just give me the answer?"

"It's Iowa, silly."

"Oh, Iowa. I suppose there is a lot of corn there." Matt gave her a crooked smile.

Their dinner continued for over an hour, until every crossword answer was completed, along with their glasses of wine.

Finally, Sohni rose, albeit reluctantly. She leaned down and kissed Matt on his lips, tasting remnants of Merlot.

"You cooked, so I'll clean. Go and relax with your bowl of ice cream."

"Am I really that predictable?" Matt selected a bowl from the shelf and a carton of butter pecan from the freezer.

As Sohni loaded their plates into the dishwasher, she noticed a blinking light on the answering machine. Matt constantly bugged her to get rid of their landline, but she resisted. Her parents were in their seventies and had trouble hearing calls made on cell phones. Plus, she liked the security of knowing there was another way for calls to come in and out, in case something happened to her cell phone.

She pushed the play button, expecting to hear a busy call center and a solicitor repeating *Hello* to an empty phone line. Instead, she heard her mom's stiff voice.

"Hi, Sohni. This is your mom. Dad and I would like to talk to you. Please give us a call."

The robotic voice that followed informed her that the message came in, only five minutes before she arrived home.

"Oh, good, you got your mom's message." Matt's voice wafted in from the family room, as he shoveled in a spoonful of ice cream.

Sohni felt her blood pressure rise. "You were here when she called, Matt. Why didn't you answer it?"

Matt set down his spoon. "You know the answer to that."

"Matt, you're a grown man. You really won't take my mom's calls because you don't like the way she talks to you?"

"Sohni, are we really going to do this again?" Matt rose and began to rinse out his bowl.

"I just don't get why you can't do this for me. She's my mom, for God's sake."

"I don't like the way she talks to you, either. I won't stand for it, and neither should you."

"My parents are who they are. They're not going to change. They grew up differently, and they see things differently. You know that."

"What I know is that you minimize their behavior. They are rude and condescending, to both of us. They act like they're making conversation, but their comments are all passive aggressive. You get off the phone with them feeling bad about yourself. Maybe you let them treat you that way, but they're not *my* parents. I don't have to."

Predictably, Matt stuck his feet into his running shoes, his earbuds into his ears, and was gone before she could say another word. She dropped into a kitchen chair, her face in her hands. They'd had the same fight dozens of times during their marriage. She'd begged Matt to play nice and try to get along with her parents, but he was stubborn and outspoken. Her parents came from a culture where elders were respected and obeyed, and children were meant to conform to their parents' wishes. Matt's parents came from one where their kids were encouraged to form their own opinions and speak their minds. The culture clash was inevitable. And Matt wasn't wrong. Her parents were not nice people. But they were still her family.

She and Matt had enjoyed a nice evening together. Why did she have to ruin it? Neither her parents nor her husband were going to budge, so why did she try so hard to bring them together? Manju had said more than once that Sohni should stop caring so much about forcing a relationship between them.

"Why do you want to bring the man you love into the black hole of self-loathing that is our parents? Admit it, Sohni. Even you and I only continue a relationship with Mom and Dad out of obligation, not because we enjoy their company. Why in the world would Matt want to subject himself to that when he doesn't have to?"

Her point was valid, as always. But for Sohni, it was a matter of principle. They were all her family, and if Matt loved her, then he had to accept that her parents came with her.

"Screw principles," Manju would say. "And sometimes, screw family."

Manju was nothing if not blunt.

Sohni grabbed her cell phone and called her little sister. Matt wasn't the only one who was predictable.

# CHAPTER 6

SOHNI HAD SPENT HOURS IN COURT WAITING FOR A CASE THAT the judge's clerk never called. The judge explained that his docket was overscheduled so he'd be moving her case, and several others, to next week. Lamenting the time she'd wasted, Sohni hung up her coat, threw her briefcase under her desk, and turned to her to-do list for Henry's case. She rubbed together her still-numb hands until her fingers could properly work the keyboard. Then she pulled up again, www. thetruthzone.com. This time she typed Curt's name into the search box, and got two hits—both articles Curt had written.

She clicked on the article with the earliest publication date. The headline read: *A Haze of Moral Ambiguity—Fraternity Initiation Rites or Criminal Acts?* It examined the practice of hazing at fraternities across the nation, focusing on the hazing practices of four fraternities on four college campuses across the country. It told of injuries sustained by at least three young men during physical hazing rituals, and further elaborated on humiliation routinely inflicted on new members by elders. Of course, most universities had strict rules about hazing. But according to Curt's article, the fraternities found ways to get around them, including forbidding new members from revealing any fraternity rituals as a condition of their membership.

Sohni wondered about Curt's sources for the article. Clearly, plenty of fraternity members were willing to break the code of silence. Notably, Curt's own fraternity, Delta Phi, was not mentioned in the article. Even so, this type of reporting would not have been well received with those in his frat. No wonder there was no love lost for Curt in the Delta Phi house.

Sohni then clicked on the second article, an undercover exposé of puppy mills. Curt described in great detail what he observed at the breeding facility he'd visited. Apparently, he had sources who'd visited facilities in other states, and related similar stories. He'd quoted ASPCA officials and prosecutors who had pursued criminal charges against puppy mill operators. There was no question he had thoroughly researched his topic. Curt then explained the distribution chain, and described how the animals that were able to be sold made their way to the pet stores, and the sad fate met by those that weren't.

As an animal lover, Sohni had difficulty making it through the text. Despite The Truth Zone's promise to present bal-anced viewpoints, the article came off as a scathing criticism of breeding facilities and their owners. She had to concede, though, that there wasn't a way to balance the horrors of puppy mills.

The information was certainly inflammatory, but was it worth killing over? Although The Truth Zone could be accessed globally, *The New York Times* it was not. How many people read Curt's articles? How much damage could they possibly do? Not to mention that the most recent of the articles had been published over five months ago. Why would someone wait so long to act? Then again, his murder could be less about damage to someone's reputation, and more about retribution. After all, revenge was a classic motive for murder, and humans were known to hold grudges indefinitely.

Sohni dialed the number listed on the website, and the call was answered in a loud tone.

"The Truth Zone, this is Tracy Zorn."

After introducing herself and confirming she knew Curt Redmond, Sohni got to the heart of the matter. "Miss Zorn ... um ... have you been notified of the recent incident involving Curt?"

"I'm afraid I don't know what you're referring to. Has something happened?

"I'm sorry to be the one to tell you, but Curt has been killed."

Silence.

"I'm so sorry," Sohni said.

The woman finally found her voice. "What happened?"

"Unfortunately, he was murdered. He was stabbed while walking on campus."

"Oh, my God! Curt is the student they keep talking about on the news. The one who was killed by the homeless man."

Sohni considered correcting Tracy and explaining that Henry was innocent until proven guilty, but figured she'd get to that later.

"Some kind of journalist, I am," Tracy said. "One of my reporters is the subject of a high-profile murder, and I'm completely oblivious."

"It's a pretty strange crime. And personally, I think there are still a lot of questions about who killed him, and why."

"Oh, I thought they arrested the guy."

"They did arrest a man and they charged him with murder. He's my client, which is why I'm contacting you. My client insists he's innocent. And frankly, I can't figure out what his motive would have been. I think someone else may have killed Curt. That's why I was hoping to talk about Curt's articles, pick your brain a bit."

"I guess so. As a journalist, I'm well-aware not everyone arrested is guilty, so I of all people shouldn't jump to conclusions."

"I appreciate that. Can you tell me a bit about The Truth Zone?"

"We're a non-profit, and we work with a couple of local colleges to offer journalism students the opportunity to research and write an entire investigative piece for publication. It's a big commitment, especially for someone taking full-time classes. Not everyone completes their articles. Thankfully, some do. Otherwise, we'd have nothing to publish." Tracy laughed loudly.

Though Sohni couldn't see Tracy, she was pretty sure she was a big woman with a big personality. Her online bio identified her as a former WBNA player, as well as an investigative journalist. She sounded like she'd be a blast to have a drink with.

"How do the students choose what to write about?" Sohni said.

"It's up to them to find topics. It might be something in the headlines that needs a more in-depth treatment, or something they've come across on their own. But my rule is that the research must be thorough and reliable, and both sides of the issue must be investigated and addressed."

"What can you tell me about Curt?"

"It was obvious from day one that Curt was not like other college students. He was passionate about making the world a better place, about righting wrongs. Many students submit articles just to get published. But not Curt. He really believed that he could change the world. He actually reminded me a of myself at that age."

"What did you think of his articles?"

"His first one, about hazing at fraternities, required quite a bit of editing. But it was well-researched and well-balanced, which appealed to me, so I published it. He was thrilled. After that, he'd come to the office to help with fact-checking, filing, or anything else that needed to be done. You could tell he just liked being a part of this."

"I saw on your site that he went on to publish another article?"

"Yes, that one was even better. He was a fast learner, and had a great future ahead of him. What a shame."

"Do you know if he ran into any problems while researching those articles, or after publishing them? Did he anger the wrong person, perhaps?"

"You think one of his articles could have gotten him killed?"

"I don't know. But right now it makes as much sense as anything else."

Tracy was silent for a moment. Sohni assumed she was thinking.

"Not that I know of," Tracy replied. "His puppy mill article was pretty damning, though. If the owners saw the article, I'm sure they wouldn't have been happy. That kid actually posed as a potential customer to get inside the place. And he wore one of those mini-spy cameras he'd purchased online. I would have been hesitant to print what he wrote if it wasn't for the video evidence he'd provided."

"Do you know what facility he wrote about? Where it was located?"

"No. He never told me."

"Do you still have the video footage he took?"

"Unfortunately, I don't. After reviewing it, I gave it back to him."

Sohni paused, out of ideas for identifying potential suspects.

"What kind of person was Curt?" she finally said.

"He was a nice guy. Ambitious. Passionate. Especially about perceived injustices. They got him fired up. Sometimes a little too much."

"How so?"

"Curt just had a chip on his shoulder about those with wealth and privilege. He really seemed to detest big corporations."

Sohni found it difficult to reconcile the conflicting information she'd obtained about Curt. On one hand, he detested wealth and privilege, and sought the opportunity to bring down the powerful. On the other hand, his best friend was a Bender, and Curt didn't seem to have a problem with sharing in the privileges of the Benders' wealth, such as hockey tickets and expensive electronics.

"Do you know if he was working on anything at the time of his death?"

"Actually, he was, come to think of it. I can't tell you what it was about though, because he didn't tell me. A couple of weeks ago, he mentioned he was investigating a new lead, he thought it could be a huge story." Tracy snorted at that. "I took it with a grain of salt, though. The kid was young, eager, always dramatic when it came to his articles. It's probably nothing."

"Do you know if Curt kept notes about his investigations?"

"From what I've seen, he took copious and detailed notes."

"Where'd he keep them?"

"I'm not sure, but it had to be somewhere close to him. He wouldn't let them out of his sight. If he was in the middle of an investigation, I would assume his notes would be among his possessions, either in paper or electronic form."

It was obvious Curt's editor didn't have the information she needed. "Thanks for your time, Miss Zorn. If you think of anything else that might be helpful, please give me a ring."

"Sure thing. If it turns out your client has been wrongfully charged with murder, maybe you could give me a call. There could be a story there." Tracy punctuated her statement with what could only be called a guffaw.

Sohni laughed. "I will definitely do that."

She hung up and reflected upon what Tracy had told her. Curt was working on a story he thought would be huge. It could just be the naïve comment of a young aspiring reporter, like Tracy believed. But what if it wasn't? What if he'd been pursuing a lead that someone didn't want pursued? Sohni needed to see his computer and phone now, more than ever.

Her desk phone rang. A collect call from the Washtenaw County Jail. In the recorded message, the caller identified himself as Henry Martinez.

"Hi, Henry."

"Hi, Missus Silver. I'm sorry to bother you, but you told me to call you if I remembered anything that could be helpful to my case."

"Sure. What is it?"

"It's something small, really. I guess I'm not even sure it has anything to do with—"

"Henry! You obviously thought it was important enough to call me, just spit it out already."

Henry chuckled. "Yes, Ma'am. It's about my bag. You know that duffel bag where the police say they found the knife and wallet?"

"Sure."

"Well, one morning when I woke up after sleeping outside, I found the zipper partly open. I didn't think much of it at the time. It was unusual because I always made sure it was closed all the way, but I figured I was just careless. I didn't think about it again until last night when I was trying to fall asleep. I'm not sure why it came to me, but I suddenly remembered it. Of course, it seems much more important now."

"That's interesting. Do you remember what morning it was?"

"I do, actually. It was the morning after Curt Redmond was killed. I know that because I was not in one of my usual spots. Remember, I left the area by the Cottage Inn after all the first responders showed up. I ended up in a place a couple of streets over, where it was quieter. But it was a place I'd never slept before. And I remember that's where I was, when I saw the zipper open. So, it had to be that morning."

"That is suspicious. Do you remember the zipper being partly open when you moved from Hill Street to the other location?"

"You know, I don't even think I looked. I was so tired and annoyed that I just grabbed my bag and threw my towel over my shoulder and marched off."

"Do you remember seeing anything else out of the ordinary that morning?"

"No. I went through my bag real quick later on, and I put away my towel, but it looked like everything was there. Nothing was missing or seemed out of place."

"Henry, assuming Curt's killer put the knife and wallet in your bag that night, how did you not notice they were there, especially since you went through it in the morning?"

"I'm not sure. I guess the knife was rolled up in my shirt, so I probably wouldn't have noticed that, until I finally took the shirt out of my bag."

"But what about the wallet?"

That had been bothering Sohni from the beginning. How had Henry not noticed a new wallet in his bag?

"Believe me, I keep asking myself that. How did I not see it for four days? The only thing I can think of is that it might have been in one of the inside pockets."

"Explain the pockets to me."

"My bag has a couple of pockets sewn into the inside. One has a zipper, and one doesn't. They were a pretty good size, so if the wallet was in one of them, I might not have even seen it."

"That does make sense."

Henry was quiet, but Sohni felt that he had more on his mind.

"You OK, Henry?"

"Yeah, I'm OK. It's just ... am I gonna beat this? Somebody set me up to take the fall. I don't know who it was, but they did a good job. I gotta admit, I'm scared. I'm afraid I'm gonna spend the rest of my life in prison for something I didn't even do."

She figured it took a lot for Henry to admit his fear, and she felt for him. The cards were definitely stacked against him. She longed to reassure him, to tell him she'd make sure justice was served, but she couldn't. Her belief that he didn't kill Curt was not admissible as evidence. And at this point, she only had the absence of evidence to make her case. The absence of blood on Henry's clothes, the absence of motive. That he wasn't five-foot-ten or taller, as the ME's report estimated.

"I don't know," she finally said. "But what I do know is that I'm going to do everything I can to get to the truth."

# CHAPTER 7

THE DELTA PHI HOUSE WAS FIRST IN A ROW OF FRATERNITY houses on Washtenaw Avenue. These houses were a little further off campus than many of the others, but consequently they were larger and more stunning than many that were closer. Sohni was saddened by the sight of these beautiful old homes now reduced to housing a bunch of rowdy college boys.

She pulled into the driveway and followed the paved walkway to the large wooden front door. It took two doorbell rings before a young man finally answered, and that young man happened to be wearing nothing but boxer shorts. He was clearly just as surprised to see Sohni in her business suit as she was to see him in his underwear.

Finally, Sohni said, "I'm here to see Zach Bender. Is he here?"

The young man opened the door for Sohni to enter, and pointed to an old couch in a sitting area.

"Feel free to have a seat. I'll go see if Zach is here."

He sprinted up the staircase, taking the stairs two at a time, an inappropriate pace for a man wearing loose-fitting boxers.

The couch he had directed Sohni toward appeared to be coated with years-worth of unidentified substances, so she opted to stand. Soon, a handsome, fit young man with short-cropped blond hair shuffled down the stairs. He was wearing only a pair of sweatpants, and looked like he had just been roused from his bed despite the late hour. Sohni blushed as she caught herself staring at his perfectly toned torso, reminding herself that he was practically a kid. After regaining her composure, she met him at the bottom of the staircase and shook his hand.

"You must be Zach Bender."

"Yeah," he mumbled, rubbing his eyes. "Who are you?"

"Uh, I'm Sohni Silver. We spoke yesterday and arranged for me to meet you here at eleven this morning."

Zach still looked confused.

"I'm with the public defender's office. I'm investigating the murder of your roommate, Curt."

She awaited a glint of recognition in his eyes. Instead, he blinked with a blank expression, then shrugged and turned to start back up the stairs. Sohni stood at the bottom of the staircase, uncertain whether to follow.

"Well, aren't you coming?" he said.

Sohni scurried to catch up as Zach led her to his sanctuary on the second level. Once the young man approached the door to the room that he and Curt Redmond had shared, he paused, his hand on the doorknob.

"I'll warn you, our room's a mess."

That was an understatement. It looked like a dresser had exploded. Clothes were everywhere, most of them dirty, by the look of them. It smelled even worse. Old food, half-empty beer cans, and sweat were the primary source of the stink.

Seeing the disgust on her face, Zach shrugged again.

"I haven't been up to doing much the last few days."

She felt ashamed when she remembered that this poor kid had just lost his best friend.

"I'm so sorry," she said.

Zach flopped on his bed and propped on an elbow. He pointed to what appeared to be a loveseat camouflaged by trash and clothes, but made no move to clear space for her. Sohni pushed a pizza box aside and sat on the corner of a cushion.

"As you've probably heard," she said, "a homeless man named Henry Martinez has been arrested for the murder of Curt. Do you know why Mr. Martinez would want to kill Curt?"

Zach tilted his head as though puzzled. "No, I just figured it was one of those random things, like he was crazy or wanted to rob him or something." He squinted at Sohni. "Why, do you think he knew Curt?"

"No, I don't. I just wondered if you knew of a connection that I didn't. In fact, I can't figure out any reason why Mr. Martinez would attack Curt."

Zach said nothing.

For the first time, she examined Zach Bender's face. He had natural good looks, including pale blue eyes and boyish features, which kept her from noticing, at first, the dark crescents beneath his lower lids. And though close-shaved, the hair on the right side of his head lay matted against his skull. His roommate's death had obviously been hard on him.

Sohni stole a glance around the room. On the nightstand by his bed were a few framed photographs. One aged photo showed Zach with a beautiful blonde woman who must have been his mother, judging by their shared physical traits. The woman squatted next to her son, smiling wide while squeezing him against her. Little Zach beamed, revealing two missing front teeth. Another depicted an adolescent Zach wearing a hockey uniform, posing next to an older man Sohni assumed to be his father.

Sohni was certain she had seen the man before, but she couldn't place him.

Though both father and son wore smiles, the obvious affection between Zach and his mother in the previous picture was missing from this one. The elder man appeared stiff, his arm thrown around his son unnaturally.

In the final photo, a teenaged Zach wore a graduation gown and stood beside an attractive young woman who pretended to plant a big kiss on his cheek while Zach grimaced in a playful manner. The young lady also resembled Zach's mother, and Sohni guessed she was his sister.

"Those are great pictures." She nodded toward the night-stand. "What a beautiful family."

"Thanks," he muttered.

"You look just like your mother."

He studied the photo of his mother, as though seeing it for the first time.

"People always tell me that. I don't remember much about her, though. She died when I was very young."

"I'm sorry."

He shrugged. "It was a long time ago."

"Do you still play hockey?"

"I used to play. But not anymore. My dad always loved hockey, so he got me into it pretty early. I was good. Played all through high school, and then made it onto the Michigan team. My dad was thrilled. He used to play for Michigan, too. But then I blew out my knee early in the first season. I had several surgeries, but they said I'd never be able to play competitively again. So that was the abrupt end to my hockey career."

"Aw, that's too bad."

Zach shrugged for the third time. "He still stays involved with the hockey program here. He gets season tickets, sometimes mingles at their practices."

Zach didn't do a very good job of masking his jealousy. The tall, handsome college student struck Sohni more as a petulant little boy vying for his father's attention.

"So, it was your dad's season tickets you used with Curt the night he died?"

The young man nodded.

"What did the two of you do after the game?"

"Well, we hung out in front of Yost Arena for about fifteen minutes, visiting with some friends we ran into. After they left, we walked a little way together and then split up. He headed toward Kelly's apartment, and I headed back here." Zach averted his gaze to the floor. "That was the last time I saw him."

Interviewing those most affected by a crime was difficult, and one of Sohni's least favorite tasks. But those most affected typically held important information, making the task a necessary one.

"Zach, can you think of anything Curt may have been involved in, or anyone he may have been acquainted with that could have made him a target?"

"You don't think his murder was random?"

"I'm exploring all possibilities. I have my doubts about the prosecution's theory."

"I can't really think of anything. You've got to understand, Curt was a straight arrow. He didn't gamble. He didn't do drugs. He didn't hang out with a bad crowd. He could sometimes make people crazy with his sense of righteousness, but I don't think that would have driven anyone to murder."

"You can't think of anyone, anyone at all who would want to hurt Curt?"

"No. No one would wanna hurt him."

But then Zach's face changed, and he paused.

"What is it?" Sohni said. "Do you remember something?"

He hesitated.

"Zach, this is important. You need to share any information you have."

The young man stared at the floor, eyes closed, until Sohni began to wonder if he was still awake. Then he sighed and slowly raised his head.

"He was in a fight the night he, uh … died. That night was such a blur, and I wasn't thinking straight when I talked to the police. I forgot all about it until now. Until you asked who would want to hurt Curt."

"Who'd he fight with?"

"Some asshole from Michigan State. He picked a fight with Curt after the hockey game. It was after our friends left. We were about to head out, and this drunk guy stumbles into Curt.

We didn't know him, but he started harassing us. Curt wasn't one to back down, so they ended up taking a few swings at each other before I pulled Curt off him, and his friends pulled the jerk off Curt. They each got in a couple of licks, but nothing too serious."

Sohni was speechless. Curt had been assaulted by another man less than an hour before he was murdered. There was nothing in the prosecution's file about that. But then again, there wouldn't be if Zach hadn't told the police. That could account for the abrasions on his knuckles and the bruising on his jaw.

"Did you catch the guy's name?"

"All I know is that his friends called him Razowski. I assumed it was his last name."

Sohni had an alternate suspect, a motive, and even a name. And she had only just begun asking questions.

"Is there anything else you can tell me about him, or about the fight?"

"Not really. The whole thing only lasted about thirty seconds."

"Where did you and Curt part ways?"

"We walked together to the corner of Hill and State. He turned left on Hill, and I headed here."

"Did you notice anything out of the ordinary? Did Curt seem upset or preoccupied?"

"No. Everything was normal."

Zach yawned then turned his head side to side, his neck cracking and popping. He checked the clock on his nightstand and turned his heavy-lidded eyes to Sohni.

"Are we almost done?"

"I just have one more thing I need to ask you. I saw Curt wrote articles for the website The Truth Zone. Are you familiar with them?"

He nodded. "Sure, I've read the ones he's published."

"So, he was pretty serious about journalism?"

Zach snorted. "He thought he was the next, Bob Woodward."

"Had he published any articles other than those?"

"I don't think so."

"Some of his articles were pretty inflammatory. Do you know if they upset anyone? Had he received any threats?"

"Not that I know of."

"His editor said he was working on a new piece. Do you know what he was writing about?"

"I have no clue."

"Do you know where he kept the notes and other materials from his investigations?"

"No." Zach sighed. "I know you're looking for someone who had it out for Curt, but I don't think you're going to find anyone. He was just a normal guy. And as far as I can tell, some desperate homeless guy stabbed and robbed him."

Sohni rose and strode to the opposite side of the room, where Curt's bed and belongings remained. Papers littered his desk. His bed was unmade, and his backpack still hung on a hook by the window. She noted the well-used items on his side of the room—an old laptop and an early model iPod. His possessions were consistent with his working-class upbringing.

Eerily, it appeared that everything remained exactly as he'd left it, as though Zach expected him to return home any moment. The scene before her left no doubt that the police had failed to search Curt's possessions, and when asked, Zach confirmed that the police had never been to their room.

"But I think my dad had something to do with that."

"What do you mean?"

Zach kept his gaze on the ground. "Well, he knew I was pretty upset and didn't want the police bothering me, asking a million questions over and over again."

Who the hell was Zach's dad that the police would abide by his wishes?

Sohni examined Zach's side of the room with a fresh eye. In contrast to Curt's belongings, Zach's practically bled money. From the state-of-the-art computer equipment to the latest iPhone, the young man had all the electronic toys he could want.

Sohni took in the closet full of designer clothes. Strewn on Zach's desk was a pair of Prada aviator sunglasses similar to the ones Sohni had fallen in love with, then cast aside after noticing the $300-plus price tag.

A brand-new high-end racing bike leaned against the wall on the other side of the couch. The cost of that bike was in the thousands, something she'd recalled from a prior case in which she represented an alleged bike thief.

The pieces were falling into place. Zach came from big money, and likely big influence.

She turned again to the family portraits resting on the nightstand. This time she studied the picture of his dad. It was obviously several years old, but Sohni was struck again by his familiarity. It took only a few seconds for realization to set in.

"Holy crap!" Her hand flew to her mouth.

"Your father is Robert Bender?"

"Yeah. The one and only. You just figured that out?" Zach gave a humorless chuckle.

Robert Bender was famous. And wealthy. He owned Bender Industries, an international auto supplier known for high-tech parts. But he was better known for his hobbies. A former hockey player, he was now a generous University of Michigan athletic booster. He also owned a minor league hockey team, which played at the suburban Bender Arena. He frequented high-profile social events, and his striking good looks made him a favorite subject of news photographers seeking social page content. Though Sohni had never met him, Robert Bender's reputation painted him as a ruthless businessman, yet enormously charismatic in social situations. Despite the quantity of press he received, Sohni was unaware that Robert Bender had children, which she found odd. She also couldn't recall hearing of a Mrs. Bender, despite her premature death, should've been fodder for the press.

Most importantly, though, Robert Bender was influential in Southeastern Michigan politics. He played a major role in funding and promoting the campaigns of hand-selected candidates. Among them was Phil Jenner, Washtenaw County's prosecuting attorney. And word on the street was that, at Phil's urging, Mr. Bender was lending his support to Phil's expected successor, Ms. Pauline Fitzgerald.

Now, the son of the powerful Robert Bender was involved, although only tangentially, in a high-profile murder. What pressure Phil and Pauline must have felt to keep the young Bender out of the limelight. No searches of Zach's room. No invasive interviews with him, and no search of Curt's electronic devices or social media accounts. Otherwise, it would be exceedingly difficult to protect Zach from an onslaught of media attention, and conceal his connection to the murdered college student.

Under normal circumstances, the police built a case against a suspect and then took the case to the prosecutor, who would decide whether or not the evidence was sufficient to support bringing charges against the accused. In this case, though, Phil Jenner must have stepped in before the police had completed their investigation. He obviously took the case prematurely, thereby shutting down any additional investigative efforts the police would have made.

What a risk he'd taken, though. Every gap in the investigation was more ammunition for the defense. Each alternative suspect or motive that Sohni uncovered that had not been eliminated by the police would weaken the prosecution's case. Phil and Pauline took a calculated risk that the knife and wallet found in the bag would be enough to convince a jury of Henry's guilt, and that nothing the defense could present would create reasonable doubt. Their failure to conduct a thor-ough investigation prejudiced Henry's rights. But coddling Robert Bender was exponentially more important to the pros-ecutors than ensuring that an innocent man was not wrongly tried for murder.

Sohni's blood boiled. She whipped her head around to face Zach, prepared with tough words for the prodigal son. But as she once again caught sight of the pain in his eyes, she remembered that he, too, was a victim. He had lost his closest friend—

like brothers, their housemates told Peter—and he should not be required to pay for the sins of his father.

Sohni bit her tongue. She nodded toward the desk bearing Curt's laptop, still open and plugged into the outlet.

"Is that Curt's computer?"

Zach glanced at the desk where the older laptop sat, then returned his gaze to Sohni, suspicion evident.

"Technically, it's mine. I let him use my old laptop after I got a new one."

"Was the iPhone Curt used also yours?"

"Yeah. I let him use it when the new model came out."

She could now identify the factor that had skewed this investigation from the beginning—Robert Bender. Having the answer, though, was both thrilling and maddening. If she wanted access to Curt's electronics, she would have to go through Zach. The prosecution would be of no assistance. She could, of course, serve Zach with a subpoena directing him to produce the computer. He was an adult, after all. But his father was a powerful man, with an entire team of attorneys at his beck and call. In his misguided attempt to protect his son, he could tie up the issue in court with motions and requests for protective orders, using every delaying tactic in his arsenal.

"Zach, I realize this seems like a bold request, but could I take a look at Curt's files on the computer?"

"Why?"

"The identity of his killer could be in that computer. It will reveal who he's been emailing, what he's been writing about, what websites he's visited, all things that could be incredibly helpful to my investigation."

"No! Absolutely not. I'm not letting some stranger go through Curt's computer."

"I understand your reaction, Zach. It must seem horribly invasive and disrespectful to your friend. But I want to make sure you understand that searches of computers and electronic devices are routine in murder cases. It should have already been done. If I request access to those items, it's a near certainty that the judge will grant it. Sure, your father has a team of lawyers that can try to stop it, or at least delay it. But eventually I will get access to at least some of Curt's devices."

The young man's pale cheeks became flushed. His devotion to his friend was clouding his reason.

"Zach, my client is fighting for his freedom. If he is convicted of murdering Curt, he will likely never step out of a prison. I take that seriously, and so will a judge. If I have to, I will subpoena the computer. And since you and Curt shared this room and so many items in it, I could reasonably request access to all of your tablets, smartphones, and any other electronic devices that Curt may have used. The forensic experts would keep them for weeks, possibly months, combing through every piece of data, including deleted data, regardless of who created it. I'm providing you with a better option. Just let me search his computer."

The young man looked pained.

"Look, I don't want to invade his privacy," Sohni said. "I'm not out to discredit or slander him. I just want to see if there's an angle that the cops haven't investigated. As you know, the police haven't even been through his things. Who knows what we might find? But if I don't find anything helpful, I'll just walk away and forget I ever saw any of it."

Zach looked like he'd been punched in the stomach. Sohni felt guilty for exaggerating. Realistically, the judge was unlikely to grant such a broad request, especially one directed at the Benders. But her words still held shreds of truth. She could, and would, use every means available to gain access to that laptop.

"I know you're grieving," she said, in a gentle tone. "I don't want to put you through all that. That's why I'm giving you the option of doing it on your own terms. All I want is to see what Curt has on that computer."

Sohni and Zach sat in silence for what seemed to her, like an hour, although it was probably only thirty seconds. The battle waging in the young man's head showed on his face.

Finally, he said, "I'm not comfortable giving you free reign to snoop through my computer. Although Curt has been using it for the last year, it still might contain information that belongs to me. Plus, I have to think of Curt's privacy. What if he has embarrassing pictures or illegal downloads, or something like that?"

Sohni opened her mouth to object—

"But I also don't want to deal with a subpoena and having computer guys going through all my stuff. So, I have a proposal for you."

"OK. Let's hear it."

"I will personally review everything on that laptop, and I'll copy Curt's emails and his documents to a flash drive. I'm sure you don't care about his pictures, his games, or his music. But if I find anything on his computer that would compromise his privacy or his reputation, and that clearly has nothing to do with his murder, I'm not going to give it to you. I don't expect to find anything like that, but I won't let him be attacked for no reason."

Zach's offer sounded fair. Most likely, anything of value would be contained among his emails or his documents. Plus, considering the uncertainty of her success, if Robert Bender challenged her subpoena, as well as the inevitable prolonged legal wrangling, she would prefer to have a potentially imperfect copy of Curt's computer files than nothing at all.

"It's a deal," she said.

She would forego exploring Curt's Internet browsing history, despite its potential usefulness, in exchange for prompt access to his files. She extended her hand to Zach. He accepted it with hesitation, and gave a limp handshake. He didn't trust her, and she couldn't blame him.

"When should I pick up the flash drive?"

"I should have it done by Saturday morning."

"Great. I'll come by, then. Zach, I really do appreciate your cooperation. I just want the truth, same as you."

Zach crossed his arms across his stomach and said nothing. Sohni took that as her cue to leave. Any further questions she had for him could be addressed when she returned on Saturday. Before leaving, she placed her business card on his nightstand and encouraged him to call if he remembered anything else, he thought might be relevant.

The house had come to life while she was sequestered in Zach's room. Now, young men were coming and going, eating, and watching TV, all seemingly oblivious to the recent death of their housemate.

She went back to her car, and once inside, sent an email to Peter: *Male MSU student with last name Razowski (sp?). Find out anything you can.*

# CHAPTER 8

ONCE SOHNI SAW IT, SHE REALIZED HOW CLOSE KELLY BUR-
gess's apartment was to the murder scene. Jake's report
had told the sad tale of a pajama-clad Kelly crying outside
her apartment the night her boyfriend was killed. The image
had stayed with Sohni, and today she would finally meet the
woman in person.

The small parking lot was filled to capacity, Sohni squeezed
her Acura into a space on the street and walked the block to the
twin, three-story red brick buildings. She climbed the stair-
way to a door on the second level and knocked. A striking
young woman wearing skinny jeans and a tight green knit top
answered the door. Her long and unruly red hair was piled atop
her head, but much like Sohni's, refused to stay in place. The
woman blew a stray piece from her face as she greeted Sohni.

"Hi. You must be Miss Silver." She held the door open
for Sohni. "Come on in. Kelly's still in the shower. She
should be out in a minute, though."

"Are you her roommate?"

"Yeah, I'm Rebecca."

"Nice to meet you, Rebecca. I'm Sohni. I'm with the public defender's office."

"Right. Kelly told me you were stopping by." Her cheery tone and perpetual smile faded. "She said you wanted to talk about Curt's murder. I still can't believe it. One day he was here, and then the next ..."

"Did you know him well?"

"Just through Kelly. But he was here a lot, so we became friends. He was a nice guy. Kelly's having a hard time with it all. It's been rough."

"I bet. What a tragedy. How long had they dated?"

"About six months."

"How did they meet?"

"Kelly and I went to a party at Curt's fraternity house. Kelly was actually still dating her high school boyfriend, Jimmy, at the time, but he goes to Saginaw Valley and wasn't here that weekend. I don't think she was looking to meet someone, but Curt swept her off her feet. He was charming. She immediately broke up with Jimmy, and she and Curt have been together ever since."

Sohni was pleased to find Rebecca chatty, and it took no prodding to elicit information from her. She considered that Rebecca may be a better source of information than Kelly. Perhaps it was Sohni's good fortune that Kelly's appearance was delayed.

"Her old boyfriend couldn't have been happy about that," Sohni said.

"Oh, no, he wasn't. I always thought Jimmy was a bit of a tool, anyway. But he got really angry and blamed Curt for the breakup. Of course, it couldn't be because he was self-absorbed. It had to be someone else's fault."

"What ended up happening with Jimmy? Did he finally accept it?"

"Not really. About two months ago, he showed up unannounced at our apartment while Curt was here. He went ballistic. Started screaming at Curt and getting in his face. He kept yelling that he was going to kick his ass. I think he'd been drinking, so he wasn't acting sane."

"Oh, my god!" Sohni said. "That must have been scary. What did you do?"

"We tried to get Jimmy out the door and away from Curt, but he was too strong for us. We finally called the police. He left before they got here, though. I haven't seen or heard from him since. Not sure if Kelly has either. You'll have to ask her."

Sohni heard footsteps in the hallway, and turned to see a short brunette with a pixie haircut and black-framed glasses. Her face was fixed in a permanent pout.

"Oh, here she is now," Rebecca chirped, seemingly oblivious to the black cloud that swept into the room with her roommate.

The two women couldn't be more different from one another.

Sohni extended her hand to the brunette.

"You must be Kelly. I'm Sohni."

Kelly gave Sohni's hand a weak shake, never changing her expression.

"Sorry I made you wait. I got back from class late."

"No problem. I've enjoyed chatting with Rebecca." Sohni smiled at the roommate, who grinned back. "Would you like to have a seat and talk?"

"Sure."

Rebecca shut herself in her bedroom, leaving Sohni and Kelly alone.

"How are you holding up?" Sohni said.

"Depends on the day."

"Well, as I said on the phone, I'm truly sorry. I won't keep you long. I just have a few questions."

Kelly nodded.

"As you know, a homeless man has been arrested for Curt's murder. His name is Henry Martinez. He often slept at the corner of Hill and Packard, right by the Cottage Inn. Maybe you remember seeing him there?"

"I do remember seeing a homeless man sleeping in that area a few times, but I have no idea if it was the same guy."

"Do you know if Curt had any interaction with him? Did they ever exchange words?"

"Not that I know of. Curt may have given him money or food. He did that quite a bit. Curt didn't have much himself, but he believed in helping people less fortunate. It was one of the things I loved about him."

"But you don't remember him doing that with the man near the Cottage Inn?"

"No. But it doesn't mean he didn't."

"Kelly, when the police interviewed you, you told them that you didn't know of anyone who would want to hurt Curt. Now that some time has passed, is that still the case?"

"Absolutely. He was such a nice guy. He didn't have enemies."

*Except your jealous ex-boyfriend.* "I know he wrote investigative articles. I read the ones he published in The Truth Zone. Do you know if he published any others?"

"I don't think so. He was proud of having his articles published, so I'm sure I would have heard about it if he had others."

"A couple of his articles exposed some unsavory practices. I could see how they could upset the people he wrote about. Do you know if he got any backlash or threats as a result?"

"If he did, I didn't know about them. We only dated for six months, so it could have happened before then. But honestly, he was just a college student writing for a website that few people know about. It's hard to imagine anyone would get upset enough to harm him."

"Do you recall Curt acting strangely or saying anything unusual in the days prior to his death?"

"No. Everything was normal." Kelly's voice cracked, and tears welled in her eyes.

Sohni paused to allow the young woman to regain her composure.

"Tell me a little bit about his relationship with Zach Bender. They seem like a mismatched pair."

"That's true. They grew up so differently, but for whatever reason they clicked. They were like brothers."

"I read Curt's article on fraternity hazing. I got the distinct impression that he was not a fan of fraternities in general."

"You're right. He thought the whole Greek system was pretty stupid."

"Then why did he join Delta Phi?"

"Because of Zach. Zach's dad was a member, and his father before him. Zach was expected to pledge Delta Phi. But he would never be separated from Curt, so he told the fraternity that he and Curt were a package deal. Of course, the frat wanted Zach, son of the rich and famous Robert Bender. So, they agreed. Pledging was important to Zach, so Curt tolerated it. Curt told me that he'd never fitted in, and that he mostly went his own way. But he got to room with Zach, and that was all that mattered."

"Sounds like Curt and Zach were close."

"They were. I admit I sometimes got a little jealous of how close they were, and how much time Curt spent with Zach. I know that sounds awful. It just seemed that he always came ahead of me. Like the night he died. Curt was supposed to be spending the evening with me. But Zach got hockey tickets, and Curt blew me off."

Tears welled in the young woman's eyes again. She continued speaking, but stared ahead with a blank expression.

"He called to tell me he had to take a raincheck on our plans. I was angry, and I told him he was selfish. I hung up on him."

Sohni placed her hand on the woman's arm.

"I'm so sorry, Kelly."

Finally, Kelly's gaze met Sohni's.

"That was the last time I talked to him. It's like a nightmare."

"So that's why he was headed to your apartment after the game ... to make it up to you?"

The young woman nodded, her chin quivering.

"After our phone call, he texted me that he'd come by after the game. But he never showed up." Her voice cracked.

Sohni paused to consider how to best ask her next question.

"Kelly, do you think Jimmy could have hurt Curt?"

Kelly's head shot up, her eyes wide behind her glasses.

"How do you know about Jimmy?"

"This is a murder investigation. It's my job to know. I also know that not long before Curt's murder, Jimmy went a little crazy when he found Curt here. He threatened to hurt him. You had to call the police."

"You can't honestly think Jimmy killed Curt. My god! He was upset because I left him for Curt. It's a normal reaction. He didn't hurt Curt when he was here. He only yelled at him. Look, I've known Jimmy since high school. The idea that he could have anything to do with Curt's death is ridiculous."

"You're probably right. But I have to explore every possibility. Have you ever seen Jimmy violent?"

Kelly hesitated. "Well, he's been in a couple of fights. Just harmless teenage stuff, though. Nobody was seriously hurt."

"What's Jimmy's last name?"

Kelly said nothing, while Sohni sat with pen poised over notepad.

"Why are you asking me about Jimmy, anyway? The police have already arrested the guy who killed Curt."

"Kelly, I wouldn't be here if I believed that."

Kelly frowned. The two women sat in silence for several seconds.

"Lincroft," Kelly finally said. "James Edward Lincroft."

Sohni thanked Kelly for her time, and trekked back to her car, where she messaged Peter with a new name to investigate. She had already found two viable alternative suspects in

Curt's killing, and a ton of reasonable doubt. And her investigation had just begun.

Later that afternoon, Peter called to let her know that he'd found both Theodore "Ted" Razowski and Jimmy Lincroft. They were college students and had no adult criminal records in Michigan. Their social media presences were typical, with viral memes and photos of parties, friends, and family.

Ted, was from a city in northern Ohio, seemed like a silly, teddy bear of a guy. She saw no hints of a darkness that could lead him to stab a man he'd argued with in a parking lot.

Jimmy's posts and tweets, on the other hand, were more inflammatory, with shades of racism and over-the-top pro-Second Amendment memes. His musings weren't overtly violent, but they left her with an uncomfortable feeling. He was from a rural area in northern Michigan, and clearly enjoyed hunting. He had posted no fewer than six pictures of him in hunting gear, holding his dead prey. His love of hunting held no significance on its own, but suggested that he may own hunting knives.

Sohni needed to know more about Jimmy. Unfortunately, neither of the men would speak with Peter, with Jimmy going as far as telling him to "get a warrant," which made no sense. But nonetheless, was revealing.

"Keep digging on Lincroft," she told Peter. "Talk to his friends and classmates if you can. I'd love to know if he was in

Ann Arbor the night of Curt's death, or if someone can verify that he was at least not in Saginaw. If you haven't already, check the darker corners of the Internet, like 4chan. I want to find out if this guy is capable of murder. And see if we can get our hands on the 911 call that Rebecca and Kelly made the night that Jimmy showed up at their apartment."

"You bet. You think we might have a psycho on our hands?"

"It's hard to know. Could very well just be the behavior of an immature young man. But we certainly can't overlook him as a potential suspect."

# CHAPTER 9

A FEW DAYS HAD PASSED SINCE HER CONVERSATION WITH
Peter, so when Sohni discovered that the investigator
had left an envelope on her desk, she assumed it was more
information about Jimmy Lincroft, dumped out the contents
and she started to peruse. She discovered, though, that the
materials were not about Lincroft, but about Henry. And they
were not good.

"Dammit," she muttered.

Spread out on her desk, were her client's criminal records
from Texas. It listed six convictions, and even more arrests.
As her gaze moved down the list of offenses, certain phrases
lunged off the page and pierced her like shards of glass: *Assault
with a deadly weapon. Assault with intent to cause great bodily
harm. Possession of switchblade knife.*

Peter had also obtained some of the police reports and
case documents connected to Henry's arrests. The story they
told was troubling. Her client had been involved in numerous

drunken altercations, some involving the use of a knife. No one was seriously injured, but he had served several thirty- and ninety-day jail sentences. During one altercation, Henry tried to attack a police officer attempting to break up the fight. He missed the officer, but couldn't avoid a conviction for his attempt. To round off the bad acts was a conviction for misdemeanor domestic violence, and a resulting restraining order entered against him on behalf of his wife. For good measure, Peter included filings from Henry's divorce case. Filings that contained the ex-wife's allegations of Henry's chronic drunkenness and increasingly volatile behavior.

Sohni rested her face in her hands. In front of her lay evidence of her client's violent nature, and his past use of a knife as his weapon of choice. She found herself torn between the two images of Henry Martinez. The violent career criminal with an admitted alcohol problem, versus the seemingly sincere man with the soulful pleading eyes.

There was one factor that could account for the different versions of her client ... alcohol. The former version was an alcoholic in free fall, whose functional alcoholism had devolved into a serious illness that destroyed everything it touched. The current version was alcohol-free, allowing him to think and act clearly.

Henry told her that he'd been sober for twenty months, which included the period during which Curt Redmond was murdered. And he had not been arrested during the three years he'd lived in Michigan. Those factors worked in his favor.

As much as Sohni tried to remain optimistic, the news of Henry's prior offenses weighed on her, not because it convinced her that he was guilty, but because it would likely convince a jury that he was. While the prosecution was allowed to introduce evidence of a defendant's past bad acts only for limited purposes, there was no guarantee that she could get the evidence excluded under these circumstances. It could be devastating to Henry's defense.

The prosecution was required to provide notice to her if it intended to introduce his past offenses as evidence at his trial. They had not yet done so, but she figured it was just a matter of time.

She'd deal with that when the time came. Now, it was time for her to leave for a much-overdue lunch with her sister.

Sohni entered the sushi restaurant at 12:14 p.m. located on Washington Street, just off campus, and it was bustling with lunch customers. She spotted Manju at a table for two in the back. Not surprisingly, she was already deep in conversation with another customer. A male customer, of course. Whereas Sohni had little experience with boys and men throughout her life, Manju drew them in like moths to a flame. Though their parents didn't allow Manju to casually date any more than they did Sohni, she became good at flirting when her parents weren't around. Like Sohni's anorexia made her feel a sense of control, Manju seemed to attain that feeling from playing flirting games, with the opposite sex. Men paid attention to her, flattered her, and she could lead them around by their noses. She wasn't cruel, though. The opposite, actually. Nonetheless, she regarded it as a game, even though sometimes she was the only one who knew they were playing.

Manju was attractive, that was true. Her facial features were similar to Sohni's … big, dark eyes and full lips. But Manju had always been fuller figured. Unlike some girls who would have perceived themselves as fat and starved themselves to achieve the waif-like look so popular in today's society, Manju embraced her full figure and dressed to accent her voluptuous features.

But Sohni didn't believe it was her sister's looks that attracted the men to her, as much as her confidence. She had always exuded self-assuredness in everything she did. Sohni knew it was a mask to hide the parental-instilled self-doubt that Manju suffered. But to everyone else, she seemed supremely confident, and men liked confidence in a woman, even if they didn't realize it.

Manju possessed a magnetic pull that caused men to pursue her, and to make fools of themselves when she finally made it clear she wasn't interested. And here she was in the back of Sushi Town, working on her next victim.

Sohni sat at the other side of Manju's table before her sister realized she was there.

"Hey, Sohni. I didn't see you come in."

Sohni smiled a knowing smile.

Manju smiled back and shrugged. "Well, I had time to kill."

A waiter approached their table and dropped off two glasses of water.

"Are you ready to order?" he said.

Intimately familiar with the restaurant's selections, Sohni had no need to crack the menu, so she nodded, as did Manju. Once the sisters sent the waiter away with an order for a cobra roll, a spicy dynamite roll—Manju's, of course—and two side salads, the sisters caught up on each other's lives.

"How are things with Andre?" Sohni said.

Manju shrugged. "Eh …"

"Manju, you mean to tell me another boyfriend has bitten the dust?"

"No, he's still around. He's just not as much fun as I thought he would be. I thought a Frenchman would be more exotic."

"He's French-Canadian, Manju. Canada is not exactly exotic."

Manju laughed. "Yeah, I guess you're right. Maybe my expectations were too high."

"Have you seen Mom and Dad lately?"

"It's been about a month since I've been over there. They bought a new couch and gave me their old one for my basement. I'd like to turn the basement into a room for entertaining, with a bar and a big TV. You know what home prices are like in Ann Arbor. I need to use all the space I have."

"That's a great idea. You do love entertaining. So how were Mom and Dad when you saw them?"

Manju shot a knowing look at Sohni. "You're trying to get me to tell you they're doing well so you don't have to feel guilty for not seeing them more often, aren't you?"

"You know, Manju, can you ever let a thought go unsaid?"

"Um, no. They're doing OK. But I do think Dad is getting worse every time I see him. He still knows who I am, but he has a hard time participating in conversations, and he repeats himself a lot."

"I was afraid you'd say that."

"Sohni, you don't have to feel guilty for choosing not to go over there that often. They re-traumatize you every time you go. They were a lot harder on you than on me, and you've suffered the after-effects of them much more than I have. No one blames you for not wanting to go. And the whole thing with Matt, and them … it's not worth it, just to feel you've fulfilled some obligation only you think you have."

"But with Dad's dementia, I feel like we both need to be there to help his memory, and I feel like I should be helping Mom more."

"They have plenty of money to hire someone to care for Dad, I swear Mom just takes on the burden so she can be a martyr and make everyone else feel bad. Stop letting her games work on you, Sohni."

"Easier said than done."

"How are things going with that new murder case? Martinez, right? That's got to be pretty crazy."

"It's still in the early stages, but I'm surprised at what I've found. You know I can't tell you too much, but let's just say there is a prominent figure pulling some strings in the prosecutor's office."

"Really?" Manju got excited over anything scandalous.

"It's going to make my job harder, but may help on the reasonable doubt front."

"Do you think he did it?"

"Who, Henry? You know I can't tell you that."

"Oh, come on. I'm your sister."

Sohni thought for a moment. "I believe there's a lot of reasonable doubt."

Manju rolled her eyes. "You're such a lawyer. And such a Dudley Do-Right. If I were you, I wouldn't be able to not gossip about my cases."

"I like rules, and I like order. I need to feel I'm in control and on the right side of the rules. You know how things can get if I feel like I'm losing control, or the threat of getting caught doing something wrong."

"Indeed, I do. It'd be like living with Mom and Dad again."

"Good point."

Their food came, and Sohni felt her cheeks redden when Manju's gaze lingered on the waiter's rear end as he left.

"Manju! Do you ever stop?"

Manju cast Sohni a mischievous look.

With her chopsticks, Manju dunked a too-large bite of sushi into her soy sauce, overflowing the cup and splashing brown drops on the table. Caring little about the resulting mess, she shoved the dripping morsel into her mouth. Sohni frowned, then laughed because she could barely resist the urge to grab a clump of napkins and mop up the mess. Instead, she ate her own food, but in Sohni fashion … small bites and no mess. Just like she liked her life.

Sohni's cell phone rang, she fumbled through her purse and hit the accept button just before it went to voicemail.

"Hello."

No response from the other end.

"Hello?"

Still nothing. But someone was there ... she heard breathing. And she was pretty sure she could hear music in the background.

Then the caller was gone.

Sohni checked her phone for the caller's number. It wasn't blocked or unavailable, but she didn't recognize it. She saved it to her contacts with a question mark.

"Who was that?" Manju said.

"I think it was just a solicitor. That'll teach me to not look at the number calling before I answer."

"Sohni, you're lying to me."

"I'm not lying. Geesh, can I just eat my lunch?"

"How many calls like that have you gotten?"

"Like what? Solicitors call all the time, if that's what you mean?"

Manju just stared. Her sister knew her better than anyone else, and could see right through her excuses.

"Well, if you get any more calls from that solicitor, make sure to report them. You know, the Do Not Call list and all."

Sohni knew exactly what Manju meant, and it had nothing to do with the FCC.

Sohni drove straight from the restaurant to the jail. Another meeting with Henry was in order.

As the officer led Henry into the consultation room, Sohni viewed him with a different eye. She tried to picture him as the out-of-control alcoholic depicted in his Texas records and tried to determine if that person was still in him today.

"Hi, Henry."

"Hello, Ma'am."

"Henry, we're in this for the long haul. You can at least call me by my first name." Henry gave her a weary smile, "OK, Sohni."

"Before we start talking about what you should expect over the next several months, we have something to discuss."

She pulled Henry's Texas criminal report from the case file and set the pages down in front of him. Henry scanned the top page until he recognized the nature of the document, then returned his worried gaze to Sohni.

"If I have this, I'm sure the prosecutor does, too. She may try to introduce this at trial. Of course, I will do everything I can to keep it out, but there's no guarantee. So, we can't ignore this. We need to be prepared to explain it. First, though, I need you to walk me through what was going on in your life at that time."

"I was out of control. My drinking went from a couple a week, to a couple a night, to all the time. I was always drunk. I knew it wasn't right and that I had a problem, but the way I was raised, you didn't see shrinks or ask for help. I lost jobs. I pissed off friends. And I lost my wife."

"How do you explain the violent behavior, Henry? You told me your sister kicked you out for your erratic behavior, so I'm guessing it wasn't new?"

"No, it started in Texas. When I'm sober, I'm an easy-going guy. I keep to myself, actually. But when I drank, I changed. I got angry about everything. Anything would piss me off. My counselor has explained to me that I was keeping all my feelings inside until they were like a time bomb. Then, when I drank, that bomb would explode." Henry sighed and shook his head. "Looking back, I can't believe the shit I did."

"You told me you've been sober for twenty months. Have you had any relapses during that time?"

"I only count months of sobriety from my last relapse. A relapse resets the clock. I definitely had some problems staying sober at first. But twenty months ago—actually, more than that now—was my last relapse. Not one since."

"That's great. Can you honestly swear under oath that you were sober at the time of Curt Redmond's murder, and had been for quite some time?"

"Yes, Ma'am."

"And the people who see you regularly will support that?"

"Definitely."

"It sounds like you've also been seeing a counselor to address the anger issues?"

"Yeah. People back home might call me a sissy for it, but I see why people do it. I had no idea I had so much shit going on inside my head."

Sohni chuckled. "I couldn't agree more."

"I also found my way back to God. I lost him years ago. My faith has helped me so much through all of this."

"If needed, do you think those closest to you would testify in court, on your behalf. Like your pastor, your sponsor, your AA leader?"

"I think so."

"OK. One more thing. I've pulled your criminal records from Michigan and Ohio, and there's nothing on them. But I want to verify with you that there's not something out there that's just not reported. Some ticket, some altercation."

"Not that I recall. I wasn't in Ohio very long. Not enough time to get in to trouble. And I've kept my head down since I've been here. No fights, no tickets. I've been doing things the right way, for once. That's why it pisses me off so much that I'm sitting in jail. What do they call it when the opposite happens of what you expect?"

"You mean, irony?"

"Yeah, that's it. This is fucking ironic."

Ironic may have been the word Henry applied to the situation, but as Sohni saw more of this mystery come to light, she opted for a different word, unjust.

Once Sohni returned to her car, she noticed a voicemail on her phone. Now driving, she played it through the Bluetooth connection. The message contained only several seconds of silence.

Then she had a thought and played it again, this time cranking up the volume. Sure enough, it wasn't silence. Someone was on the other end, she could hear the breathing, with background music.

At the first stoplight, she checked the incoming number on the screen. It wasn't the number she'd previously entered into her contacts with a question mark. She saved this number as well, with an exclamation point. One call could be dismissed, but two were no accident.

These calls were intentional. And unsettling.

# CHAPTER 10

S OHNI AWOKE AT 7:32 A.M. IT WAS SATURDAY. THE SUN
streamed through the cracks in the curtains, and she could
hear the birds chirping in the maples outside her bedroom
window. After the sudden plunge in temperatures, Mother
Nature had redeemed herself. Michigan falls were fabulous,
and Ann Arbor was especially beautiful in the autumn, with
its rolling hills, and its big old trees speckled orange and red.
The only downside of living in here in the fall, was Michigan
football Saturdays.

The University of Michigan housed the largest football
stadium in the nation, with crowds typically exceeding a
hundred thousand. While many of them were students, the
majority were not, meaning that tens of thousands of people
converged on Ann Arbor on football Saturdays, creating a
controlled chaos.

As luck would have it, this particular Saturday was the game
between Michigan and Iowa, and it started at noon. This moti-

vated Sohni to rise from her bed despite the early hour. Matt was still asleep beside her, and twice she almost changed her mind and curled up next to him instead. But she had important items on her agenda. She tugged on her robe and headed out to the kitchen for a strong cup of coffee. On her way, she almost tripped over Whiskers, who voiced his annoyance.

"Who told you to sleep in the middle of the hallway, anyway?" She stroked beneath his chin.

Two cups of coffee and a shower later, Sohni was ready to begin her day. First on her list was heading to Zach's to pick up the copy of Curt's files. In the back of her mind, she was hoping to time her visit so that she would run into Curt's parents, who, according to Zach, were visiting today to retrieve Curt's belongings. Sohni certainly didn't look forward to talking to the grieving couple, especially since she represented the man accused of killing their son. But she had to try. She figured Zach and most of his housemates would likely be attending the football game, so the Redmonds would probably arrive well before the game to access Curt's room, and also to avoid heavy traffic.

Sohni also needed to catch Zach at home to get the flash drive he'd prepared for her. She looked at her watch. *Perfect, almost 10:00 a.m.*

Although traffic was already picking up, the drive to the frat house only took ten minutes. The partying had already started at Delta Phi. At least a dozen young men were scattered around the lawn, most participating in a pickup football game. Those on the sidelines held beer cans and flirted with a few young women. They paid little attention to Sohni when she pulled into the drive. As she walked toward the front door, she noticed Zach sitting alone on the porch, holding a bottle of Rolling Rock while occasionally shouting out to the guys playing football. He noticed her just as she began climbing the front porch stairs, and jumped up like a misbehaving child caught in the act.

"I'm sorry," she said. "I didn't mean to startle you."

Zach uttered a low nervous laugh. "That's OK. I just didn't see you coming. I suppose you're here for the flash drive."

"Yeah, I wanted to catch you before the game."

"Good idea. I have it in my room. Come on up."

She followed him upstairs to the same room as before, but it looked different this time. Most of the beer and Coke cans and food containers were cleared away. The room also smelled of disinfectant. Kind of like spraying perfume on a pig, but it did look better. She was happy to see that he was pulling himself together.

As her gaze followed Zach to the desk where the computer sat, she realized they were not alone in the room. A man and woman sat on the bed once occupied by Curt and were quietly sorting through drawers. The couple was so absorbed by their task that they didn't look up when Sohni and Zach entered. She felt like an intruder. The grief and pain in the room was palpable, and these people needed their own time and space to say goodbye to their son. Sohni wondered how she had ever believed she could engage them in a discussion. She would have to forego her questioning ... at least for now.

But her decision was not needed, Zach took over and introduced her to the Redmonds.

"Mr. and Mrs. Redmond."

Cathy and Frank turned their heads toward Sohni.

"This is Miss Silver. She represents the guy who's been arrested for killing Curt."

Sohni felt the blood rise in her face, and the bile rise in her throat. The expressions on the Redmonds' faces did not help matters. Zach wore an innocent look, but she suspected he had intentionally put her in this uncomfortable position. Then again, how mad could she be. He only spoke the truth.

A few seconds of silence passed while she collected herself. Finally, she looked directly at the Redmonds.

"I'm so sorry for your loss."

Still stunned, Cathy and Frank simply continued to stare at her while her discomfort grew. She fought the urge to turn around and run to her car, and reminded herself that she was an adult, and a lawyer. Zach had invited her in, so she had as much right to be there. And she had a client to represent.

Sohni sidled to the other side of the room, where the Redmonds sat.

"It's part of my job to perform some independent investigation of your son's death. I think the police have rushed into this arrest without conducting a thorough investigation."

"Of course, you do," Frank blurted, in an unsteady voice. "That's what you people always say. Anything to get your guy off." He was blushing red, and his hands shook.

Despite her wariness, Sohni continued.

"I know you don't know me, but I can assure you that I'm not some sleazy defense lawyer. I'm with the public defender's office. I represent indigent defendants, and I don't get to pick and choose my clients. My job is not to *get them off*. It's to make sure that they receive the due process to which they're entitled." She took a deep breath. "I represent a lot of guilty people. I admit that. It's not often I say that I have serious doubts about my client's guilt, but I'm saying it now. If Mr. Martinez is guilty, justice will be done. You can rest assured of that. But I'm conducting my own investigation to see if there's something the police missed. And so far, there's been plenty."

She watched the Redmonds' faces change as her words sank in.

"Are you telling me that the police missed evidence?" Frank said.

"That's exactly what I'm telling you. As far as I can tell, they barely conducted any real investigation. I've discovered that there are legitimate suspects that the police never even spoke to."

The man still appeared skeptical. Cathy looked like she wanted to escape.

"Like who?" Frank said.

This was Sohni's chance to gain the trust and cooperation of Curt's parents.

"For instance, did you know that Curt was in a fistfight the night he was killed?"

The man glanced up at Zach. "Is that true, Zach?"

The younger man stared at his feet and nodded slightly. Frank was speechless. His mouth moved, but nothing came out.

"Why did nobody tell us that?" he finally said, to no one in particular.

"I don't know," Sohni replied. "I only found out during my own investigation."

Frank narrowed his eyes, and Sohni wasn't sure if the man's apparent anger was directed at her, or at the police.

"Curt was also assaulted by his girlfriend's jealous ex-boyfriend only a few months ago. Another fact that I wouldn't have known if I hadn't interviewed witnesses myself."

The man again looked to Zach, who still stared at his feet and offered no response.

"The evidence against my client is questionable, a wallet, and a bloody knife in a bag. I think it's a real possibility that someone else committed the crime and made it look like my client did it. The problem is that the police are being short-sighted."

She glanced at the young man standing only feet away, and lowered her voice.

"I think … a certain powerful person … may be unduly influencing the investigation. I understand that person's motivation," she subtly tilted her head toward Zach, "but the resulting failure to thoroughly investigate is abhorrent. The prosecution is convinced they've got their man, but I'm not sure they do. I think the person who killed your son may still be out there."

Cathy Redmond began to weep. Her husband glanced, but made no move to comfort her, obviously wrapped up in his own thoughts. He looked torn, unsure what to believe.

"You better not be screwing with us," he finally said, and glared at Sohni.

"I promise you, I'm not. I just want to get to the truth. I know it sounds strange, but you and I want the same thing. To find out who really killed your son."

She turned to Zach, who seemed frozen in place at the computer desk. Beads of sweat lined his forehead.

"I should be going," she said.

Emerging from his stupor, Zach pulled open one of the desk drawers, grabbed the storage device and handed it to her.

"Thanks." She then turned to face the Redmonds. "It was nice meeting you. I wish it was under better circumstances. I really am sorry about your son."

She turned again and walked toward the door. After stepping into the hall, she heard Frank call out, "Miss Silver."

She popped her head back into the room.

"Yes?"

"If it's true that my son's killer might still be out there, what can I do to help find him?"

Sohni's heart raced.

"Can I call you? We could talk more."

The man looked hesitant. Sohni understood his conflicting feelings. He was wary to trust the attorney representing the man accused of killing his son. But on the other hand, she could tell that he couldn't stand the possibility that his son's killer might go free.

Sighing, he scribbled something on a piece of scrap paper and held it out for her.

"This is my cell. I'll be expecting your call."

Back in her car, she placed Frank's phone number and the flash drive in her purse and started the ignition. Mixed emotions flitted through her mind. Excitement at having gained the cooperation of the victim's parents. Guilt for putting them through this. And uncertainty about all of it. What a fool she would look like if it turned out Henry really was the killer. Even worse, the Redmonds would think she had lied to them, used them even.

When Sohni returned home, Matt was already positioned in front of the TV, with a big bowl of pretzels and a beer. He loved college football. He started watching when the pregame shows began, and didn't leave the couch until the last game of the day was over.

"Beer before noon?" she said. "Trying to relive your college days, dear?"

He just smiled and winked, barely removing his gaze from the screen. That was one of those moments when she was reminded how boyish her husband looked, even though he was forty-two. He stood six-foot in his stocking feet, and was built long and lean, with unruly dark curls framing his face. There wasn't a stitch of gray in those locks. His bright green eyes sparkled impishly, and his sense of humor was irrepressible. He was the kind of person who made you feel good just being around him. He was always in a good mood, and his childlike excitement was contagious. No mystery why he was such a popular professor.

Sohni stepped into a sun-speckled room that served as their home office, her favorite place in the house. It was carpeted in a thick gray plush, and a dozen framed black and white photos hung on the walls, which contrasted with the burgundy paint.

The photos documented Matt and Sohni's relationship, from their first New Year's Eve together, through to the present. She had designed and decorated the room, selecting each photograph and each piece of furniture.

The room's one large window overlooked their backyard and the flowerbeds she'd tend with diligence. In the morning, sunlight streamed through that window and warmed whoever sat at the antique desk on the opposite wall. At that time of day, leaves from the mature trees in the yard diffused the sunlight, resulting in a kaleidoscope effect.

Sohni took her place at the oak desk and booted up the modern PC that sat atop it. She inserted the flash drive into the computer and began by perusing the files identified as word processing documents, where she found what one would expect to find on any college student's computer, notes and papers, Curt's résumé and some cover letters, as well as other miscellaneous and seemingly irrelevant items. While the documents provided plenty of information about Curt, they provided no insight into his murder.

Sohni had just begun reviewing his emails when she heard Matt hollering from the family room. By the sound of things, Michigan had just scored. She normally enjoyed watching football with Matt, but today she had too much on her mind. She noted, though, that her absence didn't seem to diminish Matt's enthusiasm. Football, beer, and pretzels … what more could a man want?

She located the email messages from Curt's inbox. There were fifteen in total, eight had been received before his death, and seven after. Finding nothing useful, Sohni turned to the messages the young man had saved—eighty-two—spread across five folders. Still nothing. Finally, she browsed through the three hundred messages stored in the deleted and sent folders. Just when Sohni began to think she was wasting her time, she came across a message Curt had sent to a *misley*, at a university email address. It read: *Are you sure about this? This could be huge. Let me look into it. I'll get back to you soon.*

He had sent it a week before he was killed. Unfortunately, the message did not include any additional text to help identify what he was referring to.

She again searched all of Curt's email folders but found no other messages to, or from *misley*. So, she selected the print command, and the laser printer whirred on the other end of the desk.

"Interesting," she muttered, examining the message again.

After reading the message for the third time, Sohni was reminded of Curt's comments to his editor about his latest story. Was this message about the lead he'd mentioned to Tracy Zorn? If so, who was *misley*, and why were there no other messages to or from that person? Then again, it could have been about something innocent, like a concert or a party. But there was no way to know without the rest of the email string. This isolated email didn't seem to make much sense. In fact, something seemed wrong with all of Curt's files, but she couldn't put her finger on what it was.

Sohni needed to clear her head, she wandered out to the kitchen and grabbed a bottle of Vitaminwater® before joining Matt on the couch. University of Michigan was up, 14 to 3 with less than a minute left in the first half. The minute passed uneventfully, and at halftime Matt went to the kitchen to make them both turkey sandwiches. While she was waiting, she picked up that day's *Michigan Courier.*

The tension caused by Curt's murder and Henry's arrest could still be felt in the community. The authorities reassured residents that patrols had been stepped up, both on and off campus, and that all suspicious individuals and situations were being thoroughly investigated. While this may have appeased those worried about their safety, it only inflamed the homeless rights activists, who lashed out at the mayor and the police. They argued that *suspicious individuals* equaled *homeless individuals*, and that this new policy did nothing to make the streets safer, but only resulted in the increased harassment of the homeless. The mayor assured the community that the police and campus security were doing their best to walk the line between investigating suspicious circumstances, and respecting the rights of individuals.

"It's a no-win situation," Sohni said.

"What is?" Matt returned from the kitchen with two plates overflowing with food.

"Trying to please everyone." She pointed to the newspaper article. "No matter what they do to try to make people feel safe, someone will be unhappy. Either they're doing too much, or not enough."

Then she looked up and noticed the huge quantity of food her husband had piled on the plates. The turkey sandwiches were enormous, and stuffed with lettuce, tomato, and two kinds of cheese. In addition, the sagging cardboard plates held handfuls of baby carrots and mounds of potato chips.

"How many people do you think we're feeding?" She chuckled.

Matt shrugged. "Football makes me hungry." He shoved a whole baby carrot in his mouth.

"You know that at my pace it would take me probably the entire day to eat this much."

She suspected he had intentionally overfilled her plate in the hope that she'd forget about her methodical eating style and just binge on what was in front of her. She was aware, though it was never spoken, that he hoped, one day, she'd get past the effects of her anorexia and be able to enjoy scarfing down a meal with him. With enough counseling and time, maybe she would. But it wasn't going to be today.

Sohni returned her plate to the kitchen, she cut the sandwich in half and placed one in a storage bag for later. She grabbed all but four of the carrots and put them back in their bag. All the potato chips were returned from where they came. Chips were full of fat and empty calories. They had no place on her plate.

She sat back down on the couch with a more reasonable lunch.

"That's much better." She made a face at her husband.

He smiled but shook his head. "It was worth a try."

Sohni took a delicate bite of her sandwich, wiped the mustard from her chin, and dropped a bite of turkey on the floor for Whiskers, who waited patiently at her feet.

She bolted upright. "That's it!"

Startled by her outburst, the cat retreated to a safe place under a nearby chair, obviously annoyed at having his lunch interrupted. Matt eyed her, but said nothing as she dashed back into the office. His interest piqued, he followed her.

"What is it?" he said.

She pulled up the contents of the flash drive again.

"The Truth Zone."

Matt still looked puzzled, but remained silent while she skimmed the contents displayed on her screen.

"Curt wrote for The Truth Zone. Everyone I've spoken to has told me how he saw himself an aspiring investigative reporter. His editor told me that he took copious notes. There should be notes, emails, something related to his investigative reporting on here, but there isn't. Even the articles he's published aren't here. That's what's missing."

"Is it possible his roommate just forgot to give you those files?"

"Sure, it's possible. And I'll call him to double-check. But it's more than that. You see, it's not just word processing files that are missing. There are no emails either, not from his editor, or from sources. It's as though his work for The Truth Zone didn't even exist."

"Could he have kept them somewhere else?" Matt said.

"I suppose. But I don't know where that would be."

"What if he didn't store anything on the hard drive because he was afraid someone could access it? After all, college students take their laptops everywhere, classes, coffee shops, libraries. What if he stored it all on portable media that he kept somewhere safe?"

"That's a great idea. I'll ask Zach if he knows where Curt kept his journalism materials." She flashed a coy smile at her husband. "We make a pretty good team, you know that?"

He smiled back, then looked at the clock hanging on the office wall, and a look of terror spread across his face. He made an about face and raced back to the family room, where he resumed his position in front of the TV.

"Speaking of teams ..." He turned up the volume as the athletes executed the first play of the second half.

Sohni joined him on the couch and tried to watch the game, but she found it difficult to focus. She needed to find out who *misley* was and their relationship to Curt. She also needed to call Zach about Curt's missing materials. Now was not the time, though. It was football Saturday in Ann Arbor. Besides, there were worse things than spending a Saturday with her two favorite men.

Michigan won 28 to 13. Shortly after the game, Sohni found herself all alone in a quiet house. Matt had changed his clothes and headed out for a run. And Whiskers, his belly full of turkey, snored lightly on their bed. She picked up her phone and punched in the number to Zach Bender's cell phone. He picked up on the first ring, panting.

"Hi, Zach. It's Sohni Silver."

"Oh, hey. I'm just on my way out. What do you need?"

"I'm just following up on the contents you gave me, from Curt's computer. It appears that there's nothing on the drive regarding any of the articles he wrote for The Truth Zone, including notes, emails, or even the articles themselves."

"I don't know what to tell you. I copied everything exactly like I said I would."

"Did he use external storage media, like flash drives or cloud storage, perhaps?"

"I have no idea. That wasn't part of our agreement."

"Of course. I'm just wondering if you knew."

"I don't. Besides, his parents took all his stuff home, so you'd have to contact them." Without a goodbye, he hung up.

Sohni would have no choice but to contact the Redmonds, a task she dreaded. It was better than the alternative, though, which was to serve them with subpoenas for the items. She didn't want to put them through that. She had their potential cooperation for the time being, so it would be better to try to gain access to Curt's property on friendly terms. Once again, her ire rose as she reflected on the police not taking possession of the victim's electronic data to review, as part of their investigation.

She would call Frank on Monday, but identifying *misley* didn't have to wait. Sohni got on the Internet and pulled up the University of Michigan online directory, which provided information about individuals affiliated with the university, including students, faculty, and staff. Using Matt's login information, she searched for the person who matched the email address misley@umich.edu. In seconds, the identification of Curt's mysterious email correspondent appeared on the screen in front of her, Marcus Isley, a graduate student in the material science and engineering program. And lucky for her, the listing included his phone number and campus address.

"No time like the present."

Her call went to voicemail. She left a message with her number, and asked him to give her a call back.

With nothing to do but wait, Sohni decided to confront the inevitable. She changed into nicer clothes, applied makeup, and embarked on the twenty-minute drive to her parents' house. It would raise her stress level, but assuage her guilt.

# CHAPTER 11

AFTER SEVERAL ADJOURNMENTS, THE DATE WAS FINALLY set for Henry's preliminary examination, December 3rd, which was only five days away. Despite numerous phone calls to Marcus Isley, and messages nearly begging him to call her back, it had become clear that he was not going to do so. Desperate, she called Peter with a request for some internet sleuthing.

"Hey, Peter, I need your help."

"Sure."

"I've been trying to reach a graduate student at U of M, by the name of Marcus Isley in connection with the Martinez case. He won't return my calls, so I need to get creative. I have his local address. It seems pretty likely that he'd have at least one roommate. If I give you the address, do you think you can identify the other people who live there?"

"Probably. Email me the address and I'll see what I can come up with."

"Awesome! Thanks, Peter."

Ten minutes later, Peter's reply email dinged into her inbox. Though Peter had found several people associated with the address—it was a rental property, after all—he highlighted one who appeared to currently live there, Sambhunath Patel. And Peter listed three phone numbers possibly associated with him.

She called the first, which was disconnected. The second went to a voicemail for a woman. Finally, the third number was answered by a young man with an accent that Sohni identified as Indian. The man, who called himself Sammy, informed Sohni that he and Marc shared an apartment, but that he hadn't seen Marc in a couple of months and hadn't spoken to him lately.

"Marc suddenly left school in early October and moved back with his parents in Pennsylvania," Sammy said.

"Do you remember the exact day he left?"

"I think it was around the second week of October. I don't recall the exact date, but I know it was the day after the student was killed. It was all over the news that day."

"Do you mean Curt Redmond, the student stabbed on Hill Street?"

"Right, that guy."

She informed Sammy that Curt Redmond's death was the reason she was trying to reach Marc.

"I think they knew each other," she said. "Do you know if that's the case?"

"I don't. But I did wonder if there was a connection between Marc leaving, and the murder."

"What makes you say that?"

"The way Marc acted when he heard about it. It was the morning after he died, and Marc and I were both eating breakfast, watching a morning show. It broke to the local news, and they were at the location where they found his body. We were interested, of course, because it was so close. But Marc's reaction changed once the reporter said it was Curtis Redmond."

"How did it change?"

"He froze, with his spoonful of cereal literally hanging in midair. He sat that way for several seconds. You've heard the expression when blood drains from a person's face? Well, that's exactly what happened. He turned pale. He looked like he was going to be sick. Then he got up from the table without finishing his food, and said he had to make a phone call. He shut himself in his room, and was still in there when I left for class."

"Did he ever explain his behavior?"

"No. I didn't see him again until later that day when I got home. He had packed up a bunch of his stuff and was loading it in his car. He told me he was going back home to Pennsylvania. He never gave me a sensible explanation for leaving ... just that he was going through a rough time and needed to be with his family. But I swear, before he heard about Curt's death, he was fine. Just that morning, we were joking around and making plans for the weekend. It was very strange. Based on his reaction, I had to wonder if his leaving had something to do with the murder."

"And you have no idea why he would be so upset over it?"

"Well, obviously it was concerning to both of us, generally, as students here. But I still don't have a clue why he freaked out like that."

Silence filled the line, both of them equally puzzled. Goose-bumps sprouted across her skin, all her senses telling her that Marc Isley possessed information crucial to this case. She highly doubted that the police, or Pauline, knew about Marc. Once again, it was up to her to get to the truth.

"Sammy, I think we both agree that Marc may have important information about Curt Redmond's murder, and that he may even be in danger himself. Would you mind if we put our heads together to see what we can figure out?"

Sammy hesitated. "I honestly don't know what I can tell you. I don't know how he knew Curt Redmond."

"I understand. But maybe if you just tell me a little about Marc — what he was involved in — who his friends were, I can take it from there. The way I see it, Sammy, if a homeless man truly killed Curt to take his wallet, why would that cause Marc to flee? Marc has to know something that the rest of us don't, and like I said, he may even be in danger himself. If I can figure out his connection to Curt, it helps not only my client, but also Marc."

"I agree," Sammy said. "I want to know what frightened him so badly. But why aren't the police asking these questions, instead of you. I guess I'd feel more comfortable speaking to them."

"I also wish the police were asking you these questions. Or better yet, asking Marc. But they believe they have arrested the right man. They have chosen to investigate no further. It was only through my own investigation that I came across Marc's name and an email he had exchanged with the victim. You're free to call the police and tell them what you know. In fact, I welcome it. But I don't know if they would follow the lead, especially since the case has now been handed off to the prosecutor. I, however, have significant motivation to figure out this mystery."

"All right. I'll tell you what I can about Marc. He's a good guy. I've known him since we were freshmen, and he's never been involved in anything weird or illegal, making this situation all the stranger. He's an excellent student, always got good grades. He got his bachelor's last year, and now he's a graduate student in the materials science and engineering program. His ultimate goal is to get his PhD and become a professor. He has a few other friends he hangs out with. All of them are fellow students. We all played a lot of video games. In fact, that's how he spent most of his free time." Sammy paused. "Oh, yeah, he also worked part-time as a research assistant for Professor Ito, in the material science department. Marcus performed quite a bit of materials testing for various projects submitted to the university. He really enjoyed that part of his job. He loved getting in the lab and using the equipment. He said it made him feel like a mad scientist." Sammy chuckled.

"When Marc left, did he leave a computer or cell phone behind?"

"Nope. His computer was the first thing he packed up. He always carried his cell phone, so I'm sure that went along as well."

Can you think of anything he said recently? Any off-handed comment that seemed out of the ordinary, noteworthy?"

"I really can't. But I'll think on it. Maybe I'll remember something."

"I have a cell number for Marc, but he won't return my calls."

"That's not surprising. He doesn't seem interested in talking to any of his friends, either. He called me once since he's been gone to let me know he's OK, and asked me to let the rest of our friends know as well. But that's it."

"Do you have any other numbers for him? A landline at his parents? His parents' cell phones? Do you know his parents' address?"

Sammy gave her Marc's home address in Pennsylvania, as well as a landline number at his parents' house. She then gave Sammy her own contact information.

"Call me if you think of anything," she said. "And have Marc call me if you hear from him."

After her conversation with Sammy, she felt more convinced than ever that Henry did not kill Curtis Redmond. Marc Isley's actions suggested that Curt's killer acted with forethought, that he targeted Curt specifically, and that he had reason to target Marc as well. The new information shed light on the text of Curt's email to Marc Isley. He'd written: *This could be huge. Let me look into it.* Curt's words implied that Marc had given him some significant information, maybe a lead for a new story, and that Curt was going to investigate further. A week later, he was murdered. And in response, Marc left school without explanation. That could not be a coincidence.

From her office phone, Sohni placed a call to the landline number Sammy had provided for Marc, but like all the others, it went to voicemail. After leaving a message, she hung up, but the phone rang before she moved her hand away. Hopeful that it was Marc, she snatched up the receiver.

"Sohni Silver."

Only breathing on the other end. And low music.

"Who is this?"

*Click.* The line went dead.

Sohni engaged in her usual ritual upon arriving home that evening, cuddled Whiskers to reassure him she hadn't been eaten by predators, then changed into her favorite outfit. She grabbed a Diet Coke from the fridge and settled on the couch with a Cobb salad before tuning in to an episode of Jeopardy. Matt wasn't home yet. He had a standing weekly pickle ball game with his colleague Darnell. Pickleball then led to dinner and drinks, so she didn't expect him until at least ten.

Halfway through the nine o'clock legal drama that had become Sohni's latest guilty pleasure, she was startled by the blaring of a car alarm. She moved to her front window to find her Acura's lights blinking. She snatched up her key fob and ran outside, pushing on buttons until the horrible noise finally ceased.

More than once she had found her neighbor's cat perched on the roof of her car. She assumed the animal had made a hard landing and triggered the alarm. Poor thing probably had a heart attack.

Sohni strolled around the car to verify that everything was intact. As she was about to return inside, she noticed that one of her tires was flat. She checked another, also flat. Her tires had been slashed. All four of them. She scanned the neighborhood. For the first time ever, the tall shadows of the oak trees frightened her, seeming to conceal danger in their blackness. She hurried into the house and locked the door, her heart pounding.

After verifying that every window and door was locked, she debated her next move. There was no need to call 911 because she was not in any immediate danger. But such an aggressive act needed to be reported right away, especially if the perpetrator left behind any evidence that could identify them. She called the Ann Arbor Police Department's non-emergency number. There was a car in the area, an officer informed her, and it would head over right away.

When the knock on the door came, Sohni used the peephole to verify that the person outside was a uniformed police officer. She joined him on the porch and led him to her vehicle. When he shined his flashlight on her car, they caught a glimpse of something she hadn't previously noticed. Someone had scratched a word into the paint of the driver's side door, DEAD.

Sohni started to cry.

At 10:16 p.m. the police were completing their collection of evidence in her driveway, and Matt's Volvo came to a stop in

front of their house. Sohni had forgotten to warn him of the police presence. Looking panicked, he took in the scene, then ran through the garage and into the house.

"Sohni!"

She met him at the door. "I'm here. I'm OK."

"Thank God. What the hell is going on out there?"

She brought him up to speed on the events of the last few hours.

"Why didn't you call me? I would've come straight home."

"I know you would've. I didn't want to ruin your night. The police came right away. I wasn't in any danger."

"Not in any danger! Are you serious?"

"Matt, I'm OK. It's just property damage."

Matt opened his mouth to object, but he noticed Sohni's barely held back tears. Instead, he wrapped his arms around her. She sank into him, letting a few tears fall onto his shirt. She was physically and mentally exhausted, and wanted nothing more than to take a shower, slip into her pajamas, and curl up in bed with her husband.

"Would you mind checking in with the guys outside?" she said. "I'd really like to go and take a hot shower."

"Of course."

"Please check on Whiskers, too. He's been terrified by all the excitement. I think he's hiding somewhere."

Matt chuckled. "Yes, I'll check on the cat, too."

"Thanks. I love you, Matt."

"I love you too, hon."

Sohni turned the shower as hot as she could stand, the steam rolling through the bathroom. She stood beneath the shower head as the water washed away the tension. The police were on the case, Matt was home, and everything was fine. In the back of her mind, though, she knew that she had to return to work on Monday and do her job. Though Matt had always expressed concerns about the potential dangers of her line of work, she'd dismissed them, chalking them up to his protectiveness. But she had no doubts that this night's event was connected to her work as a public defender, most likely the Martinez case. And that was something she'd have to deal with sooner or later.

When she emerged from the bathroom, she was happy to find Whiskers sleeping on her bed. Matt must have discovered his hiding spot and relocated him to his favorite place. In her robe and slippers, her hair still damp, she lay on the bed next to the warm ball of fur, and closed her eyes. Sleep came quickly.

"You know we need to talk about last night," Matt said.

Sohni, still in her robe and slippers, sat at the kitchen table with her husband, sipping on her coffee. The specter of the previous night's events hung between them.

"I know," Sohni replied.

The tow truck had hauled away her car that morning. Through the front window, she could see remnants of fingerprint dust and a forgotten latex glove, reminders of the previous night.

"I plan to speak with Helen today," Sohni said, "as well as building security. I'll be much more attentive to my surroundings, too. Plus, we'll see if the police found any usable evidence to identify the guy. There were bound to be doorbell cams or other security cameras in the neighborhood that were active at the time."

Matt said nothing, but the set of his jaw spoke volumes.

"What are you thinking?" Sohni said.

"Why didn't you tell me about the phone calls?"

"What phone calls?"

"Last night, the officer said to let him know if you received any more threatening phone calls. What was he talking about?"

She hadn't wanted him to overreact.

"Oh, those calls. I wouldn't say they were threatening. They were just odd. And there were only three of them. Just some person on the other end saying nothing for several seconds, then hanging up."

"If they were no big deal, then why did you tell the police about them?"

"Well, in light of what happened last night, they took on a new meaning. I just mentioned them in case they were relevant."

"Sohni, you should have told me. If I'd known, I wouldn't have left you alone last night."

"Did it ever occur to you that that's exactly why I didn't tell you?"

Matt opened his mouth to speak, but closed it again. Her words had hit home.

They sat in silence for several minutes.

"I'm having a security system installed right away," Matt finally said.

Sohni couldn't argue. After this week, it probably wasn't a terrible idea.

"OK."

"And Sohni, if I promise to stop being so overprotective, will you promise to not keep things from me?"

It was a discussion that was long overdue, and she was happy to finally address the issue.

"It's a deal, Mr. Silver. But you have to promise me one more thing."

"What's that?"

"No matter what I tell you, you won't tell my parents."

Matt laughed. "I'm overprotective, woman. Not insane."

# CHAPTER 12

SOHNI WAS RUNNING LATE. HER PROBABLE CAUSE CONFERence had lasted longer than expected, and Henry's preliminary examination was scheduled to begin in two minutes. She had forgone lunch, expecting to grab something between cases, but now her rumbling stomach would have to wait. After a pit stop to use the restroom and apply a cool paper towel to her face, she strode to Judge Becker's courtroom, scrolling through her unread emails that had accumulated during her conference, and noting a text from Matt that would have to go unanswered for the time being.

When she stepped through the courtroom door, she halted, her breath catching in her throat. The place was a madhouse. Every available seat was occupied. Those unable to find seats had taken to standing in the aisle. The court officers were doing their best to clear the aisle and control the crowd, but it was a daunting task that was taking a while. Sohni noticed reporters and sketch artists among the spectators in the front row.

The sheer number of people in the small space warmed the room to an uncomfortable temperature, and created a funk that made Sohni scrunch up her nose. The noise level was no better, with each person trying to be heard over his neighbor.

She cursed herself for underestimating the public's interest in this case. To her, today's proceedings was a simple preliminary examination, like so many others she had conducted. But for the public, it was another opportunity to see the accused. And to the media, it was more grist for the mill.

Sohni had never been involved in a case as high profile as this, and she found all the commotion unnerving. She was also worried about how the audience would react to Henry, and vice versa. She was relieved to see three armed deputies positioned at various locations around the courtroom, ready to subdue any troublemakers.

Sohni weaved through the crowd, thankful that the deputies had diverted spectators from the jury box, where Sohni now joined other attorneys taking refuge from the storm.

"Can you believe this?" said a fellow refugee, shaking his head in disbelief.

"I've never seen anything like it," Sohni replied.

Moments later, the court officer announced the entrance of the judge. Wearing a disapproving look, Judge Becker surveyed the mass of humanity that had managed to squeeze into his courtroom. It was obvious that the crowd and the noise made him uncomfortable. One of the deputies—a squat man wearing a blond crew cut and a holstered handgun—shouted above the din, demanding silence and threatening those who were inclined to disobey. He informed the crowd that anyone who disrupted proceedings that day would find himself in a jail cell.

The room quietened.

Judge Becker swiveled to face his clerk, who sat at his lower right. She selected a file from the stack before her and handed it to the judge, who nodded his approval.

The clerk called, *"People v. Martinez."*

Undoubtedly, Judge Becker's strategy was to dispense of the matter that drew the gawkers as quickly as possible.

Sohni hurried to take her place at the defendant's table, to the right of the podium, and felt dozens of eyes follow her. At the table, she opened her briefcase and arranged her papers, trying to ignore the undesired attention.

During her time at the public defender's office, Sohni had taken part in at least one hundred preliminary exams, or *prelims*, as they were commonly called. In Michigan, every defendant in a felony case was entitled to a prelim, an evidentiary hearing held for the purpose of determining if probable cause existed to bind over the defendant for trial. The prosecutor had to prove, by a preponderance of the evidence, that it's more likely than not that a crime was committed, and that the defendant had committed that crime. Unlike the reasonable doubt standard applicable at trial, the lower standard of proof applied during the prelim was much easier to meet. Only once has a client of Sohni's been released after a judge found that no probable cause existed to bind him over. And that was an extreme situation where the police never should have made the arrest in the first place.

It was not uncommon for defense attorneys to waive prelims, especially in a case where a finding of probable cause is a virtual certainty. But it would be crazy to do so in a case of this nature. The seriousness of the charges against Henry required that Sohni hold the prosecution to the highest standards, forcing it to prove its case every step of the way. Plus, she needed to find out if, as it seemed, the prosecution's case really revolved solely around the items found in Henry's bag. In fact, she looked forward to Henry's prelim so she could pin down the prosecution's strategy.

Sohni had not felt nervous in a courtroom in many years, so she was surprised at the butterflies in her stomach as she stood before the judge. Fortunately, the attention was not on her for long. A moment later, one of the deputies entered the courtroom, accompanied by Henry, and the room fell silent as every person in the room, Sohni included, stared at the small Mexican man accused of a heinous crime. She caught Henry's eye and smiled in what she hoped was a reassuring manner. He nodded in response, but kept his gaze to the ground, obviously startled by the courtroom scene. The deputy led Henry to the defense table where Sohni waited.

Pauline had taken her place at the table opposite Sohni, along with a younger male attorney from the prosecutor's office. She caught Pauline's eye and smiled and nodded. Pauline returned the gesture.

As frustrating as Pauline could be, she was a worthy adversary. Sohni noticed, though, that the usually unflappable prosecutor looked uneasy. Like Sohni, Pauline was unaccustomed to overflowing courtrooms and the media circus that this case had become. Sohni understood well, how even an experienced prosecutor like Pauline, or a seasoned defense attorney such as herself, could be intimidated by this barely controlled chaos.

"We are here today for a preliminary examination in the case of *People v. Martinez*," Judge Becker announced. "Are the parties prepared to proceed?"

"Yes, Judge," the ladies said, in unison.

"Good. Counsel, please state your appearances for the record."

Appearances duly noted, and stipulated matters put on the record, the judge ordered the prosecution to call its first witness.

The prosecution typically won't present all its evidence at the preliminary exam, instead they only introduce enough to meet the burden of proof, this prelim was no exception. The standard was an easy one to meet, defense attorneys can only call their own witnesses if they had contrary testimony to the prosecution. Sohni had no such witness. Over the next ninety-five minutes, four prosecution witnesses took the stand.

Pauline began by calling the first officer to arrive at the scene of the crime, Heather Sonderheim. The officer's brief testimony detailed the call she received from the dispatcher, what she found when she arrived, and how she secured the crime scene. This information was intended to set the scene. Sohni had no dispute, and saw no need to cross examine.

That was not the case for Pauline's second witness, John Townsend, the officer who arrested Henry and found the knife and wallet in Henry's bag. Sohni frowned as Officer Townsend devoted an inordinate amount of time discussing Henry's alleged assault on his partner. And the murmuring crowd fell silent as the officer described finding the bloody knife in Henry's bag. As this hearing covered not only the murder charge against Henry, but also the resisting and obstructing charge, Sohni felt compelled to rebut the image conjured by the officer's description of Henry's actions at the soup kitchen. She needed to repaint the scene to make the judge understand that Henry was startled awake, and as many homeless people do, he reacted by seeking to protect himself from a perceived danger. He did not intentionally try to punch a police officer.

"When you entered the soup kitchen, Mr. Martinez was sleeping, wasn't he?" Sohni said.

"He appeared to be."

"His eyes were closed, weren't they?"

"I believe so."

"And he was sitting still, wasn't he?"

"I believe so."

"And you woke him up by grabbing his shoulder, didn't you?"

"I put my hand on his shoulder."

"Well, actually, you gripped his shoulder pretty firmly, didn't you?"

"I don't know what you mean by *firmly*. I put my hand on his shoulder to wake him up. I wasn't rough with him, if that's what you're implying."

The workers at the soup kitchen had told Sohni's investigator that Officer Townsend grabbed Henry's shoulder so hard that his fingers made imprints on Henry's shirt. In their version of events, Henry startled into wakefulness as though he had been struck, and immediately jumped to his feet, ready to battle an unknown assailant.

"If witnesses stated that you grabbed the defendant's shoulder hard enough to make him startle awake as though in pain, they'd be lying?"

Pauline shot up like a jack-in-the-box. "Objection. Hearsay."

"Sustained," said Judge Becker.

It was hearsay, of course. But you can't un-ring a bell.

"Officer," Sohni continued, "the defendant woke pretty quickly when you grabbed his shoulder, didn't he?"

"Yeah, I would say so."

The witness answered before Pauline could object, unwittingly conceding that he *grabbed* Henry's shoulder.

"And he jumped up from the couch where he was sleeping as he awoke, didn't he?"

"Yes."

"And it was at that point that he took a swing, right?"

"Yes."

"He didn't actually hit you or your partner, did he?"

"No, fortunately."

"How far away from you was the defendant when he swung with his hand?"

"I'd say less than a foot."

"And your partner? How far away was she from the defendant?"

"She was right next to me, so I'd say the same distance."

"So, both of you were less than a foot away from the defendant when he swung his hand. But he didn't hit either of you, correct?"

"Correct."

"And the defendant did not behave in a violent manner while he was in your police car on the way to the station, did he?"

"No. But he was handcuffed."

"He could have pounded on things with his hands or the handcuffs if he wanted to, right?"

"That's true."

"But he didn't, did he?"

"No, he didn't."

"And he didn't kick, did he?"

"No."

"And he didn't yell or swear at you, did he?"

"No."

"He was a model citizen while riding in the police car, wasn't he?"

Officer Townsend cackled. "Yeah, model citizen."

"And he did not behave in a violent manner while he was at the police station, did he?"

"No."

"So, the only time you witnessed the defendant act in a way that could suggest violence was right after you grabbed his shoulder and woke him up, right?"

"That's correct."

Sohni moved on to the contents of the bag.

"As you testified previously, the defendant was asleep when you arrived at the soup kitchen?"

"Yes."

"And his bag, the one in which you found the knife and the victim's wallet, was beside him on the couch?"

"Yes."

"The bag has a long zipper that runs across the top of it, right?"

"Yes."

"Was that zipper locked?"

"No."

"So, to access the inside of the bag, one would only need to unzip the zipper?"

"Correct."

"How many people were present at the soup kitchen when you arrived that day?"

"I would say about fifty people, probably eight employees or volunteers, and the rest were guests."

"So, it was crowded."

"Yes, I would say so."

"Other homeless guests were sitting on the same couch as the defendant, weren't they?"

"Yes."

"The first time you saw the knife or the wallet in the defendant's bag was when you got back to the police station with the defendant, right?"

"Right."

"So, you didn't see who placed the knife and wallet into the defendant's bag, did you?"

"No."

"And you don't know who placed those items in the bag, do you?"

"No."

"And you don't know when they were placed in the bag, do you?

"No."

"One last question. When you purportedly found the victim's wallet in Mr. Martinez's bag, where exactly was it located?"

"It was tucked in an inside pocket."

"Did that pocket have a zipper?"

"No, it was open at the top."

"And how big was that pocket?"

"Oh, I'd say approximately six inches deep, maybe seven inches across."

"No more questions, your honor."

The crowd murmured as Sohni returned to her seat. But a "silence!" from deputy crew cut the outburst.

Sohni finally had her answer, Curt's wallet was concealed in the inside pocket of Henry's bag, which explained why he didn't find it right away. She felt good.

Pauline then called to the stand the prosecution's third witness, the lead crime scene investigator, Victor Lamott. Because the crime scene investigators and the tests they ran provided little ammunition against Henry, Pauline's questioning focused on the blood found on the knife, which matched Curt Redmond's, and the lack of any fingerprints on the wallet or knife, suggesting either that the items had been intentionally wiped clean, or that the assailant wore gloves. Pauline would later argue, that both proved Henry acted either with forethought, or at least with a consciousness of the wrongfulness of his actions. Sohni saw no use in disputing those facts—any objection would be unsupported—opting instead to demonstrate for the judge what the tests did not show.

"Your crime scene investigators collected a great deal of trace evidence from the scene of the crime, didn't they?" she said.

"Yes," replied Victor Lamott.

"And that included things like hairs, pieces of fabric, blood, and other miscellaneous items, right?"

"Right."

"And you found no evidence to suggest that the defendant had been at that location, right?"

"Well, it's a major thoroughfare. There was so much evidence it was difficult to sort through it all."

"But that's your job, isn't it, collecting and testing evidence?"

"Yes."

"And you're good at your job, right?"

"Of course."

"And, in fact, your lab, and the Michigan State Police lab, did test much of the trace evidence you found at the crime scene, right?"

"Yes."

"And your conclusion was that none of the trace evidence tested could be conclusively connected with the defendant."

"Correct."

"Your investigators also searched the scene for footprints, didn't they?"

"Yes."

"And they found no footprints at the scene matching the shoes the defendant was wearing, correct?"

"Correct."

"In fact, they found no footprints at the scene matching the defendant's shoe size, right?"

"Correct. But the guy who found the body slipped all over the place, and it was impossible to see much else."

"So, the answer is no. Your team found no footprints matching the defendant's, right?"

"Right."

"Your team also collected the clothes and shoes Mr. Martinez was wearing when he was arrested, correct?"

"That's correct."

"And those items were sent for testing?"

"Yes."

"And the lab found not even one drop of blood on any of them, right?"

"That's right."

"Of the clothes in the defendant's possession on the day he was arrested, the only item containing blood was the shirt in which the knife had been wrapped, correct."

"To the best of my knowledge, I believe that is correct."

Sohni paused to retrieve a document from the defense table, the gaze of the crowd tracing her steps.

"I'd like to direct your attention to people's exhibit number five, which you identified as a report made at the crime scene shortly after the victim's body was found."

"Yes."

"This report indicates that your team found the victim's blood as far as twenty-one inches from the victim's body, right?"

"That's correct."

"And in this report, you attribute the blood found twenty-one inches away from the victim's body to—quote—*blood splatter*?"

"Yes."

"Can you please explain what blood splatter is?"

"Sure. Blood splatter occurs when a person has suffered some kind of physical trauma, causing blood to splatter, or spray, out of a wound. Blood splatter can be found some distance from the site of the wound."

"So how do you tell the difference between plain old bleeding, and blood splatter?"

"Blood splatter is not just a puddle or a trail of blood from a wound. It has a different look. A splattered look, actually. It indicates that blood has forcibly left the area of the wound, and landed elsewhere."

"I can understand that you may find blood splatter with blunt trauma, like a beating. But how do you explain blood splatter with a precise knife wound like the one suffered by the victim?"

"Well, in this case the splatter is more like blood spray or spurt. We often see that when a knife punctures an artery, because the blood continues to pump through the artery for a short time even after the wound is inflicted. The pumping of the blood causes the blood to spurt or spray out of the artery. As a result, you may find blood from the victim quite a distance away."

"So, the blood spray you documented at the crime scene suggests that the victim's blood spurted from his wound after he was stabbed?"

"Yes."

"And, in fact, spurted twenty-one inches, right?"

"Some of it, yes. Some was much closer than that."

"So, if a person stabbed Curt Redmond with a six-inch blade and his blood squirted twenty-one inches away, the person who did the stabbing should have blood on him, shouldn't he?"

"I can't say for certain, because I don't know where the perpetrator was standing in relation to the wound."

"But it seems likely doesn't it."

"Yes, it does seem likely."

"Thank you, Sir. No more questions."

Pauline declined redirect examination and then called her last witness, Detective Jake Clarke. She walked him through the investigation and the eventual arrest of Henry.

The judge then asked Sohni if she had any questions for the witness.

"Oh, boy, do I."

"Objection, Judge. The attorney for the defense is making improper commentary."

"Sustained. No more commentary, Miss Silver."

"Sorry, Judge."

Sohni stood in front of Jake and began peppering him with questions intended to further demonstrate the lack of evidence against her client.

"Detective, shortly after the victim's body was discovered, you sent a team of officers to search a broad radius from the scene of the crime, didn't you?"

"Yes. About a mile in each direction."

"And one of the things they were searching for was discarded clothing, isn't that right?"

"Yes."

"And they didn't find any discarded clothing that contained blood matching that of the victim, did they?"

"No."

And they didn't find any discarded clothing that bore any indication that it had been worn by the defendant, did they?

"No."

"No pants?"

"No."

"No shirts?"

"No."

"No shoes?"

"No."

"No gloves?"

"No."

"Your officers also canvassed the residents living in the area in which the victim was stabbed, right?

"Yes."

"And none of the people they spoke with recalled seeing the defendant at the scene of the crime that night, right?"

"Right."

"And none of the people they spoke with recalled ever seeing the victim interact in any way with the defendant on that day or any other day, right?"

"Right."

"You also haven't found anyone who has ever seen the defendant in possession of the murder weapon prior to it being found in his bag, have you?"

"No."

"And you still haven't established a motive for the defendant allegedly stabbing a student in the back, have you?" Sohni continued.

"Well, actually we believe that the motive was robbery. We found the defendant in possession of the victim's wallet."

"About that. At the time you found the victim's wallet in the defendant's bag, it still contained cash, didn't it?"

"Yes."

"And it still contained a credit card, which, according to your investigation, was the only credit card owned by the victim, correct?"

"Correct."

"And your investigation showed that no transactions were made on that card, or were even attempted, after the victim's death, right?"

"Right."

"And the wallet also still contained a debit card issued by Huntington Bank, correct?"

"Correct."

"And your investigation showed that, like the victim's credit card, no transactions were made on the debit card, or were even attempted, after the victim's death, right?"

"Right."

"And when the victim's body was found, his cell phone, an Apple iPhone, was still in his pocket, right?"

"That's right."

"So, your theory of the case, Detective Clarke, is that the defendant murdered the victim in cold blood by attacking him from behind with no warning, just because he desperately wanted whatever of value that the victim might have had, but then once he had it, didn't spend the victim's cash, didn't use or even attempt to use his credit or debit card, and didn't take his cell phone, correct?"

For the first time since he had taken the stand, Jake averted his gaze and shifted in his chair. He was a thorough detective. Sohni knew he liked things orderly, including defendants' motives. But it was clear that he recognized, as well as she did, that the prosecution's alleged motive in this case—robbery—lacked credibility. Though she guessed he wouldn't state it outright, he looked shifty and seemed to recognize that proper police work had not been performed here. *Was it because of Robert Bender's connection to the victim? That had to bother an upstanding detective like Jake, I can exploit that.*

But before he could answer, Pauline rose.

"Objection. Assuming facts not in evidence."

"What facts specifically, Counselor?" said Judge Becker.

"Her so-called question referred to the murder as *cold-blooded*, and stated that the defendant acted *desperately*. Those are characterizations, not facts, and more commentary, I might add, on behalf of defense counsel."

Judge Becker nodded. "I'll allow the witness to answer the question. But Miss Silver, I won't give you another warning."

"Thank you, Your Honor."

The judge and attorneys turned back to the detective.

"I don't think I can answer that question the way it's asked," he replied.

"Let me rephrase. So even though the defendant did not spend the cash in the wallet, or even attempt to use the credit or debit card, or take the victim's iPhone, as lead detective, you still adhere to the theory that the defendant killed the victim in order to rob him?"

Jake paused. "I think there may have been multiple reasons why he did so, and robbery is one of them."

This was news to Sohni. She had not heard reference to any motives other than robbery. She itched to question Jake about the alleged other reasons, but to do so would break the cardinal rule of cross examination, don't ask a question you don't know the answer to. Then again, one of the benefits of prelim for the defense was the opportunity to learn about the prosecution's case. Jake's answer would likely provide helpful information, and would make little difference in the outcome of the proceeding.

"So, what do you conclude are the other reasons?" Sohni said.

Jake opened his mouth as though to answer, then closed it.

"It would only be speculation," he finally replied.

"So, in other words, there is no evidence to support that any other motive is present?"

"No, not at this time."

"Did your department conduct an examination of the victim's cell phone?"

"No."

"Did your department conduct a search of the victim's home?"

"No."

"Did your department conduct a search of the victim's computer?"

"No."

"Why not, Detective?"

Again, Sohni detected a subtle twitch in his face.

"We determined there was no need."

"But it's standard to search victims' phones and computers in a murder case, isn't it?"

"It is."

"So why wasn't it done in this case?"

"Because we knew who committed the crime."

"You mean the defendant, Henry Martinez."

"Yes."

"Mr. Martinez didn't confess, did he?"

"No."

"The only evidence you have against Mr. Martinez is that his zip-up bag with no lock contained the knife and wallet, right?"

"Well, that, and he conceded that he was in that area at the time the victim was killed."

"Anything else?"

"Not that I can think of."

"This investigation was cut short at the instruction of the prosecution, wasn't it?"

Pauline shot up. "Objection. Suggesting facts not in evidence. And leading."

"Overruled," the judge replied. "The witness can always answer no."

Sohni turned back to Jake, who looked more nervous than she'd ever seen him.

"The prosecution was satisfied with the evidence we had collected."

She stared at Jake a few seconds longer than she had to. He knew that she knew. Sohni hoped Pauline did, too.

"The defense rests."

The height discrepancy in the ME's report, as well as the other nuggets of reasonable doubt that she had unearthed, would prove valuable at trial. But she had no intention of introducing them at the prelim. Simply showing that others had motive to kill the victim, or that most likely the actual killer was taller, was not enough at this point to achieve Henry's release. The prelim was the prosecution's show. Sohni would have to wait until trial to present Henry's full defense. Despite her best efforts, there was nothing Sohni could do about the damaging fact that Henry was found in possession of the bloody murder weapon.

Not surprisingly, the judge ruled that Henry would be bound over for trial, meaning that he would be prosecuted on the murder charge. The ruling also meant that Henry would remain in jail until his trial. Sohni hadn't expected a different result. Her posturing was intended for Pauline. She wanted the prosecutor to know that she and Henry were not going down without a fight.

With the prelim over, the deputies again approached Sohni and Henry, this time to escort Henry back to the jail. Sohni quickly explained the situation to Henry, who nodded his understanding. Sohni knew he felt helpless, especially as the deputies stood impatiently waiting to take him away so they could bring in the next prisoner.

Sohni squeezed Henry's hand, then stood and strode toward the courtroom door as the deputies led Henry through a different door.

Because Henry was charged with a felony, his case would now be transferred to the Washtenaw County Circuit Court, also known as the trial court. She and Henry would make their first appearance in circuit court in a few weeks, for the arraignment on information. But that was a mere formality. Henry's plea was unlikely to change, as was the prosecution's position on a plea offer.

Trial was all but a certainty. If ever Henry Martinez needed a champion, it was now.

# CHAPTER 13

A MONTH LATER, THE PROSECUTION STILL HAD LITTLE ADDItional proof. No eyewitnesses had come forward, and the police had reached a dead end on the origin of the knife. It was purchased with cash from a high-end sporting goods store, additional lab work turned up nothing useful in the case against Henry. Yet no plea offer was forthcoming.

The defense faced a similar situation, with no contact from Marc Isley, and no solid evidence connecting Jimmy Lincroft or Ted Razowski to the crime. Sohni's motion to compel the prosecution to produce Curt Redmond's phone was languishing in the third circle of Hell.

True to her word, she didn't pursue Curt's computer, or any other electronic devices shared by Curt and Zach. But the prosecution fought against her motion, clearly wishing to not rock the Bender boat. To make matters worse, a cadre of Robert Bender's lawyers joined the party, arguing that because the victim's iPhone technically belonged to Zach Bender, who let Curt use it when Zach purchased a new one, the Benders' privacy and interests had to be considered. It was a bullshit tactic that had little merit. The phone was found on Curt's body, and there was no dispute that Curt used it as his primary cell phone. Sohni argued that Zach had given it to Curt, at which time it was no longer Zach's phone, but Curt's phone instead.

With so many lawyers involved, and the bantering about of the Bender name, the motion hearing had been adjourned several times for the filing of additional briefs, resulting in the intended unending delay.

The prosecution also filed objections to the third-party subpoenas Sohni had issued to social media companies with which Curt had accounts. She had requested his passwords and other account-related information which would enable her to perform her own search—not an unusual request in a murder investigation. But Pauline had fought them tooth and nail on this also, further impeding Sohni's investigatory efforts. Most likely, she would eventually prevail. But the time and effort required to get to that point was overwhelming. Sohni real-ized that she could no longer put off contacting the Redmonds.

From her briefcase pocket, she located the scrap of paper Frank Redmond had written his number on. With a deep breath, she dialed it. He remembered her right away and agreed to meet. He said he'd be home from work in an hour and said he could meet her at his house any time after that. It would be a forty-minute drive, but this meeting was long overdue, so she jumped at the chance. She texted Matt to let him know she'd be late for dinner.

Her email inbox notification jingled. She pulled up the new message. The sender was the Washtenaw County Circuit Court, and the attachment was a gag order. She'd never been involved in a case in which the court found it necessary to restrict the publicity surrounding the proceedings. Yet displayed on her screen was further evidence that *People v. Henry Martinez* was not a typical case. The order, entered by the trial judge without any request by the parties, prohibited anyone working on the matter from speaking publicly about the defendant, witnesses, evidence, or any other matter concerning the case.

Inexperienced as she was in complying with gag orders, Sohni printed a copy of the order and carried it down the hall to Helen's office. She knocked on the half-open door. Helen looked up and greeted her with a smile.

"Hey, Sohni. Come on in."

Sohni entered, noticing the addition of another family portrait to Helen's desk. This one showed Helen, her wife, and their two daughters, all dressed in white, standing on a balcony with a backdrop of the sun setting over a lake. She recognized the setting as Helen and Tori's cottage on Lake Michigan.

"Beautiful picture," Sohni said. "Wow, aren't the girls getting big?"

"Thanks. Yeah, the time just flies by. Can you believe they just got their driver's permits?"

"OK, that's terrifying."

"Isn't it, though? What's on your mind?"

"This just came in." Sohni gestured with the printout. "I've never dealt with one before, so I'm looking for some guidance."

Helen reached across her desk to take the papers from Sohni, and slid her glasses down from the top of her head. As Helen read the court's order, she frowned, then smiled broadly.

"I like this judge!"

Sohni couldn't help but smile along, though puzzled by Helen's reaction.

"What do you think this is all about?" Sohni said.

"I'll tell you exactly what it's about. I was meaning to come and talk to you about this."

The older woman turned to her computer and opened her browser. After a quick search, she located an audio file, turned up the volume on her laptop, and clicked on the play icon. Sohni heard Pauline Fitzgerald's voice, along with the voice of another woman, who Sohni knew to be the host of a popular local talk-radio show.

"This morning, Pauline was the guest on the *Monica Jenkins Show*," Helen said. "I happened to catch it while I was driving in to work. I couldn't believe what I heard. And apparently, neither could Judge Watkins."

Helen fast-forwarded until she reached the portion of the interview she wanted. Sohni heard Pauline's voice again, but this time the name Henry Martinez was on her lips.

"Monica, you asked me why I want to be Washtenaw County's prosecutor, and I tell you to look no further than the case everyone is talking about—the Henry Martinez case. Mr. Martinez came to Ann Arbor from Texas, of all places. Where he racked up a pretty good criminal record, I may add. We welcomed him to our county, allowed him the benefit of our assistance and services, and in return he stabs to death one of our promising young students. I am a champion for the people of Washtenaw County, and it is my mission to get people like Mr. Martinez off our streets, and to keep the county safe for our families."

Sohni sat speechless, her mouth gaping.

"You better believe I called Phil immediately," Helen said. "I hadn't even left my car yet. He got an earful. Needless to say, he wasn't aware of Pauline's comments. As you know, only the prosecutor's designated spokesperson is authorized to speak about an ongoing case. She made her comments as a political candidate, not a member of the prosecutor's office. But she was way out of bounds. Phil was furious. I suspect that he tried to control the damage, but apparently news of Pauline's indiscretion made it to the judge first. You can't blame Judge Watkins, Pauline poisoned the jury pool."

"She just outed Henry's prior criminal acts," Sohni said.

"She sure did. I told Phil that if they intend to use his criminal record in his prosecution, they'd better go through proper protocol. He agreed, and said he'd look into it right away."

"I guess that means I need to start working on my argument to keep his record out of evidence."

"Probably a good idea."

"What do I have to do differently in light of this gag order?"

"Probably nothing. You're already prohibited by this office from speaking publicly about the case, anyway. That's nothing new. Just be careful to stay away from reporters, and be extra careful where you discuss the case."

Sohni nodded.

"Speaking of being careful, have you received any more threats?"

"A couple of more calls. But nothing else."

"Have the police been able to trace them?"

"Unfortunately, they're being made from burner phones. Every call comes from a different number. They managed to track a couple of them to the stores from where they were purchased, and pulled security footage, but the person purchasing them was covered head to toe and wearing an oversized hoodie. Except for the person's height, which suggests he's a male, the police can't be completely sure of the person's gender. They dressed the same in the doorbell camera footage from my neighbor's house, the night my tires were slashed and they wore gloves."

"Who do you think this might be?" Helen said.

"I was going to ask you the same thing." Sohni chuckled.

"I think it has to be one of two people. Either someone has gotten really worked up about you representing the alleged murderer of Curt Redmond, which is scary enough, or if your instincts are correct, perhaps it's the person who actually did kill Curt Redmond. Maybe he's threatened by your stubborn insistence that someone other than Henry committed the murder."

"That's a terrifying thought."

"Could be you've gotten closer than you think to figuring this out."

"Maybe. But I'm stuck. I'm not a cop, so I can't get people to talk to me. Probably the best I can do is take what I know and use it to establish reasonable doubt at Henry's trial. Especially since the police haven't talked to any of those people, and can't account for their whereabouts the night of the murder."

"That's more reasonable doubt than many defense attorneys have. But keep working on it. Maybe you'll find an untapped source of information."

"As a matter of fact, if things go well this afternoon, I might have exactly that."

A half-hour later, Sohni was in her car, on the way to Ferndale. She sang along with an old Creedence Clearwater Revival song, but then a terrifying thought crossed her mind. What if Frank Redmond was the man behind the threats? He seemed volatile and angry when she met him in Zach's room. What if agreeing to help her was just a ruse to get close to her?

"Oh, shit! Why did I have to think of that?"

She called Helen to let her know that she was heading to Frank Redmond's home, and gave her the address, as well as Frank's cell number.

"There's probably nothing to be concerned about," she told Helen. "But under the circumstances, I thought it was wise to let someone know where I was."

"I wholeheartedly agree."

"I'll call you when I'm back on the road, heading for home."

"Sounds good. Talk to you later."

Morbidly, Sohni figured her communication with Helen wouldn't stop Frank Redmond from killing her if he was so inclined, but at least someone would know who did it and where to find her body.

At about four thirty, Sohni pulled into the driveway of a small brick ranch-style house with a postage stamp yard in serious need of mowing. Garbage overflowed from the cans next to the house. In the driveway, her car joined a Ford pickup from the previous decade, emblazoned with a bumper sticker declaring the driver a U of M parent.

With trepidation, Sohni climbed the stairs of the front porch. The door was cracked, so only a screen separated her from the Redmond's family room. She knocked delicately, respectful of the sense of mourning enveloping the home. Within seconds, Frank opened the screen door and Sohni entered into the Redmonds' private domain.

The family room, where Sohni stood, was simply decorated, with a brown faux-leather sofa against the far wall, and striped wallpaper that brought to Sohni's mind the color of burnt sienna, one she had not thought of since her days using Crayolas.

Sohni's gaze was drawn to a framed photo of Curt sitting on one of the glass end tables bookending the sofa. The opposite wall was occupied by an entertainment center that held a television, a DVD player, a Roku box, a console gaming system, and an old wooden bookcase displaying, among other items, a variety of high school yearbooks and more photographs of Curt. This room bore the mark of proud parents.

Frank Redmond awkwardly offered Sohni a seat in a tattered recliner as he sank into the sofa in a manner that belied his weariness.

"Thank you for agreeing to meet with me. It's very kind of you to welcome me into your home."

Frank narrowed his eyes. "I only invited you here because I wanted you to understand that Curt is a real person, with a real family. I wanted you to see where he lived, where he grew up, in case you were trying to manipulate me. I'm hoping you have normal human emotions, and can't lie to me here in our home."

"I assure you, Mr. Redmond, I have no intention of lying to you."

Frank crossed his tanned arms in front of his brawny chest.

"Good. And call me Frank. Mr. Redmond makes me sound old." He cracked a smile. "So, what information do you have about my son's death?"

She explained the deficiencies in the police investigation, and the role played by Robert Bender. Frank listened intently as she told him about the two men who had assaulted Curt before his death. Neither had been investigated. She also told him about Curt's strange email to Marc Isley, and Sammy's account of Marc's sudden fearful departure.

At the news of Marc's strange reaction to Curt's death, Frank raised his eyebrows.

"That sure is suspicious."

Sohni nodded. "Have you ever heard Curt mention Marc's name?"

"No, it doesn't sound familiar."

Frank stood and nearly ran down the hallway leading from the family room.

"Hold on a sec," he said, over his shoulder.

A couple of minutes later, he returned to the family room, holding a small green spiral bound book with the word *Addresses* embossed on the cover.

"This is Curt's address book," Frank said. "I found it in his room and brought it home. He kept all his friends' names and numbers in here. He had friends who had lost their cell phones and had no other record of the names and numbers stored in them. He wanted to be sure that didn't happen to him, so he scrawled them in this book. I thought it was an old-fashioned thing to do for such a young man, but it was smart."

Frank paged through the book until he came to the *I* tab.

"No one in here by the name of Isley," he told Sohni. He then turned to the *M* tab. "No Marc Isley under M, either."

Frank returned to his seat, a puzzled look on his face.

"If this Marc guy was a friend of Curt's, he would be in this book. Curt kept everyone in there."

"That is consistent, though, with what Marc's roommate told me. He said he'd never heard of Curt."

"I want to know more about Marc Isley," Frank said, "and what connection he has to my son's death."

This presented the perfect opportunity for Sohni to make her request. She recounted her conversation with Tracy Zorn.

"She didn't give much credence to Curt's comment about his new article being *the big one*. But maybe it was bigger than she knew."

Frank slowly shook his head. "Curt loved to rake the muck."

"It's possible Curt knew Marc Isley through his work on a story," Sohni said. "Perhaps even the story he was working on at the time he died. But the problem is the computer files Zach gave me didn't contain any materials related to Curt's articles. There were no notes, no drafts of articles, no emails. I suspect he may have kept them on flash drives, or on a Google drive, or something of the sort. From the materials I have, there is no way for me to determine what Curt was working on at the time of his death, or if Marc Isley was somehow connected to his investigation. And Marc will not return my phone calls."

Sohni could tell Frank's mind was working.

"Why can't the police contact him?" he said. "They can make him talk, can't they?"

"He still doesn't have to talk to them, unless they were to go as far as to lock him up for concealing information. But I don't see that happening. Plus, I highly doubt the prosecution will pursue interviewing him. Why would they go out of their way to talk to a potential witness in pursuit of an alternative suspect to the man they arrested? They have no incentive to create more reasonable doubt against my client. I can't help but believe that Marc knows something about who killed your son, but I'm at a dead end. I was hoping that maybe you'd have some information that would shed light on this situation, but it seems you're as much in the dark as I am."

Sohni had pled her case. Now she just had to wait for Frank Redmond to decide how much he trusted her.

"You know," Frank said, "I brought back a box of those little flash drives that belonged to Curt. I haven't looked at them yet. I just figured they were school papers and stuff like that. Maybe they would help."

Sohni tried to conceal her excitement.

"That's a great idea. Those could be the missing Truth Zone materials."

Frank nodded. "I've got a computer in the spare bedroom. Why don't we go in there and take a look at them? I suppose it can't hurt to try."

Sohni followed him to a room at the end of the hall, her prior suspicions of Frank all but forgotten in her excitement. The room was filled with exercise equipment, including a weight bench, a rack of dumbbells, and a rowing machine.

"They were Curt's," Frank said, as Sohni took in the scene. "Bought everything himself. He bussed and waited tables, saved up his money. Pieced it all together one at a time."

Looking out of place was a computer stand. The computer it held was obsolete by today's standards, but when Frank flipped the power switch, the computer began to boot. He pulled a small plastic bin from the stand's built-in cupboard. The bin held about eight flash drives, each of which was labeled in black marker applied to a strip of masking tape.

Together, Sohni and Frank sorted through them. One of them bore the notation *Zone*, which Sohni and Frank interpreted to mean that they contained materials relevant to Curt's work for The Truth Zone. Sohni was grateful that Curt was so well-organized.

Frank inserted the Zone drive into the computer. The device contained three folders labeled *notes, emails*, and *articles*.

"Shall we try emails?" Frank said.

"Sure."

He clicked on the folder icon, only to find that it contained numerous subfolders. Each subfolder appeared to be labeled with a person's first initial and last name. Frank rushed to click on a folder named *M. Isley*. They stared in silence when twelve email messages appeared.

"Well, I guess they knew each other, after all," Frank said.

# CHAPTER 14

SOHNI AND PETER REVIEWED THE PAPERS SHE'D BROUGHT from the Redmond's house. In addition to the twelve email messages exchanged between Curt and Marc, she and Frank had found eight pages of notes, all generated in the three weeks before Curt was killed, relating to what they believed was his latest investigation.

Starting with the emails between Marc and Curt, she sorted them from oldest to most recent. Marc's first message told Curt that he had some inside information that needs to be made public, and that he'd selected Curt to share it with, based on his previous Truth Zone articles, and because he was a fellow U of M student.

"Inside information," Peter said. "I wonder what that means?"

"I have no idea. But those words imply he had access to non-public info from somewhere. But where?"

"It doesn't look like he provides any detail in his messages. They're vague."

"Yeah, but in these later emails, the two men made arrangements to meet in person. If they followed through, seems like whatever they discussed should be in Curt's notes."

Peter pulled out the notes.

"Well, let's take a look," he said.

"His editor was right. He did take detailed notes. Look at that, at the top of each page, he indicated the source of the information and the date."

Peter found the page inscribed with the same date as the planned meeting.

"These must be the notes from his meeting with Marc," he said.

The hope they'd soon know what was discussed during that covert meeting was quickly dashed. Tracy had failed to mention that Curt wrote his notes using his own shorthand, which made them undecipherable to anyone else.

"You've got to be kidding!" Sohni said. "I finally get hold of these, and I can't even read them."

"Let's see if we can make out anything," Peter said. "There are multiple references to *TE's*, and the word *Intact*. The abbreviation *FLAM* appears several times, too."

"Yeah, but I have no idea what any of them mean."

Sohni turned to the next few pages of notes, labeled *Internet research*, dated the same day as the meeting.

"The initials DAE show up several times on this page," she said. "And these, look like years. And here at the bottom, he wrote *Big K's*, with a colon, and then *FMC 50 mil* and *Toy–25 mil*.

"Mil could stand for million, maybe."

"If so, that's an awful lot of money, and an awful lot of reasons to kill. But that's all we have right now, and we're not even sure he was talking about money." Sohni closed her eyes, frustration mounting. "Wait a minute. The reference to K's ... I remember that from law school. K is an abbreviation for contract. He could have been referring to two contracts, one for fifty million, and one for twenty-five million."

"That makes sense. But who are FMC and Toy?"

Sohni opened up her browser and typed *FMC* into Google.

"Geez," she said. "Who would've thought there'd be so many FMCs? There's the Federal Maritime Commission, Fox Movie Channel, some chemical company, a technology company, and a dialysis services provider, just to name a few."

"Don't even bother trying *Toy*," Peter said. "But how about DAE?"

She plugged it into the search engine.

"Damn, same problem. There are just too many."

Sohni flipped to Curt's final pages of notes, which were labeled *Review of MI's records*.

"These must be Curt's notes about the actual evidence Marc showed him," she said.

"Holy crap! These are even worse than the previous pages. Are these, like, math equations?"

Peter was right. All she could identify were math symbols and numbers. The remainder was gibberish to her.

"I don't know what it means," she said, "but I do know that it can't be a coincidence that Curt made these notes only two days before he died. The more I learn, the more convinced I am that Curt's article was the motive for his murder. But what the hell was he investigating?"

As far as she could tell, only one person knew, other than the killer. But Marc Isley wasn't talking. At least, not to her.

"You know, Peter, let's go back to Marc's comment about inside info. Maybe we can figure out some aspect of his life that would give him access."

Sohni flipped her notepad until she came to the page containing the scrawled notes from her phone call with Sammy. She reviewed each line, looking for any additional leads to follow. Her hope rose as she came across a detail she had forgotten.

"Hey, Marc worked as a research assistant for a professor in his department. I don't know exactly what research assistants do in that context. Do you think he could've accessed sensitive information that way?"

"I suppose it's possible," Peter said.

"Darn. I didn't note the professor's name."

Sohni again opened her browser. She found the university's online directory and searched for professors in the material science and engineering department. She scrolled through all the resulting listings until one rang a bell.

"Professor Shinji Ito. That was the professor Marc worked for. Maybe he knows something. I would assume he had access to the same information as Marc." Sohni scribbled on her legal pad the number for Professor Ito, then punched the numbers into her phone.

The phone was picked up on the first ring, and Sohni heard a man's harried voice on the other end.

"Shinji Ito." He sounded distracted.

When Sohni identified herself, Professor Ito apologized for his abruptness.

"Things are a bit chaotic here," he said.

"Is everything OK?"

"Oh, yeah. It's just one of my research assistants. He left town without warning, in the middle of his research. He's really left me in the lurch."

"You aren't, by chance, referring to Marc Isley, are you?"

The line was silent for several seconds.

"Yes, actually. How did you know that?"

"Marc Isley's sudden departure is exactly what I'm calling about. I think I may know why he left. But I need your help in putting the pieces together. I'd like to meet with you in person. How is tomorrow?"

With surprise and confusion in his voice, the professor agreed to a 9:00 a.m. meeting at his office. Sohni hung up the receiver and gave Peter a fist bump.

"This might be our last chance to figure this out. Wish me luck!"

Once Sohni saw the state of Professor Ito's office, she better understood his mental state on the phone the previous day. When she first entered, she thought it was empty, that Professor Ito had not yet arrived. But as her eyes adjusted to the gloom—*why doesn't he buy some bigger lamps*—she noticed a small Asian man hidden behind giant piles of haphazardly stacked papers.

The dry-erase board on the far wall was covered with equations and notations. She noticed one beat-up plastic chair—which she was pretty sure used to be yellow—set to the right of the professor's desk. That, too, was covered with a stack of papers. Sohni wondered why he had suggested that she meet him in this visitor-unfriendly hovel.

The professor sat at his desk, on a three-wheeled leather desk chair with a back so high Sohni could only see him from the side. He was reading from a textbook and scribbling notes on a yellow pad. Reading, scribbling. Reading, scribbling. Sohni found it mesmerizing. Then she realized she was standing in Professor Ito's doorway, staring at him, observing his idiosyncrasies like a voyeur, so she cleared her throat.

"Excuse me. Professor Ito?"

The small man started, clearly annoyed at the interruption.

"Yes?" he barked, spinning on his oversized office chair until he faced her.

Taken aback by his abruptness, Sohni took a step back. This only seemed to annoy the man more.

"Yes?" he said again, this time with even less patience.

Sohni recovered and flashed him a smile.

"Professor Ito, I'm Sohni Silver." She extended her hand to him. "We spoke on the phone."

The professor's face transformed into a toothy grin that seemed disproportionate to the size of his face. He rose and took Sohni's hand in his, pumping her arm, all annoyance apparently gone.

"Please have a seat." He gestured to the occupied once-yellow chair.

When Sohni hesitated, the professor recognized the problem, and in one fell swoop, scooped up the offending stack of papers and placed them in one of the few open spaces on his desk. He was obviously skilled at shuffling stacks of paper.

Once Sohni took her place on the now-vacant chair, Professor Ito returned to his own, crossed his legs and clasped his hands in his lap. His transformation into an attentive, friendly host was complete, Sohni thought with wonder.

"Miss Silver, you said you may know why Marc ran off?"

"I believe I do, Professor."

"Call me Shinji, please."

"OK, Shinji. This is going to sound a little crazy, but bear with me."

He chuckled. "Well, that's a mysterious way to start a conversation."

"Yes, it is. But you'll understand soon. Do you recall the student who was killed, stabbed to death, near campus in October? His name was Curt Redmond."

"Yes, I do. It was all over the news."

"It was. Well, a homeless man named Henry Martinez was arrested for the murder. I represent Mr. Martinez."

"Oh. I see." Shinji's smile faded.

"It's my job. As a public defender, I am assigned to represent defendants who can't afford attorneys. Every defendant is entitled to an attorney and a fair trial."

She was tired of having to explain that.

"Of course, of course. I'm sorry. Please continue."

"There is a gag order in place in this case, so I can't tell you much about the case itself, or the evidence in it. But I can tell you that I have been conducting my own independent investigation. I do request that you please keep private any information I provide to you."

Shinji nodded.

"Marc's roommate told me that the morning after Curt's murder, Marc saw a story about his death on the news, freaked out, and immediately packed up his car and left for Pennsylvania, where his parents live."

"That seems odd."

"I agree. You see, Curt was a journalism student who had written a couple investigative articles for an online news site called The Truth Zone. You can check it out for yourself. I found out that Marc had been secretly meeting with Curt, providing him information, which Curt was further investigating in the hopes of turning it into another article."

"What kind of information?"

"I'm not exactly sure. I have Curt's notes, but they're in his own type of shorthand, and I can't interpret them. But Curt and Marc met only three weeks before Curt was killed. Then Marc hears about Curt's death, and he freaks out and skips town. I can't help but think those things are related. And now Marc won't answer anyone's calls. I think Marc was scared that he'd be killed, too."

"You're right. That is a crazy story. But I have to agree that it seems more than a coincidence."

"I've shared with you what I know. I was hoping you could share with me what you know."

"I'd be happy to, but I don't know anything. This is the first I've heard about any of this."

"Why don't you start by telling me a little about the research Marc Isley was working on?"

"He was conducting research on a new thermoplastic elastomer."

Apparently noticing the frown on Sohni's face, Shinji chuckled.

"In laymen's terms, a thermoplastic elastomer is a rubber-like compound that can be used for a number of manufacturing applications. In this case, the compound Marc was studying has been touted by its developer as a great new breakthrough for the automotive industry."

"What was the purpose of Marc's research?"

"The university was contacted by the Department of Defense with respect to this purportedly fabulous new thermoplastic elastomer. This new compound is a polymer blend. Specifically, in this case, a plastic, and a rubber, which is nothing new. But what's so special about this product is that it supposedly can be used to create weather stripping for automobiles and other vehicles that performs head and shoulders above any product currently used in the industry. Apparently, the sound reduction aspect alone is incredibly impressive. The car companies are salivating over the potential benefits of this product, and some of them even entered into advanced contracts with the manufacturer. All the hype piqued the interest of the DOD, which is considering requiring its contractors to incorporate the weather-stripping products in military vehicles for better protection from the elements."

"Do you know which auto manufacturers had entered into contracts for this product?"

"If I recall correctly, I think it was Ford and Toyota."

"I think those were the contracts referenced in Curt's notes for the article! *FMC* is Ford Motor Company, and *Toy* is Toyota. See, you've already been helpful."

"Good to hear."

"Please continue," Sohni said.

"Before agreeing to use the product, the DOD insisted that more rigorous testing be performed. Not wanting to turn away government business, the manufacturer agreed to provide some of the weather stripping to the university, specifically the materials science and engineering department, to conduct the additional testing."

"What kind of testing are we talking about?"

"Well, the DOD was especially concerned about endurance, especially the ability to withstand harsh elements such as extreme heat and cold, pounding sandstorms, and hurricane-like conditions. Marc was performing tests to simulate these types of conditions. He was noting the short-term and long-term effects of extreme weather conditions, as well as testing the thermal capabilities."

"Meaning, how well it stood up to extreme temperatures."

"Correct. Marc had only been working with the product for a couple months. We hadn't had a chance to sit down and go over his findings. Unfortunately, I've been too busy since he left to track down and review his results. Not that it really matters. For quality control purposes, we're going to have to start all over. That is, unless Marc returns soon."

"From what I've seen of Curt's notes, I think it's possible that the information Marc provided to him had to do with his research on this product. Is it possible that Marc learned something significant during his research?"

"It seems unlikely. It's just routine testing on a mundane product."

Sohni pulled Curt's notes from her briefcase and handed them to Shinji.

"Please take a look at these notes. Does any of it mean anything to you?"

He studied Curt's notes. "I do see the references to FMC and Toy that you mentioned. I also notice references to TE, which could mean thermo elastomer. Oh, here he mentions *Intact*. That's the brand name the product is being marketed under."

"Wow!"

"Oh, one more thing. I see *DAE* here. I believe that's the name of the company that manufacturers the product." Shinji set down the papers. "I guess you've proven me wrong. It sure seems that Marc was giving Curt information about the product he was testing. But what information?"

"I was hoping you'd know. Did Marc mention anything to you? Did he seem concerned about something?"

Professor Ito's eyes went wide. "Wait a minute! Come to think of it, Marc called me the day before he left. He told me he needed to discuss some test results with me. Said it was important. Unfortunately, I was out of town at a conference, but I told him to come by my office the next morning. He never showed. I later discovered that he'd left town. I had almost forgotten about his phone call."

"Do you think he'd speak with you if you called him?"

"No. I've tried calling him. Other than a brief voicemail he left for me in the middle of the night, he won't call me back."

"He's scared."

"You might be right.

"Where are Marc's test results, his notes, the product of all his work?"

"For tests such as these, the individual performing the tests keeps written notes, as well as computerized records. Every detail of every test is noted, as are the results. The written notes are maintained in a notebook, which is locked in a cabinet in the lab when it's not in use. The computer records are stored on our department's server, but are password protected. Quality control is extremely important in these situations. There are only a few people who have access to any of the records."

"I assume you're one of those people?"

"Naturally. But like I said, I haven't had a chance to review them since Marc left."

Sohni bit her tongue. She wanted those test results, but she wanted it to be Shinji's idea.

"You want to know the results of Marc's testing, don't you?" he said.

"I truly believe those test results hold the answers to our questions, and why Marc ran off so suddenly. Why a young journalist was murdered. Most importantly, though, I think those test results could help prove my client's innocence."

Shinji stared at Sohni and blinked twice. Three times. Sohni felt she would burst if the professor didn't say something soon. But she couldn't push him, only wait for his response.

Finally, he said, "I can't let you see the results."

Sohni's heart sank. She was so close to solving this puzzle. So close to obtaining the information that would set Henry Martinez free. Yet with one sentence, this man had snatched away any chance she might have had to learn the crucial information.

"But—"

Shinji held up his hand. "However," he drew out the syllables, "I will look at the test results myself. If I notice anything significant, anything ... worth killing over," he smiled, "I will contact you."

Sohni realized she had been holding her breath, and exhaled audibly. The professor had come up with a satisfactory solution. He had to restrict access to the data to preserve the integrity and confidentiality of the testing. She understood that. But by reviewing it himself and alerting her to any significant information, she could still get the information she needed and proceed with her investigation.

Sohni stood up from her rickety plastic chair and placed her business card in Professor Ito's hand.

"Thank you."

Shinji smiled and bowed slightly. Sohni headed toward the doorway that led out of this claustrophobic office. Before exiting, though, she turned to face the professor one more time.

"I hope I hear from you soon. As does my client."

# CHAPTER 15

TWENTY-SIX HOURS HAD PASSED SINCE SOHNI LEFT PROFESsor Ito's office, and every time her cell phone rang, she grabbed it, hoping it would be Shinji calling with important information. It wasn't.

She turned her attention to other cases. The prosecutors had sent over plea offers that she needed to review and discuss with her clients. She couldn't deprive her other clients of the zealous representation to which they were entitled just because Henry's case was such a mystery.

Just as Sohni had focused her full attention on the offers before her, the ringing of her cell phone made her jump. She snatched it up, almost dropping it, and was elated when she saw Professor Ito's number on the screen.

"Sohni Silver."

"Sohni, it's Shinji Ito. I told you I would call if I found something relevant in Marc's notes."

Sohni's heart pounded.

"Well, I found something. Something that could be important."

Here was the moment of truth. This is when she would finally find out what Curt was writing about, what the murderer didn't want exposed.

"Thanks so much for calling," Sohni replied. "Please tell me what you found."

The professor remained silent.

"Shinji? Are you still there?"

"Yes. I'm here. I guess I'm just not certain that I should be sharing this with you. I admit I'm torn. On one hand, the integrity of our research and our university is of great importance to me. The desire to preserve that integrity tells me to keep this information confidential until all the research is complete, and then only present it to the DOD as part of our final report. However, I also realize that a young man is dead, and a potentially innocent man on trial for his murder. That is a powerful motivation for breaking the rules."

"Indeed, it is. To be honest, Shinji, you're my last hope. You are the only other person who knows what both Marc and Curt knew." *Well, except for the murderer.* "Without this information, my investigation is finished. I have nowhere else to go."

Sohni's words hung in the silence that followed. Several seconds passed with only the sound of Shinji's breathing.

"It's highly flammable," he finally said.

"What?"

"The thermoplastic elastomer. It's highly flammable. Completely unsuitable for automotive use."

"Oh!"

"Quite shocking, actually. Even basic testing by the manufacturer should have revealed this significant defect. It makes me wonder whether those behind the development of this product didn't bother to test for flammability, or if they knew all along the significant risk posed by their product. Either way, by promoting this product as a safe alternative for use in motor vehicles, they have acted in a highly unethical and possibly illegal manner. Use of this product could injure, or even kill, thousands of people."

"But admitting to the defect would mean starting over," Sohni said. "The manufacturer would have to go back to the drawing board and either find a way to correct the defect, or scrap the product altogether, either of which would probably cost millions of dollars, especially since they had already entered into contracts with auto manufacturers. Plus, its reputation would likely suffer a blow from which it might never recover."

"I think you see now why I had to pass this on to you," Shinji said. "It's not only your client's life at stake, but potentially thousands of other."

"You did the right thing, Shinji."

"I wish I could do more, but my hands are tied. You know I can't publicly reveal the test results. But between you and me, if I'm asked about them, let's just say I won't deny them. The public has to know about this. Let me know if I can do anything else to help."

"I will. But you've already done more than you can know. I appreciate it, Shinji. I know this wasn't easy."

"Good luck, Sohni."

When Sohni finally came down from her high, reality began to set in. An hour after her call with Shinji, she sat paralyzed.

"Now what?"

She had been so focused on finding out what Curt was writing about, she hadn't thought about what she would do with the information once she got it. She had acquired some investigation skills over her years as a defense attorney, and the staff investigators were impressive, but they were all in over their head with this. She knew little about the auto industry, and even less about thermoplastic elastomers. She needed help. But her office also didn't have the funds to hire an investigator for a full-blown inquiry into the Intact product and who may have killed Curt.

An idea flashed into her mind. Just as Curt was intrigued by this subject, other reporters would likely be as well. And of course, the mystery has thickened since one reporter is already dead, and a source is in hiding. Any professional investigative reporter worth his salt would salivate over this story.

Just as Sohni's excitement peaked, she was again deflated as she remembered that a gag order was in effect for this case. While revealing to the press the results of Marc's testing would likely not violate the court's order, explaining her theory about the connection between the test results and Curt's murder would. Without knowing about the possible murder connection, any reporter's investigation would be incomplete and not as beneficial to her. Sohni was left with a dilemma, how to get all the information to a reporter without disobeying the court's order.

Skirting rules was not Sohni's strong point. Complying with the court order to the extreme, which would be her usual approach, may condemn her client to an unfair trial, and possibly life in jail. But directly violating the order was also not an option.

A solution popped into her head. She picked up the phone and punched in Frank Redmond's cell number. She was about to gain some practical experience in rule bending.

Sohni's call had caught Frank under the hood of a 2018 Jaguar. She waited impatiently while he walked to another room.

"OK, it's quieter here," he said. "What's up?"

"I know what Curt was writing about. And I believe it got him killed."

Silence filled the line.

"Are you there, Frank?"

"Yeah, I'm here … I guess … I just wasn't expecting this."

"Can you meet with me after work tonight? I'll come to Ferndale. Just tell me where."

More silence.

"Are you OK?" Sohni said.

"Yeah, yeah. It's just a lot to take in. How about Como's at six thirty?"

"Sounds great. I'll see you then."

Sohni wondered at Frank's seeming hesitance. Was it really just surprise, or had something changed in his attitude? In her prior dealings with him, she had gotten the impression that

Cathy Redmond did not support her husband working with Sohni, which was understandable. But Sohni sensed that he not only wanted, but needed, to be a part of this investigation. In her experience, men like Frank couldn't stand feeling help-less. She could see that helping to solve this mystery made him feel useful, gave him a purpose. But if it was sowing dissen-sion in his marriage, he may have determined it wasn't worth it. After all, with his son gone, Cathy was all Frank had left. He wouldn't want to risk losing her, too.

Whatever his thinking, he at least agreed to the meeting. But would he agree to what she was going to ask of him?

At 6:23 p.m. Sohni slid onto a bar stool at Como's, a popular restaurant and bar operating in downtown Ferndale for over fifty years. She waved down a bartender and ordered a ginger ale. While she waited, her cell rang. It was a number she didn't recognize, so she let it go to voicemail. By now, she had learned not to answer unknown calls. Her stalker always left breath-ing on her voicemail, but she could at least deprive him of the satisfaction of doing it while she was on the line, and make him leave a message.

Despite the police's attention, the harassment had contin-ued. She felt like she walked on eggshells, never knowing when the next incident would occur. After her tires were slashed, she and Matt had taken to parking in the garage. It took some doing, moving the kayaks, bikes, and other miscellanea to the basement. But it was worth the peace of mind. And Matt had insisted on installing a security system. She was still vulnerable in numerous ways, though. If Matt had his way, she'd never leave the house. But he'd been true to his word. She let him know right away when the calls came in, and he refrained from overreacting.

Sohni caught a glimpse of Frank as he entered the restaurant. He looked tired, with dark circles under his eyes. She waved until she caught his attention.

Frank took a seat on the stool next to her and asked the bartender for a Miller Light.

He turned to face Sohni. "What did you find out?"

She pulled papers from her briefcase and mopped up any wet spots before spreading the documents on the bar in front of him. Sohni spoke for several minutes, filling him in on Curt's notes and her interpretations, gesturing and pointing to specific portions of the papers. She told Frank about her conversations with Professor Ito, and the damning information Marc Isley's research had uncovered.

When Sohni had finished, Frank just stared at her.

"A thermoplastic elastomer?" Frank finally said. "You think Curt was killed because of an article about a car part?"

"Not just any car part, Frank. This new elastomer was touted as revolutionary. Car companies had already placed advanced orders in the tens of millions of dollars. The Department of Defense was considering incorporating it into their military vehicles. A defect in that product, especially a defect as significant as this, would be its death knell. Not to mention possible humiliation of the people involved in developing the product."

Frank took a swig of his beer, but said nothing.

"Think about it, Frank. There were very few individuals who knew about the flammable nature of the elastomer, namely Marc Isley and Curt. Marc had not even told his professor yet. And there was only one of those individuals who planned to write about it, expose it to the world. And he's conveniently dead."

Frank winced.

"Oh, geez! I'm sorry. That was incredibly insensitive."

"Do you really think somebody would kill to keep that a secret, though?"

Sohni shrugged. "Apparently, Marc Isley thought so."

A minute passed in silence as Frank digested the information.

"Assuming this is all true," he said, "what is it you need from me?"

"You need to go public with this information. You need to go to the press, make a big stink about the inadequate investigation the police conducted, and give them the new evidence. Explain to them that there is a solid and credible lead that the prosecution has missed, one that not only could solve Curt's murder but could blow the lid off a major scandal."

Sohni explained that even if the first possibility didn't persuade the press to run with this, the second would.

"If you can convince the press to take up this story, the public pressure would likely force the hand of the prosecutor and the police, compelling them to look into this new theory of the killing, which is ultimately what we both want."

When Sohni stopped talking, silence took over once again. Frank stared over Sohni's head and out the window, where people hurried by on Woodward Avenue. A brisk wind began stirring, so the passersby clutched their coats around them and picked up their pace as they hurried to their destinations. He took a gulp of his beer. And then another.

"Why do you need me? Why can't you do this?"

She noticed how ragged his voice sounded.

"I wish I didn't have to ask this of you," Sohni replied, her voice soft. "But the judge put a gag order in place that prohibits everyone involved in the case from speaking about it publicly. I would be in contempt of court if I went to the press with what I know, which would jeopardize my client's ability to receive proper representation and a fair trial. Not to mention that I could lose my license to practice law. You, however, are not subject to that order."

Sohni scanned her surroundings, then leaned toward Frank.

"By giving you the information, I have," she whispered, "and asking you to go to the press, I am already doing more than I should. If the judge found out I was behind it, she might still hold me in contempt. But the way I look at it, the information I have was already in your possession, and you could have just as easily put it all together. I haven't given you anything you didn't already have." She leaned back into her bar stool and stared into Frank's eyes. "You're the only one who can do this. My office doesn't have the resources to pursue these leads, and I wouldn't even know where to begin. Besides, the press would be more interested in talking to you."

Frank sneered. "No kidding. Those vultures have been calling our house ever since the news broke of Curt's death. I just hang up on them. Sometimes I leave my phone off the hook. For the first few days, news vans were parked out in front of our house. Do you know those bastards actually filmed me and my wife as we left for Curt's funeral?"

His face flushed, and his hands shook. He took a deep breath and gulped his beer.

"I always hoped Curt wouldn't be *that* kind of journalist." His face softer now, but his eyes full of pain.

"I'm sorry, Frank. I've been so wrapped up in solving this puzzle that I forget you've suffered a devastating loss. Maybe this is a mistake. I shouldn't have called you. I'm so sorry."

Sohni gathered the papers on the bar and shoved them into her briefcase. She then removed her coat from the back of her barstool, grabbed the handle of her briefcase, and began to scoot off her seat.

"Just forget about it, Frank. I'll find another way. You need to move on with your life. It wasn't fair of me to ask. I'm just gonna leave now. You go home. I won't bother you anymore."

She dropped money on the bar to cover the tab, and started to walk away. Frank just gazed at the floor.

It had just occurred to Sohni the pain she was causing Frank, and the rift this would cause between him and his wife. The black hole she was trying to drag him back into. How selfish had she been, thinking only of herself. My God, the man had lost his son. What was she doing?

He grabbed her arm. She turned, surprised, to find that he looked surprised as well. They stood poised like that for several moments, Sohni standing next to Frank with a startled look, and Frank clutching her arm like a drowning man grasping for a lifeline.

"Leave the papers," he rasped. "I'll do what I have to do."

# CHAPTER 16

DANIEL DALMAKIS SAT SPEECHLESS, PHONE STILL IN HIS hand. For twelve years, he had been an automotive reporter for the *Michigan Courier*. But he had never gotten a call quite like this one. Never had anyone called him to discuss a murder, especially one as high profile as the Curt Redmond case. Why would they? He wrote about cars, not murders. If the caller had been anyone else, he would have chalked him up as a quack and not given it a second thought. But Curt Redmond's murder was frontpage news, and he had been asked to get involved personally by Frank Redmond, the murdered boy's father.

Although he tried to direct Frank to another reporter better suited for the job, Frank was adamant. He wanted Daniel, and said he'd understand why once they'd had a chance to talk.

Daniel was wary. He didn't like what he was stepping into. But he was curious, too, and his inquisitiveness had won out. He was scheduled to meet Frank at a local Coney Island restaurant in half an hour. After rousing from his stupor, he grabbed his coat and headed to the parking garage.

Daniel checked his reflection in the mirrored door of the elevator. In his opinion, he looked every bit of his forty-six years, and then some. He still had a full head of wavy black hair, but it was peppered with gray. His legs were still lean from his days of running, but the extra weight around his midsection detracted from his former athletic physique. Though naturally olive-toned, his skin appeared pallid, almost translucent. Most shocking to Daniel, though, were the crow's feet that had bracketed his eyes like misshapen quotation marks. He could have sworn they weren't there last week.

"God. I look like my father," he muttered.

He had no one to blame but himself. When he should be in bed, he was instead surfing the Internet, reading and researching, absorbing everything he could learn about cars and the auto industry. He wrote obsessively, not only for the newspaper, but also magazine features and blogs. His existence was a virtual two-way highway of information.

He knew from a young age that he was destined to write. From the time he first learned to put pencil to paper, he was hooked, writing stories, poems, plays, anything he could. His teachers raved, but suggested that perhaps he should devote a little of that time to math and science instead, advice he didn't heed.

In high school, he was appointed editor of the school newspaper. As a section editor in college, his musings on campus life earned him a following and local fame. It was only after entering the workforce that he realized he could combine his two favorite things, journalism and cars.

After twenty-four years as a writer, he still loved what he did, and his passion and devotion to his chosen field showed in his writing. He was a national expert on all things with four wheels and any company that made them. But years ago, his love became an obsession, and as obsessions tend to do, it left room for little else in his life. Lately, he had begun to realize what his dedication had cost him. He had no wife, no children. He owned no real estate, because he convinced himself that the large time commitment that comes with home ownership would cut into his work. And that simply wouldn't do.

At least he committed to a dog. He wanted a German Shepherd—he loved large dogs—but his apartment complex frowned upon that. He settled for a Shih Tzu. The damn thing looked more like a mop than a dog, but Benz was a great companion who tolerated Daniel's strange hours and lack of a yard.

His physical well-being had also suffered. Exercise was a thing of the past. Living by himself, he had little motivation to cook, so he ate poorly, too much take out. And he had a little too much fondness for the old happy hour. He wasn't an alcoholic, mind you. Some drinks after work with friends just seemed preferable to returning home to an empty apartment night after night.

His lifestyle showed on his face in the form of purplish crescents under his lower lids, and in his midsection, which got thicker with each passing year. He had recently started questioning some of his choices, and wondered if it was too late, if he was too far gone to make up for lost time. Boy, would his mother be thrilled if he found himself a wife.

Catching another glimpse of himself in the mirrored door, Daniel realized he was going to have to make some changes before that was going to happen. He looked like death warmed over.

The elevator dinged as it reached the parking garage, bringing him out of his cloud of self-doubt. Once in his vehicle, he entered a destination into his cell phone GPS. A diehard purist, he wouldn't dream of desecrating his classic Mustang with a dashboard GPS, so his cell phone would have to do. But he didn't mind. Hell, he couldn't even remember the last time he drove a vehicle with power locks.

Daniel pulled his car into a spot near the Royal Oak location of Leo's Coney Island, a popular chain.Notebook in hand, he entered through the exit door of the restaurant, almost knocking over two senior citizens deep in discussion about their acid reflux medications. They cast him dirty looks, but never stopped their conversation.

"Sorry." He made a beeline for the only open booth in the place.

He had arrived ten minutes early, so he figured Frank Redmond wouldn't be there yet. He was wrong. Daniel had barely set his butt in the cold hard booth when a man slid in across from him.

"Frank Redmond?"

"Yeah. Nice to meet you."

Frank didn't look pleased about meeting him. In fact, he looked downright terrible, with his face pale and sallow, and his eyes sunken into dark circles. His clothes hung from his body like he had just escaped from a refugee camp. Daniel reminded himself that this man had just lost his only son.

After his initial assessment of the man he came here to meet, Daniel opened his notebook and picked up his pen.

"So Frank," he said, hand poised over his notebook, "I can't wait to hear what you have to tell me."

Frank reached into his bag, and pulled out a sheath of papers. To Daniel, they looked like a stack of computer printouts.

"These are for you. Your copy." Frank handed him the stack bound by a red rubber band. "These were my son's. He was an aspiring investigative journalist. Wrote for a website called The Truth Zone. He always thought he'd break the next big story. Always looking to right the wrong."

"What are these?"

"They're his notes. Some emails, too."

Daniel nodded.

"After his death, I started looking through his things. I was never totally convinced of the cops' story about his death. Why would some homeless man randomly kill my son, not use the cash in his wallet, and then just go to sleep with the evidence in his bag? It just didn't feel right."

It was puzzling, indeed. But Daniel still didn't see what this had to do with him.

"I started asking questions, and I found some suspicious stuff. I found out that my son was working on an article. He told his editor it was really big. Curt could be a bit of a sensationalist, so at first, I didn't think much of it. But then I saw these." Frank gestured to the papers.

Daniel spent the next fifteen minutes listening while Frank explained the details he had discovered. The source in hiding was particularly intriguing. When Frank finally got to the results of Marc Isley's research, Daniel was hooked.

He couldn't believe that neither he nor any of his colleagues had an inkling of any of this information, but some college student had managed to unearth a potentially huge scandal in the automotive industry.

Then it hit him.

"Are you suggesting that this is why your son was killed?"

Frank's stare pierced right through him.

"That's exactly what I'm suggesting."

Daniel mulled over this information for a minute or two.

"But who would do this?"

For the first time, Frank looked less certain. He slowly shook his head, exhaustion seeming to take over his body.

"That's what I'm hoping you can find out."

As Daniel drove back to his office, he questioned whether he should have agreed to tackle this investigation. While he was intrigued by the subject matter, and would love to be the journalist to break the story about the defect in the elastomer, he also realized that his commitment to this investigation implied to Frank Redmond that he would find his son's killer, and Daniel didn't know if he could do that. Didn't know if he even wanted to try. But he had committed anyway.

He thought about the information provided by Frank Redmond. There was little question in Daniel's mind as to which thermoplastic elastomer was the subject of Marc Isley's research. As of late, a new elastomer developed by a relatively unknown supplier called Detroit Automotive Elastomers—commonly referred to as DAE—had received a great deal of press. Indeed, the new elastomer, when molded into weather stripping, was touted as the most noise resistant variety ever developed. Consistent with Frank's infor-mation, Daniel knew that several auto manufacturers had in fact pre-ordered the weather stripping, which was to be sold under the brand name Intact, to the tune of tens of millions of dollars.

Daniel knew how devastating a revelation like Marc Isley's could be to the manufacturer. DAE might never recover from the financial and reputational damage. But he remained skep-tical that Marc's discovery had led to Curt Redmond's murder. DAE was, after all, made up of scientists and businessmen. Not hit men. Then again, people had been killed for far less.

Daniel knew that if he broke the story of this deadly defect in the highly touted new product, it would be a huge boon for his career. Of course, if he also broke the story of the real killer of Curtis Redmond, his career could take on a whole new dimension.

Daniel had worked his way to a comfortable columnist posi-tion, his face displayed with every article he published, and he was happy right where he was. He was doing what he loved, and had a great deal of discretion in choosing the topics of his articles. Many reporters aspired to editorial positions, but not Daniel. He did not want the responsibilities that came with a promotion. Being an editor also meant more management and less writing, a sacrifice he was unwilling to make.

But he could move upward as a writer. Acquiring more fame and accolades would bring the benefit of more freedom in his journalistic choices, as well as opening doors to new opportunities, including television. But if he could really identify a murderer—one whom even the cops couldn't identify—he could write a book. Maybe he'd get a movie deal, too.

Daniel caught a glimpse of himself in the rearview mirror, bringing him back to Earth.

*Slow down.* He chuckled. *First things first.*

He didn't even know if the information this kid had was solid. Plus, the only informant he knew of was apparently in hiding. He needed to take a closer look at the elastomer, the testing, and the evidence in Curt Redmond's murder. He needed to call DAE, Professor Shinji Ito, and of course, Marc Isley, if he could find him. Daniel would also need to arrange for his own testing of the elastomer to confirm the results achieved by Marc Isley.

A lot of research was ahead of him. His movie deal would just have to wait.

After his call to both the public defender's office and the prosecutor's office proved fruitless, Daniel called the number he'd been given for Marc Isley, his home number in Pennsylvania. The phone rang and rang, but as expected, only the answering machine picked up. He left a message, but wasn't hopeful he'd receive a call back. He contemplated hopping in his car and taking a road trip to Marc Isley's hometown in hopes of haranguing him into talking. But he realized that he had no way of knowing if Marc was even in Pennsylvania. He could be anywhere. Without proof of Marc's whereabouts, and without knowing whether he'd even talk, driving to Pennsylvania would probably be little more than a wild goose chase, and a huge waste of time. Daniel concluded that unless he got incredibly lucky and Marc returned his phone call, he would just need to verify through other means whatever information Marc had shared with Curt Redmond.

Professor Shinji Ito was the obvious next step. Daniel called the material science and engineering department offices, where someone gave him Professor Ito's office phone number. He punched in the number, but once again got only a voicemail. He left a message asking the professor to call him when he got in, and placed a checkmark by Shinji's name on his scrawled list of tasks.

He knew that regardless of what Professor Ito eventually disclosed, Daniel would still need to arrange for his own testing of the Intact product. As an automotive reporter, he had developed relationships with various individuals at companies within the auto industry. At times like this, those relationships came in handy. In particular, he was well-acquainted with Gerry Atkins, the owner of Macomb Comprehensive Testing, an independent, materials testing laboratory in Warren, Michigan. Gerry would expedite whatever tests he requested, and give him a good deal to boot.

He put a call in to Gerry Atkins's cell phone, but once again, the call went to voicemail. Daniel left yet another message. *For God's sake, doesn't anyone answer their phone anymore,* he thought while placing another check on his list.

The next entry on his list would not be as simple. He needed to get his hands on a sample of the Intact product. DAE was likely to provide samples to prospective purchasers, namely those companies that manufacture vehicles. Manufacturers would have the capacity to test the product as it was intended to be used, installed in the vehicles. But journalists like him would typically have no use for a small component such as weather stripping, without a vehicle to test it on. DAE was bound to deny such a request, but he figured there was only one way to know for sure.

He typed *Detroit Automotive Elastomers* into Google. The first hit was the official website for the company, which Daniel clicked on. The website that came up was little more than an advertisement for the Intact weather-stripping product. It was obvious that Intact was the company's only product, and that the fate of DAE rested on its success, thus giving credence to Frank's theory that Curt's article could have devastated DAE.

Daniel located DAE's phone number on the website, and dialed it. Refreshingly, his call was answered on the second ring by a pleasant-voiced woman who promptly transferred his call to the public relations department. However, that was where the pleasantries ended. DAE's PR director, who introduced himself as Carlo Moretti, was not only unwilling to provide Daniel with a sample of the Intact weather stripping, but also left Daniel with the distinct impression that DAE had exercised poor judgment when selecting the head of its public relations department. Mr. Moretti was an arrogant ass.

"And who exactly are you?" Moretti said.

"Daniel Dalmakis, automotive reporter for the *Michigan Courier.* Your Intact product is the talk of the town. I'd like a sample to work with for an upcoming article."

"A sample? You do know that Intact is weather stripping, right?"

"Of course."

"I hardly see how a small sample of the product alone would be necessary or beneficial to a reporter. The product serves no purpose without being installed in a vehicle."

"I understand. Nonetheless, I would find it useful. I'd like to see it, touch it, compare it to other similar products."

"Mr. Dalmakis, you're wasting my time. That request is just silly. We've performed demonstrations of features of the product installed in vehicles, including comparisons of our product to its competitors. I believe there is a video on our website. I can send it to you if you'd like. But there's nothing you can do with just a sample. If there's nothing else?"

Daniel's unfortunate interaction with DAE made him even more curious about the fledgling company behind this wondrous new product. It also left him exploring other options for obtaining a sample of Intact.

An idea struck him, and Daniel dialed the phone once again. This time, he called Ed Bigsby, a writer for *Motor Times* magazine. Daniel met Ed years ago at an automobile trade show, and they hit it off right away. Even though Ed lived in Chicago, the two men, both lifelong bachelors, made it a point to meet up for golfing weekends at least a couple of times a year.

Ed started off as a newspaper reporter, just like Daniel, but about eighteen months ago moved to *Motor Times*, a monthly magazine. Daniel recalled that Ed had wrote a column about the Intact product, back in May. Ed would likely be able to tell him more about DAE.

Ed's cell phone had not even completed the first ring when he serenaded Daniel with his usual greeting.

"How the hell ya' doin', Danny Boy?"

Ed had an annoying habit of referring to Daniel as *Danny Boy*. Even his own mother didn't call him Danny. Plus, he was Greek, not Irish.

Daniel smiled anyway. "Not bad, Ed. How 'bout you?"

"Can't complain. Cold as hell here, though. So much for global warming."

Daniel chuckled. Same old Ed.

"Hey, Ed, I'm actually calling on business. I've got a question for you."

"Sure. Shoot."

"I remember you wrote an article about the new Intact product, several months back. What can you tell me about DAE?"

"Not much, really. Small company with a lot of capital. Not really sure where the money came from. Some silent investor, I would guess. The reporter curiosity in me wanted to learn more about DAE, especially how the new kid on the block managed to cause such a stir in its first outing. But the scope of my story was limited to the product itself, not DAE, so I focused only on Intact."

"I seem to recall your magazine performed some independent testing in connection with your article."

"We did. But only after it was installed in a vehicle. Our testing was limited to addressing the claims of DAE regarding the phenomenal performance of Intact when it comes to protection from wind, rain, and sound."

"How did you get a sample to test?"

"Got it from one of my contacts at General Motors. GM was evaluating whether to begin using the product in its vehicles, and had been provided samples, which it installed into vehicles for testing purposes. My contact allowed me access to one of the trucks with Intact installed, but only after DAE signed off, which wasn't easy. DAE needed to verify my credentials, inspect the vehicle to ensure the product had been installed properly, and was not damaged, and they practically interrogated me regarding the scope of my article."

"Did you have the pleasure of meeting Carlo Moretti?"

Ed chuckled. "Ahh. I see you've had the pleasure as well."

"You could say that. So how did Intact perform?"

"Fantastic. Best weather-stripping I've ever seen. Didn't you read my article?"

"Yeah. But it was months ago. I can't remember that far back. You don't still have any of the product, do you?"

"Nope. Sorry. The car was just a loaner, and we never had a piece of Intact separate from the car. Hey, Danny Boy, do you know something I don't? What are you keeping from me?"

"It's probably nothing. Just following up on some leads. But if I find out something juicy, you'll be the first to know."

"Yeah right, ya' damn liar."

The men laughed again. But they both knew Ed was right. If Daniel found Marc Isley's research to be accurate, Daniel alone would break the story. And Ed would do the same if the tables were turned. It was dog eat dog, in the world of news reporting.

"Thanks, Ed."

"Yer welcome, buddy. Let's hit Myrtle Beach for some golfing this winter."

"You bet. I'll email you some dates. Talk to you later."

Daniel ended the call, but before he could set down the phone, it rang. His ringtone set to full volume, Sammy Hagar's, "I Can't Drive 55," blasted through the office, causing more than a couple heads to turn toward him.

He hurried to answer the call. "Daniel Dalmakis."

"Mr. Dalmakis, this is Professor Shinji Ito from the University of Michigan. You left a message for me earlier."

"Of course, Professor Ito. Thanks for returning my call. I was hoping to discuss with you some research your department, and in particular, your student Marc Isley, has been performing with respect to the new Intact weather-stripping product. I'd like to ask you a few questions."

"Mr. Dalmakis, I'm not sure I'm in a position to answer all of your questions, but I may be able to confirm or deny certain information. However, you have to promise that you will not name me or the university as your source for this information."

"That's no problem. This call is just to confirm what I've already been told about Mr. Isley's research. I will need to perform independent testing, anyway. Confirmation from you will just make sure I've got good information before I move forward."

"OK, then. Go ahead."

"Can you confirm that Marcus Isley worked for you as a research assistant?"

"Yes."

"And he was working on a project for which he was conducting testing of a thermoplastic elastomer commonly known as Intact."

"Correct."

"Is it true that during his testing, he discovered—or at least, reported to have discovered—that the Intact product is highly flammable?"

"Uh … I can only confirm that Marc's notes reflect that finding. I have not spoken to him about it, nor have I performed the test myself."

"Is it true he suddenly left town after Curt Redmond was murdered?"

"I'm not going to talk about that. If you want information about Marc, you'll have to contact him directly."

"But he's not answering anyone's calls, right?"

"Again, I'm not talking about Marc."

"OK, OK. So, to summarize, is it correct to say that if Marc's findings about Intact's flammability, as reflected in his notes, is correct, the Intact product is much more flammable than one would expect it to be, for vehicle use?"

"Correct."

"One last question, Professor. Do you have a sample of the Intact product you could share with me so I can conduct my own independent tests?"

"Um … I'm afraid I can't do that. We agreed to only use it for our specified purposes."

"Oh, well. It was worth a try. Thank you, Professor Ito. I appreciate your time."

"You're welcome."

The call was short and sweet, but it served its purpose. Marc's supervising professor confirmed what Frank Redmond had told Daniel. It was time to move forward with a new round of testing. All he needed now, was something to test.

Time to call in a favor.

# CHAPTER 17

SOHNI FINALLY GOT THE INFORMATION SHE HAD FOUGHT SO hard for, and it confirmed she was on the right track. After months of legal wrangling, the judge had granted her motion for an inspection of Curt's cell phone.

The expert's analysis of the phone's activity showed mostly what you'd expect from a college student, with a couple important exceptions. Curt's browsing history indicated that he had visited DAE's website and accessed articles about thermoplastic elastomers generally, as well as the Intact product specifically. His log also showed several calls and texts made to Marc Isley's cell phone during the weeks just prior to Curt's murder.

On her second read through of his log, a series of calls caught Sohni's attention. Eight days before Curt was killed, he had started receiving calls from numbers that weren't in his contacts, and that she could not otherwise identify. Each lasted between six and ten seconds. There were no outgoing calls to those numbers, indicating that Curt did not call the person, or persons, back. He received the final one on the day he was killed.

Sohni grabbed her own cell phone and scrolled through her contacts until she found the numbers of the burner phones from which she had received the threatening calls. She had received twelve calls from five numbers.

"Holy shit!"

The numbers matched. Curt had also been receiving calls from the person threatening her. She no longer had to wonder if her caller was someone angry at her representation of Henry, or someone threatened by her investigation. If Curt was receiving the same calls, it had to be because of his investigation into Intact. The caller probably thought the matter had been taken care of after Curt's murder. But then she had picked up where Curt left off.

Sohni was both excited and terrified. Excited because this was evidence that Henry did not kill Curt. He was instead killed to prevent him from revealing the defect in the Intact product.

Terrified because the killer now had her in his sights.

She hurried to Helen's office. Other than the calls, there had been no more incidents since her tires were slashed. But she now knew that she couldn't wait for the next one to get serious about this threat. Though Matt had bought an alarm device for Sohni carry with her, that was not going to keep away a madman hellbent on killing her.

"Helen, can we arrange a security escort to and from my car each day?"

"Has something else happened?"

Sohni explained her discovery. "I now believe I need to take this threat more seriously."

Helen nodded. "I agree."

She called the building's security office. A quick word with the manager, and arrangements were made.

"Call Tom when you arrive in the morning. He'll send someone to meet you. Stay in your car until he gets there. He'll walk you into the building. When you're ready to leave in the evening, give him a call and he'll have someone walk you to your car."

"Thank you, Helen. That makes me feel a lot better."

"You're welcome. I'm glad you came to me. Now remember, no exceptions. Don't go to and from your car alone, OK?"

"OK. I'm still going to have to leave the building to walk to court or to get lunch, though. What do you recommend?"

"The buddy system. If you have to leave, take someone with you. I'll alert everyone to the situation and encourage them to accompany you, if requested. I would guess that the more people you're with, the safer you'll be."

"That's probably true."

"I also think you need to update the police about this new development. They are already aware of the calls and the tire slashing. But at the same time, I understand the situation is awkward. You would essentially be accusing the police of arresting the wrong man."

"Yeah, that could be a little weird."

"But you still need to let them know. You don't have to make any accusations. Let's also call the prosecutor's office. The evidence you've gathered has become pretty compelling.

They need to know that they are likely prosecuting an innocent man."

"I don't look forward to that call," Sohni replied.

"Yeah, me either. Let's just get it over with."

Helen punched in Pauline's cell number. As the line rang, she transferred the call to speakerphone so Sohni, sitting across Helen's desk, could participate.

"Pauline Fitzgerald."

"Pauline, it's Helen Sorenson."

"Hi, Helen."

"Sohni is here with me, and we have something important we want to bring to your attention. Is this a good time to talk?"

"Yeah, I'm in my office. What's going on?"

"Pauline, I know this is unusual," Sohni said, "but I have accumulated a great deal of evidence that strongly suggests that someone other than Henry Martinez killed Curt Redmond."

"Well, that's your job, isn't it?"

"Of course. But this is different. I have been receiving threats. A dozen or so calls, and my car was vandalized."

"Oh, yeah, I heard about that. But what does that have to do with the Martinez case?"

"I found out today, when going through Curt Redmond's cell phone records, that he was also receiving calls during the days leading up to his murder. They were from the same number that has been calling me. You see, Curt was an investigative reporter. I have mounds of evidence showing that he was working on an investigation at the time of his death that threatened to destroy a corporation. I believe that's why he was killed. And I believe the same person who killed him, is now threatening, me."

Silence on the other end of the line.

"Are you, actually serious?" Pauline said.

"Of course, we're serious," Helen replied. "We wouldn't be calling you if we weren't."

"Let me get this straight. You want me to drop the charges against the man who was indisputably in the area where Curt was killed at the time of the murder, and who was found in possession of the murder weapon, and the victim's wallet, because the victim—who was a college student, by the way—may have been writing an article?"

"What we want is for you to sit down with us and go over what we've found," Sohni said. "I think you'll find it compelling."

"I don't have time for this. If you think you have evidence to create reasonable doubt, then present it at trial. The police have conducted their investigation, and we've arrested the man we believe is responsible."

"But that's not true!" Sohni yelled. "The police barely conducted an investigation. They didn't search Curt's phone, his computer, or even his room. You don't even have a motive. And all for what? To appease Robert Bender?"

Helen frowned at Sohni. She'd gone too far, and she knew it.

"OK, we're done with this conversation," Pauline said. "I'll see you in court."

The line went dead.

"Well, that went well," Helen said.

"Yep." Sohni dropped her head into her hands. "Just super."

As she drove home, after being seen off by a security officer, she saw threats at every stoplight, a menace in every shadow. How was she supposed to live her life normally, knowing she was in the crosshairs of a person who had already killed once. Especially when no one with authority to protect her took her seriously.

She had called the police, as Helen instructed, and spoke with the same detective who had looked into the previous incident. He took down the information and said he'd continue his investigation, but she could tell that some hang up calls were not his priority, even when she explained the connection to Curt. Everyone in the county believed Henry Martinez killed Curt, and her assertions to the contrary were, to everyone else, nothing more than the tactics of a desperate defense attorney.

Her thoughts turned to the reporter Frank had entrusted with Curt's notes, Daniel Dalmakis. If he finally disclosed to the world the secret the killer was so desperately trying to keep hidden, then all of this would be moot. There would be no secret left to protect, and no remaining reason to target her.

The waiting left Sohni restless and on edge. She had no way of knowing whether the reporter was even pursuing the story, and if he was, whether he would be publishing it any time soon. Or even better, whether he had found anything that could help Henry. The gag order in place prevented her from contacting the reporter directly, and her own personal ethics stopped her from bothering Frank. She would never forget the pain he exuded at their last meeting. She vowed that she would not be responsible for inflicting any more torture upon that man. He had done everything she had asked of him, she would not ask for more.

It left Sohni with no choice but to wait and prepare for the worst-case, which is that the threats would continue unabated, and Henry would go to trial on murder charges.

Sohni barely heard her ringtone over the P!nk song she had cranked up on the car radio. Like she had conjured him, Frank was on the other line. She connected the call through her car's hand-free system.

"Hi, Frank. How are you?"

"Doing OK. Is this a good time to talk?"

"Of course," Sohni replied, too enthusiastically, her heart rate increased.

"I'm sorry to bother you, but I feel like I'm ready to jump out of my skin. I haven't heard anything from the reporter, one way or the other. I've read every issue of the *Michigan Courier,* cover to cover, but—"

"Nothing?" Sohni said.

"Exactly. Nothing."

"Well, he did call me shortly after you spoke with him. So that's something. Of course, I couldn't speak about the case, but I was happy to learn that he was at least investigating."

"That is good!" Frank said. "That's great, actually. But I was hoping to hear something more by now."

"I understand."

"I hate the waiting, the not knowing. And I can't do a damn thing about it."

"Have you followed up with the reporter?" Sohni said.

"I didn't know if I should. I figured I needed to let him do his job without me hanging over his shoulder. I assumed if he needed to talk to me, he'd call."

Silence filled the phone line, both lost in their thoughts.

"I-I'm not exactly sure why I called," Frank said, sounding sheepish. "Sorry to bother you. I just didn't know who else to talk to."

"Don't apologize. I was just sitting here in my car, feeling the same sense of helplessness, which is a pretty horrible feeling."

"Maybe I will give Dalmakis a call. If he's decided not to pursue the story, then I can take it to someone else. If he has, and can't talk to me about it, then at least I know."

"That's true. He very well could be in the middle of his own investigation. He'll need time. You dropped quite a bomb on him, remember."

Sohni was surprised to hear a thin laugh from the other end of the line.

"You're right. You should have seen the look on that poor guy's face. I don't think he knew what hit him."

Sohni felt the corners of her own mouth turn upward. She was imagining the meeting between Frank Redmond and the reporter, Frank strung out and clutching Curt's notes like a lifeline. The reporter debating whether to give in to the intrigue, or run like hell.

"I would say check in with him," Sohni said, "then let him do his job. That's my advice, for what it's worth."

Frank grunted his agreement. "Let's just hope he does it quickly."

Sohni pulled her car into the garage, happy to see that Matt was already home, and made sure the garage door was shut before exiting her car. She found Matt in the office, grading papers, and wrapped her arms around him from behind.

"Hey, hon. Smells good in there. What magic potion do you have in the Instant Pot?"

"I'm trying out a new vegetarian chili recipe. It has egg-plant, which seems a little weird. But I figured, what the hell?"

"Well, I look forward to trying it. I'll just go change my clothes and then be right back down to set the table."

As she stepped into her sweatpants, a crash echoed from below, followed by the sound of glass tinkling, then the shrill siren of an alarm. But this time it wasn't her car. It was the house alarm.

She galloped down the steps, taking them two at a time, and met Matt at the bottom, who'd come looking for her. Together, they searched the house until they found the gaping hole in the sliding glass door that led to their fenced-in backyard. In the middle of the living room lay a large rock, looking like a meteorite crashed to Earth. Shards of glass had sprayed through the room, landing several feet away from the door.

"Don't touch anything!" Matt said. "Call the cops."

Sohni dialed 911.

The police arrived quickly and inspected the inside and outside of the house. They found no one. The door to the fence that surrounded their back yard hung open, though Sohni recalled that it was shut when she arrived home.

"Damn!" Matt said. "I didn't think about the fence when I had the security system installed. It should have had a sensor to let us know if someone opened it or jumped over it. This guy was able to just enter our backyard and come right to our patio door without us knowing. That was stupid of me."

"Matt, this isn't your fault. Stop beating yourself up. We've never had to live like this before. What do we know about securing a house? We're both OK. It's just a window."

One of the investigating officers said, "Mr. and Mrs. Silver, we found something you need to see."

They followed him back to the living room, where officers were taking photographs of the scene. The police had discovered a folded paper attached to the rock with a rubber band. The officer unfolded it and held it up with gloved hands, for the couple to see. The text was made up of letters cut out of magazines, like ransom notes from movies. But this was not a ransom note.

As Sohni read the message, she gripped Matt's arm.

*U R NEXT.*

# CHAPTER 18

DANIEL'S CONTACT AT GM HAD COME THROUGH FOR HIM. HIS old friend, Todd Billings, happened to manage GM's materials testing department. Their friendship had paid off for Todd several years ago, and as a result, Todd owed Daniel big.

During the Great Recession, when GM suffered devastating financial difficulties, Daniel had learned some inside information concerning GM's expected downsizing, including measures that would have devastated Todd's department and jeopardized his job. The non-public information Daniel had shared with Todd enabled him to act offensively. Todd had never forgotten Daniel's kind gesture. Now it was Todd's turn to return the favor. Luckily, Todd Billings had an extra sample of the Intact product, and he was willing to share it with Daniel.

GM had completed its testing of the weather-stripping product and no longer needed the sample. The testing a car manufacturer performs on a minor part such as weather stripping was basic, and according to Todd, the Intact product performed spectacularly. For the more thorough testing, like flammability, a company such as GM generally relied on the testing conducted by the product manufacturer itself.

Fortunately, Todd was also willing to provide Daniel with copies of DAE's own testing documentation. According to DAE's reports, the results of their comprehensive testing, which was performed in-house, was within normal parameters. DAE's testing was not as extensive as some Daniel had previously seen. Several tests often found in this type of report were missing, including flammability. The omissions obviously did not concern the automobile manufacturers. They must have found the testing sufficient for their purposes. But they did concern Daniel. Were those tests omitted because the results would be incriminating? Or did DAE, like the auto companies, simply consider them unnecessary? Although the question of whether DAE knew about the product's flammability fascinated Daniel, it was largely academic. Whether or not DAE knew of the defect prior to Curt's discovery didn't change that the product was dangerous. Either way, DAE had a lot to answer for. Assuming Marc Isley's results were accurate.

That morning, a message from Gerry Atkins had been waiting in Daniel's voicemail box. Gerry had completed testing on the Intact product, and had invited Daniel to meet him at the testing facility later that day. When Daniel entered the Macomb Comprehensive Testing offices, Gerry greeted him with his usual wide smile and vigorous handshake. Gerry was hard to miss, with his prominent handlebar mustache and wide girth, and a personality to match. Daniel had found him likeable and kind-hearted, and he was a blast at happy hour.

After his warm and boisterous greeting, Gerry got down to business.

"I have your test results." He raised his eyebrows. "They're rather interesting."

Daniel raised his eyebrows too. "Oh, that sounds juicy."

"Come with me."

Daniel followed Gerry to his office, which was little more than a cluttered storeroom with an old beat-up desk.

"The CEO doesn't even get a window?" Daniel said.

"I get no respect around here," Gerry said, doing his best Rodney Dangerfield impersonation. "It's pretty much just a place to store papers." He chuckled, gesturing to the array of papers strewn about the office.

"So, what did your testing show?" Daniel said.

"Well, I'll tell you, I'm pretty damn curious as to what this product is you brought me. It has some serious problems."

"Like what?"

"Like, it failed miserably in the flammability portion of the testing."

Daniel's heartbeat quickened. Marc Isley was right, after all.

Gerry handed Daniel a sheath of papers that summarized the testing and the results. Sure enough, under the flammability testing section, the product achieved abysmal scores.

"This appears to be intended for use as weather stripping," Gerry said, "but I can't imagine an application for this product for which this level of flammability would be acceptable. It is inherently unsafe. Virtually any contact with flame, or even extremely high temperatures, would cause it to catch fire."

Gerry noticed the smile that had crept across Daniel's face.

"Well, I didn't think that would be good news, but I see I was wrong."

"Let's just say it makes for good journalism."

"Glad I could help. I'll keep my eye on the headlines for your next big story. And for mention of my stellar testing services, of course." Gerry winked.

"You can count on it. If this story is as big as I think it's going to be, everyone will know the name *Macomb Comprehensive Testing*."

Gerry's face lit up with his contagious smile. "That's what I like to hear!

Daniel was eager to return to his office to compare Gerry's testing results with DAE's own. He also needed to learn more about DAE, the newcomer to the auto supply game, with a revolutionary new product and suspiciously flawed test results. He pressed harder on the accelerator of his Mustang and watched the needle on his speedometer edge a little over eighty. Police be damned, he was hot on the trail of a huge story.

Based on what Gerry had told him, no halfway competent lab could possibly miss such a glaring defect. That took Daniel back to his two alternative conclusions, and neither was good for DAE. Either DAE was negligent in its design of the product, and then in its failure to test properly, or DAE covered up the Intact product defect and intentionally omitted the poor test results from the reports provided to the auto manufacturers.

Daniel entered the parking structure, parked with his right front wheel well over the white line, and hurried to his desk. There, he found the DAE testing reports that Todd had shared with him. Daniel perused the papers, comparing them to the ones provided by Gerry. As to the tests conducted by both DAE and Macomb, the results were similar. Only the absent information was damning.

Intentional or not, DAE's omission could be incredibly costly. The first time a car turned into a fireball, the truth would come out. Lawsuits would ensue, as would an investigation. The auto manufacturers would cancel their contracts and probably be forced to recall all cars made with the Intact product. DAE would be ruined.

Daniel needed to obtain more information about DAE. He started with the Internet. On the State of Michigan's website, Daniel was able to view copies of corporate filings for all Michigan corporations, so he searched for Detroit Automotive Elastomers. A list of DAE's filings appeared on his screen, along with links to images of the actual documents. He clicked to open DAE's articles of incorporation, which were just filed the previous year.

As he scrolled down, he was surprised to find that DAE was incorporated by Robert Bender, a well-known local businessman who owned the highly successful auto supplier Bender Industries.

Daniel wondered why Robert Bender would form a separate corporation to manufacture and market Intact, instead of doing so through the well-established and well-respected Bender Industries. He was also surprised to find that Robert Bender associated with fraudulent activities of this sort. The reputation of Bender Industries, as well as that of Robert Bender, was spotless. Why would he engage in such reckless behavior that would jeopardize not only DAE, but Bender Industries as well?

Daniel's gut told him there was more to DAE than met the eye. He continued searching through the corporate records. DAE's first annual report, filed earlier that year, identified the corporate officers. Not surprisingly, Robert Bender was listed as the president and treasurer. However, a new name showed up as vice president and secretary, Carlo Moretti.

Daniel repeated the name *Carlo Moretti* to himself several times, trying to remember where he had heard that name before. Finally, it occurred to him. Carlo Moretti was the ass he spoke to when he called DAE to obtain a sample of Intact. So DAE's public relations director was also its vice president and secretary. Daniel was pretty sure he had never heard of this Moretti guy prior to his phone call to DAE. What was he doing in cahoots with an established businessman like Robert Bender?

Daniel typed *Carlo Moretti Michigan* into Google. The first few hits didn't appear relevant, but the fourth listing drew his attention and he clicked on the link. The resulting article turned out to be, of all things, a wedding announcement from a local community newspaper. The blurb, which totaled three sentences, read as follows:

*On Saturday September 8, 2001, Vincent Mancuso, son of Mr. and Mrs. Salvatore Mancuso, married Maria Zarrella, daughter of Mr. and Mrs. Giuseppe Tucci, at St. Crispin's Roman Catholic Church in St. Clair Shores, Michigan. A reception followed at the Italian American Club of Macomb County. The couple will reside in St. Clair Shores.*

Carlo Moretti's name didn't appear in the announcement, but Daniel located the search term in the caption under the accompanying photograph of the wedding party.

> *From left to right: Sophia Tucci (sister of the bride), Angela Moretti (sister of the bride), Celia Zarrella (daughter of the bride), Maria (Zarrella) Mancuso, Vincent Mancuso, Anthony Mancuso (brother of the groom), Carlo Moretti (nephew of the bride), David Moretti (brother-in-law of the bride)*

"Holy shit!" Daniel sputtered.

He had not recognized the name Moretti, but he sure as hell recognized the names Salvatore Mancuso and Giuseppe Tucci. They were the heads of the Detroit Mafia. Robert Bender, Daniel concluded, was in bed with the Mob.

By the time Daniel arrived in Della Stanford's office, the chairs were all occupied, as were all four of the walls and Della's desk. Daniel stood in the doorway until Della gestured to an open space against the window, which Daniel filled.

Della Stanford proudly served as editor-in-chief of the *Michigan Courier*. She held her reporters to the highest standards, and cherished the reputation of her newspaper above all else. Della, like Daniel, was one of the old-school idealists, and her emphasis on quality over sensationalism did not always please her publishers. After all, sexy sells. But her reporters won awards and gained access where other reporters could not because of the tight ship she ran. And Della was tough. The editor, who stood barely five feet tall, and typically wore her white hair assembled in a neat bun, looked grandmotherly. But she had won many a battle of wits with tough-guy reporters and bully publishers.

Della had practically grown up in a newspaper office, learning the business from the inside out while passing her summers in her father's own editor's office during her youth in Indiana. She was a black woman in a white man's world, but nobody knew the business better, and she was damn good at what she did. Once they figured that out, her bosses mostly let her run things the way she wanted, which was by the book, with a touch of creative genius.

This explained the overcrowded office full of suits. Daniel recognized an entire hierarchy of editors, as well as a publisher's representative named Don, and one of the newspaper's lawyers. Della was taking no chances. After all, Robert Bender was a powerful person.

All gazes turned to Daniel as he detailed his investigation and the story, he anticipated writing. Reactions around the room varied. All present recognized the potential journalistic impact of his discoveries, but those paid to protect the newspaper's legal and financial interests showed concern. Daniel understood. Like it or not, it took money to run a paper. While the investigation and series of articles Daniel planned to write could be a boon for the paper, any explosive article could lose advertisers and piss off the wrong people.

"Do you feel your investigation might damage your relationships with the auto manufacturers and suppliers?" Della said. "The manufacturers will be caught with egg on their faces when you let the world know that they had almost allowed a major safety hazard to slip by their radars."

"That has occurred to me. I don't want them to think I've become a new industry watchdog, someone they have to be wary of instead of working with."

Della nodded. "It's a concern. But I don't think that alone should prevent you from doing this story. Viewed another way, you're actually doing the manufacturers a favor by alerting them to the problem with this product before they install it into their cars. Canceling orders is much easier than recalling vehicles."

"Good point," Daniel said.

More concerning to the suits, though, was any potential loss of advertising revenue, and of course, the potential lawsuits. No one wants to be disparaged in the press, even if the facts reported are entirely true. Some targets will stop at nothing to prevent the truth from being revealed, including litigating the newspaper into bankruptcy. Robert Bender was one of those.

"Robert Bender will fight tooth and nail to keep Daniel's investigation from ever seeing the light of day," said the lawyer. "I know for a fact that he has a team of lawyers on retainer, ready to strike at the first sign of trouble. More than likely, Bender will have us in court before the first article is even published."

"That's pretty much inevitable with that man," said Don. "But we'll have a team assigned to ensure that no mistakes are made, fact checkers, researchers, editors, lawyers. And Daniel's work will be analyzed under a microscope before it's ever printed. A lawsuit will cost us money and possibly slow us down, but as long as what we're publishing is the truth, we won't lose. Plus, a high-profile lawsuit will only bring more attention to Daniel's articles."

Everyone nodded, seemingly satisfied.

"Is anyone going to talk about the five-hundred-pound elephant in the room?" said an editor. "The Detroit Mafia, really?"

"I don't think it makes a difference," Don said. "We just report the facts."

"But why is the mob involved in this company?" the editor replied. That seems so strange to me. Does this have to do with the Teamsters? Is it all some kind of money laundering scheme? Should we be looking further into that aspect?"

"Right now, I think we need to keep our focus on the Intact product," Della said. "I agree that the Mob's involvement is bizarre and warrants further inquiry, but let's put that on the back burner for now."

"But the Mob's ownership of DAE can't be avoided when you look at the murder angle." Daniel said.

Every head in the room turned toward him.

"Murder angle?" Don said.

"There's no murder angle," Della replied. "This article is about the defect, and only the defect."

"Well, actually," Daniel said. "Curt Redmond's murder is what this entire investigation has been about. It's how the whole thing started."

"Daniel, you are an automotive reporter, not a detective," Stella said. "I know the connection between Curt Redmond's murder and his investigation into Intact is intriguing, but we are not the cops, and we don't accuse people of murder."

"But it needs to at least be mentioned! The last reporter about to break the story of the defect was murdered, and his source is in hiding."

"But the police arrested a man for his murder, one whom has nothing to do with the Intact product."

"Many people think they have the wrong guy."

The others in the room listened in silence, their attention moving from Della to Daniel and back, as though watching a tennis match.

"Daniel! What is going on with you? You know we can't interfere with the prosecution of Henry Martinez. Not without more than what you have."

"What the hell are you guys talking about?" Don said.

Daniel explained how the case came to him in the first place, and the unavoidable connection between Curt's death and the Intact product.

"But Daniel, you simply do not have enough evidence to print such a serious accusation. You are asking to be sued."

Daniel sighed. "You're right, Della. I don't have enough."

But he thought of Frank Redmond and his suffering. He knew Frank trusted him to get at the truth about his son's murder, not just the Intact product. Just because he agreed to leave any references to Curt's murder out of his Intact articles, didn't mean he would stop digging into Curt's murder.

After assigning roles and reviewing protocols, Della dismissed the horde. Only Della, Daniel, and the automotive editor remained, as the rest streamed into the hallway, sucking in breaths of cooler air and fanning themselves with their legal pads.

Then the meeting turned more interesting, with the three of them strategizing a promotional campaign for Daniel's story. Della proposed that Daniel turn his article into a three-part series. The first article, to be published soon, lest it be stolen by another reporter, would detail Daniel's investigation, and his findings regarding Intact. The second, to follow a couple of weeks later, would focus on DAE, Bender Industries, and the effects of the scandal on both suppliers, as well as the auto industry. The third and final article was undecided, and would be largely determined by the course of his investigation. The editors discussed the internet and promotional campaigns, and instructed that more testing be performed, this time in the presence of *Courier* photographers, who would snap com-pelling photos and video of the Intact product bursting into flame. Daniel rolled his eyes, but agreed. He could live with the new expectations of modern technology, as long as he got to write his story.

Finally free, Daniel bolted from Della's office. He flapped his arms like a crazed bird, trying to dry the sweat circles that had formed under his armpits, but caught a glimpse of himself in a window and stopped. He made a beeline for his desk, where he began what he anticipated to be the most frus-trating and futile part of his investigation. First, he would again call Carlo Moretti, with a formal request for a meeting, which would undoubtedly be denied. He would then prepare formal, written questions for DAE, which the company would never answer. It was standard journalistic procedure. But in this case especially, he felt confident his efforts would be a pure waste of time.

Which is why Daniel was speechless when Moretti returned his call an hour later, with an invitation to meet with Robert Bender at the Bender Industries office later that week. Of course, Daniel had stated only that he was intending to write an article about Intact, and that he would like an opportunity to first discuss the product and his article with DAE.

He was no stranger to Robert Bender. They'd met numerous times, but had formed little rapport. It was Daniel's observation that Bender had little rapport with most people. The man attracted a following due to his striking good looks and dynamic showmanship, and he was a skilled businessman. But even a scratch beneath the surface revealed an arrogant, haughty man who was impossible to get close to. Daniel would have liked to believe that it was his reputation that led DAE to grant him an interview, but he knew it was more likely to be Bender's propensity to show off, and his desire for free press coverage for his new product.

This time, Robert Bender's arrogance was going to be his downfall. He was about to let down his defenses and welcome the wolf into his henhouse.

Daniel conveyed the news to Della, who was equally surprised, and bade him equal parts good luck and caution. He had two days to prepare, to research, and to find the most efficient use of the time he would be graced with Bender's presence. Once he started asking questions, he knew his welcome would be revoked. He needed to get on the record as much information from Bender as he could before the man became aware of the article topic.

Walking that line would be a challenge, and Daniel only had one shot.

# CHAPTER 19

DANIEL'S MUSTANG IDLED IN BUMPER-TO-BUMPER TRAFFIC on I-75. He was headed to the Bender Industries office in Auburn Hills, a northern suburb of Detroit, but based on the snaking trail of brake lights ahead of him, he was going to be late.

The traffic jam broke sooner than expected, so he arrived only five minutes late to the Bender offices. True to the company's image, the building gleamed in the morning sunlight, all steel, and sharp angles. Above the third-floor windows, a large script B dominated the façade. Daniel paused and took in the structure with a keen reporter's eye, from the brushed nickel front door to the meticulously pruned shrubs and Japanese Maples lining the front walkway. The building exuded an aura of precision, the perfect image for an auto supplier specializing in high-tech, cutting-edge components. He wondered, though, if the cold precision of Bender Industries said less about the *industries*, and more about *Bender*. The company's owner was much like his building, perfect and precise, all shiny metal and sharp edges.

Daniel took a seat in the building's lush lobby as he waited for the receptionist to notify Bender of his arrival. He didn't wait long. A middle-aged woman wearing a tan business suit and trendy, black-framed glasses soon emerged from the elevator and strode towards him. She was Robert Bender's assistant, and she had been sent to escort him to the conference room, where her boss would be meeting him shortly. She led him to a room as imposing as the building's exterior. The room's centerpiece was the ten-foot-long, three-inch-thick granite slab that functioned as a conference table, which was surrounded on every side by roomy gray leather swivel chairs. Two walls were entirely made up of floor to ceiling windows, providing stunning views. Daniel observed high-tech electronics throughout the room, including a video-conferencing system and a seventy-inch flat screen attached to the back wall. Original oil paintings adorned the pale blue walls, and the peaked ceiling bore two rectangular skylights, which cast rays of sunlight onto the conference table. The room inspired awe, or intimidated, depending on the context. Daniel felt both.

Even though he had arrived late, Bender kept him waiting. Seventeen minutes passed while Daniel arranged and rearranged his papers, and reviewed and re-reviewed his notes. What was it about that man and this place that made Daniel so unsure of himself? He'd conducted countless interviews, some adversarial, but he had never let his nerves get to him. Bender was different, though. The man was a robot, never showing emotion and always in control. Conducting the interview he'd planned, would not be easy.

When the CEO finally arrived, he was impeccably dressed, from the perfect pleat in his pocket handkerchief to the mirror-like shine of his black Italian leather shoes. Not a hair was out of place. Walking ramrod straight with an unmistakable air of importance, he entered the conference room and offered his hand, with perfectly manicured nails, to his guest. Daniel rose from his seat to exchange a firm handshake, now feeling frumpy in his wrinkled sports coat, which he kept stashed in the backseat of his Mustang for just an occasion. His first miscalculation, he allowed himself to be outdressed and outclassed by a mile.

Still standing, Bender offered him a drink, gesturing to the beverage cart parked nearby. Daniel thanked him, grabbed a Diet Coke, and emptying it into a glass of ice. He returned to his seat and swiveled in his luxurious chair to face Bender, who had sat in the chair next to Daniel, which also happened to be located at the head of the table. Daniel felt confident that was no accident. Miscalculation number two.

Bender crossed his legs and settled back into his seat, flashing a disarming smile. The epitome of confidence.

Daniel realized that he'd been duped. Bender had never intended to answer Daniel's questions. The meeting was nothing more than an in-person press release. The man would tell him what he wanted printed, with the expectation that the *Michigan Courier*, his marionette, would publish the company line. In his childlike giddiness over Bender's willingness to meet with him, Daniel had abandoned his journalistic instincts. He should have known better. The man was a master at the art of manipulation. He knew how to work a room, how to persuade others to do what he wanted, while allowing them to believe it was their own idea. He always got what he wanted. Why would he believe this meeting would be any different? He expected Daniel to be so awed by the experience that he would do his bidding.

This realization made Daniel's blood boil. He was being treated as nothing more than another Bender minion. More maddening was that he had begun doubting himself, even after all his years of reporting. Bender's expensive suit, perfect coif, and million-dollar conference room were nothing compared to the bomb Daniel came armed with. Regardless of what the man believed, Daniel was the one with the power, a lesson Bender would soon learn.

"You'd like to know more about Intact?" Bender said. "It's absolutely revolutionary. There's nothing else like it out there."

He slid a press packet across the table, and was clearly prepared to speak at the reporter indefinitely. But Daniel intended to take control of the meeting. They were working from his agenda, not Bender's.

"I've read the press releases and spoken to third parties who've installed it in vehicles," Daniel said. "I understand the sound reduction is amazing."

"Absolutely. But sound reduction is just the beginning. Its ability to maintain internal temperature and block out external pollutants is also very impressive. Intact will be the new standard, no doubt about it."

"By all public accounts, the reviews have been positive. But have you run into any problems? Have any of your customers expressed concerns about the product? Have there been any test results that weren't as glowing?"

Bender was far from intimidated by Daniel's questions, but they threw him off his stride. His gaze became distrustful.

"Of course not," he replied.

"I understand the Department of Defense is interested in Intact for their military vehicles."

"Correct. The weather stripping will be unbeatable for vehicles to be used in extreme temperatures, high winds, sand storms, hurricanes, and the like. I expect the DOD will soon be placing a large order."

"But U of M is testing the product first, correct? Precisely because of the extreme conditions in which the vehicles may be used?"

"Yes. Standard procedure for the DOD."

"I'm assuming that those types of conditions were not contemplated in the original testing performed by DAE."

"Of course not. If they had been, the DOD would have no need to perform additional testing. DAE's testing focused on general automotive use, not military use. Although certainly, the product is also well-suited for it."

"To your knowledge, has the U of M lab's testing raised any concerns about the Intact product?"

"As I said before, there have been no concerns raised about the product. Before DAE put Intact on the market, it conducted thorough testing. It passed with flying colors, and those test results have been distributed to all potential customers. I'm sure U of M's results will be no different."

"So, you feel confident that Intact has no defects, and is completely safe for use as weather stripping both in personal and military vehicles?"

"My answer to that, and you can quote me, is a resounding yes. It is absolutely safe." Robert Bender uncrossed his legs and leaned toward Daniel, one elbow propped on the table. "Off the record, what are you implying? Is this some kind of fishing expedition? Do you intend to attempt to disparage the Intact product to boost sagging readership and make a name for yourself? If so, you'd better be damn careful."

"Mr. Bender, I assure you that I am not some rookie reporter, and I do not write for a tabloid. We publish nothing but responsible journalism."

"Good. Then you know that the Intact product has been extensively tested by DAE, and installed and run through its paces by others, and has received nothing but glowing reviews."

"And you have confirmed that you have heard nothing to the contrary. Got it."

Daniel removed from his notebook copies of DAE's testing reports provided to him by Todd, and showed them to Bender.

"Are these the official testing reports that DAE provided to the auto manufacturers?"

Bender studied the papers. Not surprisingly, his wariness had grown.

"I can't say for certain. I'd have to check our own records. I can tell you that they are in the format we use, and seem to include the signature of our testing manager. However, I simply cannot verify their authenticity without comparing them to our own copies."

"Can you easily access your copies so that we can compare?"

"No. They are kept at DAE."

"I'm surprised you didn't bring your Intact papers with you, knowing that was the subject of our meeting today. In fact, I was surprised that we weren't meeting at DAE offices instead."

"First, you were not specific as to what you wished to discuss. I brought along a press packet, assuming that would suffice. I couldn't know you would have so many questions about DAE's testing. Second, this office is where I spend the majority of my time, so it was much more convenient for me to meet with you here."

"That's fair. Perhaps then, you could have your assistant fax me the official testing reports." Daniel reached into his shirt pocket, withdrew his business card, and tried to hand it to Bender.

The man remained motionless, so Daniel slid his card across the table until it touched Bender's hand. Still, he didn't move.

"Perhaps you could tell me why you need them?" Bender said. "Certainly, all the information you need to write an article about Intact is available to you in our press packet. And I'm here as well to answer questions you may have about the product and its performance. I've already told you that there are no concerns regarding the testing of Intact. That should be the end of the issue."

"I can tell you that I obtained these testing reports from a source at an auto manufacturer, who states that he received them from DAE. Surely that's something you should be able to confirm."

"I already told you that I don't have the copies here."

"I understand that. But I'm sure you could make a phone call that would get me the information pretty quickly."

"I'm sure I could, if I was so inclined." The man's glare spoke volumes.

The power rested with him, lest the reporter forget it. Daniel wrote as he said, "So on the record, DAE is unwilling to provide the *Michigan Courier* with copies of DAE's testing reports for the Intact product, and also unwilling to confirm or deny that the reports we have were those officially issued by DAE. Is that correct?"

Bender swallowed hard, his face unchanging.

"I will talk to our testing department and our public relations manager and find out if that's something we can provide."

"Also, I see there are certain tests routinely found on such reports, that are not included on yours. For example, if you compare your reports to ones provided by other suppliers, you will see that the other suppliers included several more testing categories."

Daniel pulled more sheets from his notebook and placed them beside DAE's reports. With his pen, he pointed to several test results listed on the sheets that were absent from DAE's report. Bender listened closely and reviewed the portions identified by Daniel.

"Again, I cannot say for sure if the reports you claim to be DAE's are authentic," Bender said. "Even if they are, DAE's testing manager is the one who determines which tests are necessary for a particular product. He makes his decisions based on the type of product, its intended use, and the requirements of the end purchasers. I'm sure he selected the tests that he considered to be the most important and relevant for Intact. I can't speak to why he selected the tests he did, but I can assure you that he is highly experienced, and I trust his decisions. Moreover, the auto manufacturers are satisfied with the reports we've provided. They obviously have no problem with what tests were and were not performed."

"May I schedule a meeting with your testing manager? I'm sure he can ably answer my questions. What's his name? I can't quite make it out from his signature."

"That would be highly irregular. He does not do interviews on behalf of DAE. And his name is irrelevant."

"Then perhaps I should send DAE some written questions. You can obtain the information from your testing manager and provide me with written answers."

"Mr. Dalmakis, you are free to do what you deem necessary. But you are currently squandering the one and only opportunity you will have to obtain information about Intact. I will waste no more time on this once I leave this room."

Daniel slid the testing results from Macomb Comprehensive toward Bender, and placed the report next to DAE's own report.

"Mr. Bender, I had a third-party lab perform testing on Intact. Some of the tests were the same ones performed by DAE, and for those, the results were quite similar. But the lab I used, also performed standard tests that were oddly not included in DAE's report, such as flammability. Please note the results of that test."

Bender sighed in a condescending tone as he skimmed the report. Then he frowned.

"Well, obviously this is wrong. I frankly have no idea what you tested. It might not have even been our product. I also have no knowledge of the integrity of these tests or this lab. This is ludicrous."

The flush that slowly appeared on Robert Bender's face was the only sign of his irritation. His demeanor remained cool as ice.

"I assure you, Mr. Bender, that the result of the flammability test is accurate. In fact, the U of M testing revealed the same defect. Do you have any comment?"

"Damn right I do. It is your testing that is defective. I suggest you tread carefully, Mr. Dalmakis. I will own your paper by the time I'm done with you." The man gracefully rose from his chair. "I will show you the way out."

But Daniel remained seated. "Just one more question."

Bender sighed loudly. "Get on with it, then. I have a great deal of work to do."

"Do you know a former U of M student named Curtis Redmond?"

Bender jerked his head around to face him, confusion on his face.

"Curt? What does Curt have to do with this?"

"You knew Curt Redmond?"

"Of course I did. What kind of reporter are you?"

Daniel winced inside. He was asking himself the same thing.

Robert Bender's cheeks showed more color, and his volume increased.

"Curt was my son's roommate, his best friend. My son is reeling from his death. Now you come in here invoking my son's dead friend? You'd better have a damn good reason for bringing up Curt's name."

Daniel was stunned, confused, his thoughts racing. The facts suggest that Curt Redmond was going to expose Intact's defect to the world, and in doing so ruin his best friend's father. Maybe Curt hadn't gotten far enough in his research, to discover that his friend's father owned DAE. Or maybe he did, and just didn't care. Could Robert Bender or his mobster partners have found out? It would have been easy enough if Curt roomed with Bender's son.

Daniel was hoping to leave this meeting with answers. Instead, he now had more questions. But he would have to collect his thoughts later. Right now, Robert Bender was waiting for an answer.

"Curt Redmond was also writing an article about Intact. He had learned about the highly flammable nature of the product. But he was murdered before he could complete it."

The color drained from Bender's face. Though he tried to maintain his composure, it was obvious that the man was shaken.

In a raspy voice, he whispered, "Why are you telling me this?"

"It's just interesting, that's all."

Bender scoffed. "Interesting? A young man is dead, and it's *interesting*?"

Daniel's brain spun as he processed what he had just learned. Bender's close connection to Curt was a curveball he hadn't expected. The question he wanted to ask Bender sat on his tongue, but he knew making such an allegation was reckless, especially to a man like Bender. But he also knew that after he left that room, he would most likely never have another opportunity to get Bender on the record, to make him address the allegation. It was now or never.

"Did you, or your silent partners, know he was writing an article about Intact?"

Bender looked at Daniel as though he had sprouted two heads. Then he replied calmly, despite the turmoil obviously raging inside.

"I have no idea where you're getting your information, but that is the most ridiculous thing I've ever heard. And what exactly are you suggesting? That I had him whacked to prevent him from writing some amateur article about Intact? You, Mr. Dalmakis, are not only out of line, you are insane."

The man straightened his jacket, pressed his slacks with his palms, and strode to the door. He turned back to face Daniel, and the look he cast made Daniel want to hide under the giant granite table.

"You should leave now, Mr. Dalmakis. Our time is done."

Della was waiting for Daniel when he returned to the office. And she was not happy. She pounced as soon as he entered.

"What the hell were you thinking accusing Robert Bender of murder?"

The chatter and keyboard clacking stopped. Everyone's attention turned to Della and Daniel. He halted and took a step back as Della approached him, all flushed skin and wild eyes. Daniel sometimes compared angry Della to a puffer fish. She was a sweet-looking petite woman most of the time. But when enraged, she seemed to grow to twice her size and ten times fiercer.

Before Daniel could respond, Della's head snapped around to the gawkers.

"Get back to work!" she yelled.

They did.

Della grabbed Daniel's upper arm and nearly dragged him into her office, where she slammed the door so hard the photo of her granddaughter leaped off her desk and onto the floor, face first. She delicately picked it up and repositioned it on her desk. Then she swung back around to Daniel, who stared at his feet like a naughty schoolboy. Della breathed in deep, closing her eyes, then exhaled slowly. Calmer, Della directed him to sit in one of two chairs in front of her desk.

"I will ask you again. What the hell were you thinking accusing Robert Bender of murder?"

Daniel looked sheepish. On his way home from Auburn Hills, he realized he'd gone too far bringing up Curtis Redmond's murder, and was crazy for suggesting—even through a vague implication—that Robert Bender may have been behind it. A good way to get himself sued, or worse yet, killed.

"I wasn't thinking, Della. I was running on adrenaline. And I feel it in my gut that DAE is behind Curt Redmond's death. I really do. But I realize that I accomplished nothing by going about it the way that I did."

Daniel's sincere repentance seemed to mollify Della.

"You're not a cop, Daniel." She scoffed. "You're not even a crime reporter. You're a car guy. What are you doing out there chasing a murderer? Especially when the police have already arrested the man who supposedly did it?"

"I've read about the evidence in the case. I don't buy it."

Della rolled her eyes.

"Really, Della. The more I learn, the more I believe they've arrested the wrong guy. The police don't have the evidence I have. They don't know that at the time of Curt Redmond's death, he knew about Intact's defect and was planning to reveal it, and that his source is in hiding. They also don't know that DAE is partly owned by members of the Detroit Mafia. Curt Redmond was interfering with the mob's livelihood. He was a threat, and now he's dead."

Della studied Daniel in silence for several seconds.

"You really think the Mob may have killed Curtis Redmond?"

"I do. I really do."

"Daniel, I sympathize with your plight. I understand your reporter's urge to seek the truth, to right injustice. But we simply cannot make unfounded accusations. You know that as well as anyone."

He nodded. "Of course."

"Not to mention, the obvious dangers of making accusations against mobsters."

He nodded again.

"You see, with the auto component we have something tangible that we can test. We can obtain empirical data. Murder isn't so easily proven. And it isn't our job to prove it. We have to trust our justice system to do that."

Daniel had let his emotions run away with him. He wanted so much to help Frank find his son's killer that he'd made promises he could never keep. As Daniel thought of the distraught man, he had met at the restaurant only weeks ago, he was overcome by guilt. Guilt for leading on Frank. Guilt for not being able to find his son's killer. He wondered how he would tell Frank that he had failed him.

"But that doesn't mean that you can't take the evidence you have to the police," Della said. "They may be interested in hearing what you've learned. You should at least give them the opportunity to pursue that theory, if they so choose."

"I've been told that the police and the prosecutor are dead set that they've got the right guy and won't consider other suspects. I didn't think it would do any good to ask them to look into DAE."

Daniel's interest in pursuing the murder aspect of the story was derived not only from law enforcement's lack of interest in doing so, but also from his obligation to honor an ill-conceived promise to a grieving father. Once again, he was struck with guilt. He would proceed to write his story about Intact, and probably make quite a name for himself in the process, and Frank Redmond would still have no answers. In other words, he would use the information which Frank had entrusted to him, for his own gain and give Frank nothing in return. Boy, he felt lousy for a reporter about to send shockwaves through an industry.

"You wield more power than you think, Daniel. If a reputable reporter brings information to the police, they may very well take it seriously. Even if they are reluctant, they will be aware of the fact that any failure on their part to fully investigate the lead you've provided may end up on the front page. Not only would that reflect badly on them, but it could even result in enough reasonable doubt for an acquittal."

"I hadn't thought about it that way."

There *was* something he could do to help Frank. Daniel had obtained evidence that no one else had. Evidence that strongly suggested the police had arrested the wrong man for Curt Redmond's murder. Shared with the right people, that evidence could lead investigators to the real killer. He took some comfort from knowing he could at least do that much for Frank.

As he left Della's office, he formulated a plan. His first call would be to Frank Redmond. His second to the Ann Arbor Police Department.

Daniel found Frank Redmond lying on the tattered vinyl couch in the employees' lounge, with an ice pack held to the crown of his head.

"Oh, no! What happened to you?" Daniel said.

"You happened to me." Frank's attempt at a laugh made him close his eyes and moan. "I was under the hood of a Jaguar, wrestling with a stubborn screw, when you called. I was so surprised to see your number on my display, I bolted up and clocked my head on the latch of the car hood. You literally knocked me on my butt. This had better be worth it." He tried to laugh again but winced.

Frank struggled to sit up, then ceased trying.

"If you don't mind, Daniel, I'll just stay right where I am. I assume you'd prefer that to my throwing up on you."

"Yes, actually, that does seem preferable." Daniel chuckled. "I'll make this quick, then. I can't provide too many details because the investigation is ongoing, but I have obtained information that supports your theory that Curt was targeted because of the article he was writing about the Intact product."

"I knew it!"

"I can't tell you specifically who did it, and I don't know if I will ever know. But there's one piece of information that suggests a great deal. The company that makes the product is owned by the Detroit Mafia."

"No shit? Wow, that says a lot, doesn't it?"

"I would have to agree with you."

"Did Curt know?"

"I don't know. I didn't see anything in his notes, so it's impossible to say."

"It probably wouldn't have stopped him. That kid was like a dog with a bone."

Frank closed his eyes, feigning pain in his head, but Daniel was pretty sure he was hiding the tears in his eyes.

"Anyway, what I really need to talk to you about is where I go from here. I've made progress in the overall investigation. I've confirmed the defect in the product. Confirmed that Marc Isley knew and told Curt about it. And I've verified that the manufacturer omitted the damaging results from the official testing report it distributed to potential customers. In other words, the only way the auto companies would have known about this dangerous defect was through Curt's article. Thus, making him a target. I've also learned about the Mob's connection to the business. What I have put together is a pretty good theory of who likely killed Curt and why. But—"

"There's always a but, isn't there?" Frank said.

"But ... I'm not a detective. I write about the auto industry. I will get sued, and probably fired, if I make murder accusations against citizens without more proof."

"I get it. You're finished. You're going to take my son's investigation and print it yourself, and wipe your hands of anything else."

"Please let me finish, Frank. I've been thinking long and hard about this. It is not my intention to walk away. But at the same time, I don't have the resources to pursue a killer. I have an idea, but I'd like you to be on board with it."

"OK, let me hear it."

"I'd like to take everything I have—Curt's notes, the testing results, my own notes—to the Ann Arbor Police."

"They're not going to do anything! I already told you that. They are so sure they've got the right guy they won't even pay attention to you."

"I don't necessarily agree. Remember, I'm a reporter, and I can publish what I know at any time, which would not only make them look bad, but could mess up their case against Henry Martinez. Nothing is stopping me from bringing everything I know to the defense attorney as well. She can't share information with me, but there's nothing stopping me from sharing it with her."

"Yeah, maybe you should take it to Sohni."

"Sohni?"

"Uh, Sohni Silver. The woman who represents Martinez."

"You know her well?"

"No. We've just spoken a couple times."

He stared at Frank, trying to read his face and wonder why he was on a first-name basis with the attorney defending the man accused of killing his son.

"My thought is that if what you seek is a more thorough investigation into your son's death, the police are in the best situation to do that. They are the only ones who can do that. Not me, not the defense attorney. And if I keep pressure on them, make sure they know that if they do not explore these leads I will out them in the paper and to defense counsel, they are more likely to do the right thing."

"I guess that makes sense," Frank said. "And you promise you will stay on them."

"I do. To me, this story isn't just about a defective weather stripping. It's about your son, too. I want to see the whole story told."

Frank closed his eyes and rested in silence. Daniel thought he had fallen asleep.

"I agree with your plan," Frank said. "Take it to the police."

Daniel nodded. "But I have one more question for you. I want to move ahead with publishing my investigation into Intact, and I want to write the article Curt set out to write. I will give your son proper credit. Though I don't technically need it, I'd like your approval. You trusted me with this, and I want to do right by you, and your son."

"I appreciate your integrity. I trust you will do right by Curt." Frank's voice cracked, and he cleared his throat. "I can't wait to see it in the paper."

For the first time since Daniel stepped foot in the employees' lounge, Frank gave a smile that met his eyes.

# CHAPTER 20

JAKE STARED AT THE STACK OF PAPERS IN HIS HAND. WHEN Daniel Dalmakis called and told him he had some information about Curtis Redmond's murder, he never suspected a story like the one he had just heard. At first, he considered the reporter's theory laughable, that Curtis Redmond was executed by the Mob. But then it became clear that Dalmakis had done his homework. By the time Dalmakis left the station, Jake was questioning whether they had arrested the right guy.

An even more unpleasant thought was the phone call he would have to make to Pauline. The prosecutor was preparing for the upcoming, high-profile trial of Henry Martinez. She had assured the public repeatedly that the killer was off the street and would be prosecuted to the fullest extent of the law. Pauline hadn't admitted it, of course, but she fancied the prosecution of Henry Martinez as her big break, the case that would make her career. In the wake of a successful high-profile prosecution such as this, a victorious campaign would be a piece of cake. But what if Martinez was not the murderer? Jake didn't want to think about it. Pauline would be humiliated, and he knew that she wouldn't bear the brunt of the blame alone. If she went down, she was taking him with her.

He released a long sigh, closed his eyes, and massaged his temples.

"Damn," he muttered. "How did we miss this?"

It didn't matter *how* they'd missed it, only that they did. Even if there was no merit to Dalmakis's theory, the evidence carried enough weight to create reasonable doubt. And Dalmakis made it clear that if the police did not adequately pursue this alternative theory, his next stop would be Martinez's defense counsel. There was no question that Jake had to pursue this lead.

He would have to work cautiously, of course. The reputations of powerful people were at stake. Neither Robert Bender nor his silent partners would take kindly to rumors that they were being investigated as possible murder suspects. Plus, a leak that the police were pursuing alternative leads could impact the trial against Henry Martinez. Jake would have to use the utmost care in his investigation.

He reached for the phone, then stopped, his hand in midair. He debated whether Pauline needed to be informed of this latest development. If there was a legitimate alternative suspect in Curt Redmond's murder, then of course Pauline must be told. But at this point, Dalmakis's theory was merely conjecture. There was no hard evidence that Redmond was killed by anyone other than Henry Martinez. Jake could begin investigating, and then only call Pauline if he found information worth reporting.

He knew he was just putting off the inevitable. The truth was he dreaded alerting Pauline to his own oversight. But he dreaded even more the possibility that Pauline might find out about his surreptitious investigation before he told her about it. So, with a grimace and a sigh, he picked up the phone.

He caught Pauline as she was leaving for court, she had little time to talk. But what she lacked in time, she made up for in volume. Jake pulled the phone an inch away from his ear as she berated him.

"How could you have missed this!" she shouted. "You're supposed to be a detective. Didn't you actually do an investigation?"

It took great restraint for him not to point out that it was Pauline who had rushed the investigation, not the police. That she was the one who believed Mr. Martinez made a perfect suspect, and had instructed the police not to look any further. But he held his tongue. Nothing good would come of it.

"Do you have any idea what this will do to my case against Henry Martinez!" she said.

Yes, he knew well. But he was pretty sure she also meant, *Do you know what this will do to my career?*

Jake was unsympathetic. As far as he was concerned, Pauline had gotten herself into this. Granted, Mr. Martinez had the murder weapon and the victim's wallet in his possession, but he insisted that he didn't even know they were there. Other aspects of Curt's life had warranted investigation but had been ignored, as a favor to Robert Bender. But Pauline didn't want to hear that. She saw her chance at the spotlight, and she took it, truth be damned.

What made Jake most angry was that she was going to take down the Ann Arbor Police Department with her. The department was made up of hard-working men and women who took pride in their work. Based on these investigative failures, Jake and his fellow detectives would come off as bumbling idiots. The press would have a field day with this. He swore that if he and his colleagues took the blame for those failings, Pauline would not escape unscathed.

Before hanging up, Pauline left him with instructions to do what he had to do, in order check out the information Dalmakis had provided, but to *keep his investigation as quiet as humanly possible.*

Relieved the phone call was finished, Jake turned his attention to the evidence Dalmakis had turned over, a sheath of cryptic journalist's notes, two sets of testing reports for the Intact product, DAE business records, and the reporter's notes summarizing his conversations with Professor Shinji Ito and Robert Bender.

Jake shook his head, contemplating whether Dalmakis was brave, or just crazy, for implicating DAE in Curt Redmond's death during his meeting with Bender. He wished he could've witnessed that meeting. Dalmakis mentioned that Bender had lost his cool, which revealed a lot, because Bender was definitely not the type to lose control.

Jake had met Robert Bender once before, at a fundraising event. Most memorable was Bender's charm and poise. He was unflappable. Like a magnet, he drew others to him. People wanted to be near him, share his space, as though the mere nearness would imbue them with the overwhelming confidence that Bender exuded. He was a natural-born leader. No question why he was so successful. Interrogating a man like that would be no easy task. If indeed Robert Bender was involved in the murder, getting him to break would be next to impossible.

Dalmakis seemed to believe that Bender's partners were the more likely murder suspects. Jake didn't agree. His years as a cop had made him more cynical. In his experience, people as seemingly perfect as Bender were all too often psychopaths. Not to mention that Robert Bender had a relationship with Curt Redmond and easily could have learned what Redmond was up to. He may have shared the information with his mobster friends and let them do the dirty work. Regardless of how it went down, he believed that Bender had to have been part of it. That is, if Henry Martinez did not actually kill Curtis Redmond. And that conclusion was still a long way away.

Although he did not look forward to it, Jake would have to meet with Bender. The Redmond file contained Zach Bender's home number, which was also Robert Bender's. But a workaholic like Robert Bender would not be at home at 10:00 a.m. on a Thursday. Because the police never found it necessary to interview him in connection with Redmond's murder, the file did not include any other numbers for him.

Jake obtained the main number for Bender Industries from the company's website, and soon found himself speaking with a haughty secretary who informed him that Mr. Bender was out of town that week. She suggested that Jake leave a message for Mr. Bender, and he could get back to Jake when he had a chance. Probably next Monday, when he returned to the office. Monday was seven days away.

Robert Bender's secretary played her role as Mr. Bender's gatekeeper well, protecting him from all sorts of intrusions. Her attitude and tactics were required in her line of work, and probably encouraged by her employer. But Jake was not about to be blown off by Robert Bender, and certainly not by his secretary.

"With all due respect, Ma'am, this is Detective Jake Clarke of the Ann Arbor Police Department, and I am calling on official police business. Let me make it clear that I will not be waiting a few days for a return phone call."

The secretary tried to interject, probably to explain what a busy man Mr. Bender was, but Jake cut her off.

"I assume that Mr. Bender carries a cell phone, correct?"

The secretary stammered, but Jake did not allow her time to respond to his rhetorical question.

"I strongly suggest that you get hold of Mr. Bender immediately on said cell phone, and tell him to call me within the hour. If I do not hear from Mr. Bender within sixty minutes, I will dispatch an officer to bring him to me. Do you understand?"

A pause on the other end. No doubt, she was unaccustomed to being spoken to in such a manner.

"Of course, Sir," she finally replied.

Jake left his cell number and hung up. He felt bad being rude to the secretary. She was just doing her job, after all. But his meeting with Daniel Dalmakis had left him in a sour mood. He was not going to be pushed around by Robert Bender, or anyone associated with him.

Jake had just returned to his desk with a fresh cup of coffee, when his cell rang. He couldn't help but smirk when the caller identified himself as Robert Bender. He addressed Jake politely, but arrogantly, his tone making clear that the phone call was a huge inconvenience.

"I do hope this is urgent, Detective. I was forced to step out of an important meeting with a customer."

Jake almost laughed at Bender's self-importance, but he figured doing so would not help the already strained exchange.

"I apologize for any inconvenience, Mr. Bender, but I need to meet with you as soon as possible. I'm investigating the death of Curt Redmond."

"A meeting is unnecessary, Detective. I assure you that I have no information about Curt, or his death, that would be of any help in your investigation. He was my son's friend, not mine."

Jake realized his jaw was clenched. Bender's arrogance was astounding. But this time, he wasn't in charge.

"With all due respect, Mr. Bender, I will determine what is and isn't necessary in this investigation."

Bender was a shrewd man. He knew that Jake's call coming on the heels of Dalmakis's accusations was not a coincidence. It was obvious from Bender's silence that he was debating whether to deny Jake the requested meeting. Ultimately, though, he had to know that refusing to answer the detective's questions would cause much more trouble, so he agreed to meet.

"However, I'm afraid I'm in South Carolina at present. I won't be home until Friday evening. My flight doesn't get in until 5:00 p.m. The soonest I could possibly get to Ann Arbor would be the next day, Saturday. But I have a standing tennis

match at 8:00 a.m. every Saturday. It would be at least noon
before—"

"I will come to your house tomorrow, after your flight
arrives," Jake said. "You should be home by seven, right?"

"There is no need to drive all the way to Bloomfield Hills,
Detective. I'm happy to come to Ann Arbor. Like I said, noon
on Saturday would work fine."

"It's no inconvenience at all, Mr. Bender. I will see you at
seven on Friday."

"Friday it is."

After they ended the call, Jake thought how fortuitous it
was that Bender was flying home late, at the end of the week.
He would have no excuse for not meeting at his house, since
surely, he would be tired after his trip, and would head straight
home from the airport.

Jake wanted Bender in comfortable surroundings, where his
guard might be down. It wouldn't hurt that he would also be
fatigued. Meeting the man at his home, instead of his office,
would also have the advantage of privacy. He didn't want word
getting out that Bender was meeting with the police.

Scheduling the meeting for Friday also provided Jake four
days to do his research. He grabbed a pencil from the lopsided clay pencil jar atop his desk. Despite his rotten mood, he
smiled as he took a second look at the handmade art project
his seven-year-old son had gifted him last Father's Day. The
words *World's Best Dad!* were scrawled in the clay in uneven
second-grade handwriting. He also glanced at Tyler's picture
on his desk. It was times like this, Jake remembered why he
kept it there. It did wonders to lighten his mood.

Jake used the pencil to scribble out a to-do list. He listed the items in no particular order:

1. Talk to Professor Ito.
2. Meet with Frank Redmond to review victim's files.
3. Call Gerry Atkins to verify the results of his testing.
4. Call Marc Isley.

Apparently, Marc was refusing to speak with anyone, but Jake intended to call the local police near Isley's Pennsylvania home. Perhaps a visit from law enforcement would change his tune. Jake did not want to leave any stone unturned before he headed into the lion's den that was the Bender interview.

According to Dalmakis, his first of a series of articles about DAE and the defective weather stripping would be published in eight days. That gave Jake a short window to conduct his own investigation before all hell broke loose.

He looked at the ugly gray clock on the station wall, 10:15 a.m. no time like the present.

After trying to locate Frank Redmond at the dealership where he worked, Jake was directed to his house, he had taken a few days medical leave. The look on Frank's face made clear that Jake was not who he expected to see on his porch. In fact, Jake reached out and grabbed Frank's shoulder, afraid the man would pass out. He realized that he should have called first. The last time Jake had appeared at the Redmonds' door, he had pulled them from their sleep, into a living nightmare.

With his mouth open, Frank stared at Jake for several seconds.

"Mr. Redmond, Detective Clarke of the Ann Arbor Police Department."

Frank shook himself out of his stupor.

"Of course, of course. Come in, please." He stepped aside to allow Jake to enter the house.

His hands were shaking as he closed the door and offered the detective a seat. Frank hurried to return to his place on the couch, and gestured for Jake to take a seat as well. The detective parked his large frame on the other end of the sofa, and crossed his right ankle over his left knee.

"How are you doing, Mr. Redmond?" Jake said, his forehead creased.

Apparently realizing he must look a fright with his matted hair, tattered clothes, and two-day stubble, Frank mustered a wan smile.

"I've been better. Got a concussion at work. I'm off until my doctor clears me to return."

Jake nodded.

"I stopped by the dealership to speak with you, but I was told that you were home on medical leave. That's why I came here. I hope your injury isn't too serious."

"Nah, just a bump on the head. But I am about to die of boredom. You know, it's bad when I'm thrilled to receive a visit from a cop."

"Indeed." Jake laughed.

"As much as I welcome the interruption, I'm curious, why are you here?"

Jake paused, appearing to search the floor for the proper response. Finally, he raised his gaze to meet Frank's.

"You know that we've arrested a man believed to be your son's killer, Henry Martinez."

"Of course."

"The prosecution of Henry is ongoing. He had the murder weapon and your son's wallet in his possession. He is our only suspect."

"Right."

"But recently, some new evidence came to light that suggests that others may have had a motive to murder Curt."

Jake chose his words carefully, and measured Frank's reaction as he spoke.

Frank said nothing.

"But you already know this, don't you, Mr. Redmond?"

"Yes, I do. I am the one who gave Mr. Dalmakis Curt's materials. I'm going to allow Mr. Dalmakis to write the article Curt didn't live to write. And in exchange, he got me a step closer to finding my son's real killer."

Jake narrowed his eyes and studied Frank.

"You never believed Henry Martinez was the killer?" Jake said, although he knew the answer.

"No. It never seemed right to me."

"Well, I'm here now. Show me what you got."

Frank stood, and without saying a word, headed toward the spare bedroom, where the computer and Curt's flash drives still sat. Jake followed. Frank booted up the computer, and as the machine whirred and beeped, he gave an account of how he learned about what his son was investigating, an account which, Frank would later realize, omitted Sohni's involvement.

When the desktop icons finally appeared on the screen, Frank inserted the first flash drive. A list of Curt's files appeared, and Frank handed over the reins to Jake. For the next two hours, Jake maneuvered the mouse, clicking and scrolling, until he had reviewed every email and Word document. By the time the detective finally rose from the chair, his knees cracking and popping, Jake was satisfied that every page Daniel Dalmakis had turned over was indeed derived from Curt Redmond's original files.

"Thank you, Mr. Redmond, for taking the time to go through these with me. Your assistance has been invaluable."

"Of course. Anything you need, you know you can count on my help."

"Well, now that you mention it, I'm afraid I'll have to take all these flash drives with me as evidence. The printouts won't be enough. I will need the originals if the evidence will ever hold up in court."

Frank looked sick, and Jake recognized that Frank hated to part with these last vestiges of his son, but at the same time, wanted justice for him.

Jake remained silent while Frank's inner battle raged.

Finally, Frank said, "Can I copy the files for myself first? I just want these to remember Curt."

"Those are now evidence, Frank. I'm required to take them immediately. No one else, not even you, can be allowed to handle these flash drives. I will be required to account for chain of custody, and to the extent they were out of my control, even momentarily, a defense attorney can claim contamination."

Jake was also fighting an internal struggle. He did things by the rules and felt compelled to comply with his duty to seize the evidence immediately. But he was also compassionate, and a father. He was caught between being a good detective and a good person. Ultimately, the good person prevailed.

"Tell you what," Jake said. "I will do it for you. I will copy the contents of the flash drives onto your hard drive. That way, I can honestly say they were never out of my custody or control, but you will be able to keep Curt's files."

"I appreciate that."

Due to the age and slowness of Frank's computer, the process was not a quick one. But he took the time needed to ensure Frank would always have his son's words. When finished, he put on his coat, picked up the box of flash drives, and moved to the front door. Before leaving, he paused.

"You know, there is one question I keep coming back to," Jake said.

"What's that?"

"Did your son know he was about to ruin his best friend's father? Or had he not yet figured it out?"

Frank stared at Jake with a look of complete confusion.

"Robert Bender?" Frank said. "What does he have to do with this?"

Jake felt like a man trapped in a hole he had dug himself, as he searched for a response to Frank's question.

"Well, I thought you knew," he finally said.

"Knew what?"

"Robert Bender owns DAE, the company that manufactures the allegedly defective product."

Frank stood with his mouth hanging open. "But Daniel told me that DAE was owned by the Mob. That the Mob killed Curt. He didn't say anything about Robert Bender."

"The Mob does own DAE. They do seem the most likely suspects, absolutely. But Robert Bender is a partial owner as well, so he stands to lose a lot if your son's article is published. That's all I meant."

Daniel Dalmakis had intentionally omitted any mention of Robert Bender during his conversation with Frank. Obviously, Daniel realized that Frank was less likely to do something stupid if he thought the murderer was part of an organized crime family. But if he thought the murderer might be a man he knew, who was to say how a grieving father might react.

Frank dropped onto the nearest chair.

"Frank, listen to me. All of this information is preliminary. We don't even know that anyone connected with DAE had any involvement in Curt's death. You have to promise me that you will not say one word to anyone about this investigation. And for God's sake, do not even utter Robert Bender's name. If you do, you will jeopardize this investigation." Jake squatted until he was face to face with Frank, and stared directly into his eyes. "And I'm sure I do not have to tell you to stay away from Mr. Bender. Do not contact him in any way. Let us do our job. Do you understand?"

Frank looked him in the eye, and nodded. "I understand. I will leave it to the police."

After a moment, Jake stood and left the house, acknowledging Frank with a nod.

On the porch, with the door shut behind him, he released a long breath and hoped to God that Frank was telling the truth.

# CHAPTER 21

THE FENCE HAD BEEN REINFORCED WITH SECURITY SENSORS. The glass pane in the patio door had been replaced, and her personal escort saw her to and from her car each day. But Sohni still didn't feel safe. After the rock incident, the police took her worries more seriously. But despite their best efforts, they had found little evidence to help them identify the perpetrator.

The general consensus was that the suspect was a man, probably under fifty and physically fit. He was quick, completing his crimes and leaving the scenes without being spotted by neighbors. He had a good pitching arm, too, according to the strength he had thrown the rock with. Most frightening, though, he was excellent at not leaving evidence behind. Police confirmed that he must have worn gloves while preparing for and carrying out his acts, because not one fingerprint was found, and no identifying features were visible on any security camera footage. They did find a couple footprints in

Sohni's backyard, though. Size 11, likely a Timberland boot. Hardly distinctive.

While the uncertainty weighed on her, it took an even greater toll on Matt. He could barely sleep at night, certain that every creak of the house was someone breaking in. He kept a baseball bat under the bed, positioned for him to quickly grab the handle in an emergency. He even proposed buying a gun. The old Matt was anti-handgun, quick to quote statistics demonstrating that someone in the household was far more likely to be killed by a gun than an intruder. He'd even become especially protective of Whiskers, which was sweet in its own way, but also a sign of his worsening obsession, which worried Sohni.

The situation was also not good for their relationship. All pretenses of Matt trying not to smother her with overprotectiveness were gone. She sometimes felt the need to escape from his watchful eye, and would use a visit to her sister's as an excuse. He resisted letting her leave, but she was not about to be a prisoner in her own home.

On this day, the sisters painted Manju's living room. With Manju blasting Imagine Dragons, Sohni taped, rolled, cut in, and did everything but think about the threats. The work was therapeutic, and so was the company. She smiled at her sister, who winked back.

The ladies declared a five-minute break, so Sohni checked her phone. And regretted it.

"My God! Matt has texted me three times and called twice. Manju, what am I going to do with him?"

"Have you ever seen him act this way before?"

"He's always been overprotective, but nothing like this. This is neurotic behavior. It's not healthy, but he doesn't seem to see anything wrong with it."

"Maybe the two of you should see a counselor. You could tell him it's because of the trauma you've experienced. In other words, make it sound like it's more about you."

"That's a good idea. But right now, I need to reassure him that I'm not dead."

*At Manju's. I'm fine! We had music playing. Couldn't hear your call. I'll let you know when I leave.*

Just as she hit Send, her phone rang. She assumed it was Matt, with yet another check in, but the screen displayed Frank's name instead.

"Hi, Frank."

"Hey, Sohni. I wanted to give you a heads up. The reporter came to see me today."

"Really? What did he have to say?"

Frank filled her in on the article Daniel intended to write, and his plan to take the evidence to the police, with a promise to expose their failure to investigate if they didn't follow through."

"That's wonderful!" Sohni replied. "Maybe this time the police will get it right."

"He also told me something that we didn't already know, and that I think you need to be aware of."

"What's that?"

"The company that manufactures Intact, DAE, is owned by the Mob."

"So, he thinks the Mob killed Curt?"

"He does."

"Frank, I haven't told you this, but I've been getting threats. My tires were slashed. A rock was thrown through my window. Dozens of phone calls with silence on the other end, all coming from burner phones."

"Oh, geez. I had no idea."

"At first, I didn't know whether I was being targeted by someone very upset that I was representing Henry Martinez, or by the person who actually killed your son. Then I discovered something else. Curt's cell records revealed that he had been receiving similar calls from the same numbers. I think whoever was threatening Curt is now threatening me. That makes me think that there's someone out there who desperately wants to keep the information Curt had—that we now have—from being revealed. What you just told me, about the Mafia, it all makes perfect sense."

"It does," Frank said. "I can't believe Curt got himself messed up in this. Please be careful."

"I will. Thanks for the call."

Sohni turned to find Manju staring at her, wide-eyed.

"The Mafia?" she said.

"You know I can't talk to you about my cases."

"Bullshit, Sohni. Is that who's been threatening you?"

Sohni sighed. "It's possible."

"Maybe Matt isn't as crazy as he seems, then. Maybe you should buy a gun."

"Manju, not you, too."

"You need to tell Matt, and the police, immediately. Tell your boss, too."

"OK, OK. I will. Don't get carried away."

"Carried away? Maybe it's time you took these threats more seriously. I know that we weren't raised to speak up for ourselves. We ate our feelings. Or in your case, threw them up. We were trained to be stoic, not to complain, not to seek attention. But if you don't demand more protection, Matt and I will do it for you."

Sohni rolled her eyes. "Don't you think you're being a bit dramatic?"

Manju had ignored two back-to-back phone calls during her argument with her sister, but the third call got her attention. She held up a finger to Sohni.

"Speaking of dramatic, it's Mom." Manju slid her finger to accept the call. "Hi, Mom."

Sohni could hear loud chatter from the other end of the phone, though it was pressed against Manju's ear, and she observed her sister's face change from annoyed, to confused, to concerned.

"Mom, slow down. U of M Hospital? Sohni's here with me. OK, we'll be right there." Manju ended the call.

"What the heck's going on?" Sohni said.

"Dad's in the ER. We need to meet Mom there now."

Sohni's father was belligerent. Dementia did that to people, turned mature adults into bratty children. And that's exactly what he was acting like today.

"Adarsh! Stop it, Adarsh." her mother said.

But her father ignored his wife and continued shoving his belongings back in the empty boxes. Adarsh was a dominating man, and for decades he had run his household with an iron fist. A man of little emotion and an overblown sense of righteousness, he'd exercised control over every aspect of his wife and daughters' lives, expecting them to live by old-fashioned religious and cultural standards, and obey him as the male of the household. Now, he was a mere shadow of that man—physically and mentally weak—but his strong will had not dissipated. After his visit to the ER, his family realized he was too much for his wife to handle, which is why they had made the difficult decision to move him to a memory care unit.

"Why are all my things here?" he said. "Take them home now, Raima! Take me home now."

"You can't go home, Adarsh. You scalded yourself, thinking you could make rice. What were you thinking? You never cook. You won't listen to me or your doctors. You're always wandering off, hurting yourself. I don't have a choice. I can't keep you safe."

Adarsh pointed to Sohni. "You, girl, don't just stand there. Take these to my car."

She stood motionless, looking to her mother for guidance.

"Ah, you've always been useless," he said. "Get out of my way. I'll do it myself."

His wife cajoled him into putting down the box.

"Manju, why don't you show your father around the place," she said.

"Actually, why don't *you* show him around the place," Manju replied. "I'll take care of things in here."

Her mom shot her a look that could've frozen water.

"Your poor mother. Such insolence. I ask for so little." She took her husband's arm and led him out of his room.

Sohni slid down the wall until she sat cross-legged on the floor, breathing deep. Manju joined her and took Sohni's hand in her own. For years they'd been terrorized by that man, and every day still lived with the emotional scars. Their mom's abuse was more subtle. The seemingly innocuous comments dripping with private meaning. The putdowns, and constantly playing the martyr.

Sohni flashed back to when she and her sister were children, and they sat just like this, providing emotional support to each other, and dreaming of the day they were grown and free of the abuse. Yet here they were.

Moving her father was a major decision, and they knew it had to be done as a family. So, for the last week, she and Manju had helped their mom pack his things surreptitiously, and move them into his new residence. Today, though, was the day they would walk away and leave him there.

Sohni felt nauseous. "I need some fresh air."

She walked outside, the brisk air was exhilarating on her face. Every cell in her body screamed at her to get in her car and drive as far away from there as she could. But she couldn't leave Manju there alone.

Sohni's phone rang. It was Frank.

Even before he revealed his reason for calling, Sohni sensed the change in Frank's demeanor. For the first time in the few months she had known him, Sohni heard hope in his voice, and she dared allow her hopes to rise as well. The news Frank conveyed, though, was even better than she could have imagined.

"Jake Clarke was at your house, looking at the same computer files we looked at?"

"Yep. He spent hours reviewing them. And he took the originals. He's pretty serious about this investigation."

"That's wonderful. Was it Dalmakis? Did he force Jake's hand?"

"Yep. The detective figured out I was the one who alerted the reporter, so I admitted it. But I kept your name out of it."

"I really appreciate that."

"Oh, yeah. There's one other thing."

"What's that?"

"The Mob isn't the only owner of DAE. Robert Bender is also an owner."

Frank's upbeat mood had disappeared.

"What does that mean?" Sohni said, but she had already started wrapping her head around the possibilities.

Frank responded with silence.

"Frank, you can't really think Robert Bender had anything to do with Curt's death."

She knew that was exactly what Frank thought.

A chill coursed down her spine. Frank was a desperate man. And desperate men were also dangerous.

"Frank, talk to me! You have no evidence that Robert Bender knew anything about this. You already said the company was owned by the Mob. Isn't it much more likely that they killed Curt?"

"You're right. But I just can't get past Bender's involvement. I'm finding it very difficult to write it off as coincidental."

Sohni would never say it to Frank, but the same thought had crossed her mind. Bender was the father of Curt's best friend. That would give him easy access to Curt and the information concerning his investigation, especially since Curt used Zach's computer. But it was a huge leap, from reasoning that Robert Bender might have known of Curt's investigation, to concluding that he would have killed him over it. Of course, what if Robert Bender mentioned Curt's investigation to his partners? Perhaps Robert Bender was indirectly and inadvertently responsible for Curt's murder by sharing the information with the wrong people.

"I don't know what to think." Frank's words jarred Sohni from her thoughts. "I'm just glad the police are investigating. It's exactly what both of us wanted."

"Yes, it is," Sohni replied. "Let's not jump to any conclusions until the police have completed their investigation. I'm sure they will make the same connections we have."

Frank uttered a throaty laugh. "Don't worry. I'm not planning to go off half-cocked. I intend to let the police do their job."

Sohni's laugh was one of relief. "Good to hear. Well, it's great to know about the investigation. Thanks for letting me know."

"No problem. I'll give you a call if I learn anything else."

"Thanks, Frank. Talk to you later."

Their relationship was a strange one, but they had an inexplicable bond. Frank needed Sohni, which is why he kept calling her, even though he had no obligation to do so. Perhaps it was because she was an outsider and wasn't bogged down in the pain of Curt's death. But most likely it was because she was the one other person who believed that Henry didn't kill

Curt. And Frank's presence in her life kept Sohni focused on what was really at stake here. While her first priority was achieving an acquittal for Henry, Frank was a reminder that a young man was dead and that justice had not yet been served.

Sohni punched in the number for the Washtenaw County Prosecutor's Office. Pauline had no idea she knew about Jake's investigation, and her call took the prosecutor completely by surprise.

The receptionist informed her that Pauline was gone for the day, so Sohni opted for her voicemail. Sohni's message left no doubt as to why she was calling. She demanded that Pauline agree to adjourn Henry's trial until Jake's investigation could be completed. Especially since the police are no longer confident they even have the right guy.

Sohni marveled at how well she had orchestrated this. For someone who never broke the rules, and possessed very little guile, she had succeeded in stunning fashion.

Her hands were numb, she walked inside and returned to her father's new home, a twenty-by-fifteen-foot room. A far cry from the glass-fronted lakeside house he had resided in this morning.

Sohni could hear the arguing from down the hall, her father barking commands, thinking he was still in charge, and her mother trying to calm him. It was all pointless. She didn't need to be there, and neither did Manju. They could do nothing for either of their parents, and the trauma of it would send the sisters to extra therapy sessions for months.

She found her sister standing in front of a dresser, folding and re-folding their dad's shirts, her hands shaking.

Sohni approached her and whispered in her ear, "Let's get out of here."

At first, Manju looked concerned and glanced toward her parents, who were still bickering. Then she flashed a big mischievous grin that lit up her face. She grabbed her coat from the doorknob, took Sohni's hand, and the two of them walked out without a word.

"Girls, where do you think you're going?" Raima yelled. "Don't walk away from me!"

But the women continued to Sohni's car, got in, and drove away.

When they reached Sohni's house, where Manju had left her car, they found the squad car parked at the curb, in the same spot as when they'd left. Sohni waved to the officer inside, and so did her sister, but with a more suggestive smile. Sohni rolled her eyes, but Manju laughed, starting her ignition. Before pulling out of the driveway, she rolled down her window.

"I feel like we just escaped from prison, and that US Marshals will be coming for us."

"Yep, that sounds about right," Sohni said.

Her father's move had taken most of the day, so Matt was already home.

She planted a kiss on his cheek. "Hi, hon. I see our friend is still outside."

"Yeah, he's leaving soon. But another car will come by later. They can't provide a twenty-four-hour presence, but their boss has asked them to stop by when they can, more as a deterrent than anything else."

"Does that make you feel a little better?" she said.

"It does."

"I have some other news that might make you feel even better."

"Oh, yeah? I could sure use some of that."

"The police have reopened the Redmond investigation. They're following the new lead I found. They might actually find the guy who's doing this."

"That's great news. Even just having the cops asking questions might get him to back off. I'm sorry I've gone a little crazy. I just want this to be over."

"I know. Me, too."

Sohni heard her ringtone, and pulled her phone from her purse. The screen displayed a question mark.

It was her mystery caller.

# CHAPTER 22

J AKE HAD FINALLY FOUND MARC ISLEY. ACCORDING TO THE
Pennsylvania State Police, all indications were that he and
his family still lived where they had for decades, on a back
road in Myrtleville, Pennsylvania. And a drive-by performed
by local police confirmed that Isley's Ford Focus was parked
in the driveway.

Traveling to Pennsylvania himself seemed unnecessary, when all he needed was a conversation with Isley. Jake
requested the assistance of the local police, who agreed to bring
Isley to their station, put him on speakerphone with Jake, and
record the interview.

Jake's cell phone rang at 8:15 a.m. as he was just arriving to
work. The screen identified the caller as Officer Henry Perkins
of the Myrtleville Police Department. Perkins had obviously
made fast work of rousting Mr. Isley.

Jake rushed to pull into a parking spot, and accepted the
call.

"Detective Jake Clarke."

"Good morning, Detective. It's Hank Perkins from the Myrtleville Police Department. We've got your guy here. Are you ready to talk with him?"

"That's great. Thanks. I am ready, but I was wondering if you could give me your impression of him first."

"My impression? Well, he's a chubby towhead who looks fourteen." Perkins laughed. "In all seriousness, though, he's pretty scared. I thought he was gonna pee his pants when he saw me at his house. He insisted on having his dad come with him to the station, so I've got 'em both here."

"That's fine. If having his dad with him makes him more comfortable, I consider that a good thing." Jake hurried into an open interrogation room, where he'd be able to hear better, and grabbed his notebook. "OK, I'm ready whenever you are."

Thirty seconds later, he was talking to the elusive Marc Isley. After some prodding from Officer Perkins, and some comforting words from Isley's dad, Jake was able to pull the story from Marc. And it was quite a story.

"The weather stripping just burst into flames. I couldn't believe it! I tested it twice to be sure, but there was no doubt that the product was dangerous. I documented all my research for Professor Ito to review. But it nagged at me. I just kept thinking that this terrible product was about to be installed in cars. People could die. I knew the school's only obligation was to report back to the DOD about the testing results. There was no way I could be sure that the public would learn about it unless I let them know."

"And that's when you contacted Curt Redmond?"

"Yeah. A friend of mine is a journalism major, and I remembered her telling me about The Truth Zone, and that students were given the opportunity to write real-world investigative articles. It sounded like the perfect solution. I checked out its website, and I noticed that this student named Curt Redmond had written more articles than anyone else. He seemed quite serious about it. So, I looked him up in the student directory, and there he was, still at U of M. I sent him an email, and from that we arranged a meeting. I was really happy with his response. He understood the urgency involved, and seemed excited about exposing the company peddling this crap. I trusted him."

"What do you know about Curt's work on the article? How far had he gotten?"

"He didn't tell me specifics about his work, but he continued to check in with me periodically to ask additional questions or get my thoughts on something. It seemed to me that he was moving quickly."

"Did he mention anything odd, like somebody following him, or threats he may have received?"

"No. But after I met with Curt and told him everything I knew, I started getting weird phone calls. They were from numbers I didn't recognize, the first few calls I answered anyway. You never know. It could be a professor or a classmate whose number I don't have in my contacts. But the caller never said anything. I knew he was there. I could hear him breathing right into the phone. It wasn't a butt dial. Someone was on the other end trying to intimidate me. I finally stopped answering calls from numbers I didn't recognize. But he left voicemails."

"What did he say on the voicemails?" Jake said.

"Nothing. He just stayed on the line, breathing into the phone, same as when I picked up. I felt someone was threatening me. And I mean, I'm just a normal guy who goes to classes all day and plays video games all night. The only possible reason anyone would come after me would've been the information I gave to Curt. I got spooked."

"You refer to the caller as *he*. Do you have a reason to believe the caller was male?"

Marc thought for a few moments. "I guess I don't really know for sure. The way he was breathing, though, made me think he was male." He chuckled. "I guess that sounds kind of silly."

"No, not at all. Anything you can tell us is helpful."

"The breathing was heavy. Heavy mouth breathing. It's just not the kind of thing you usually hear from a woman."

"Did you tell anyone about the phone calls? Maybe Curt?"

"No. No one. I just kept hoping they'd go away."

"Did the calls eventually stop?"

"Yes … after Curt was killed."

"Do you still have the numbers these calls came from?"

"I probably still have them in my phone log. It would take me a few minutes, but I should be able to identify at least a couple of them."

"That would be great. Officer Perkins, could you please email me those numbers?"

"Sure thing."

Jake continued. "Marc, what about the voicemails? Did you keep those?"

"No. I deleted them. Sorry."

"If you would sign an authorization for us, we can get your cell records from your carrier. They may be able to pull your deleted voicemails as well. If you could specify the time frame during which the calls came in, that would be helpful."

"Sure. No problem."

"Other than the phone calls, did you notice anything else strange? Anyone following you?"

"Not that I recall."

"Marc, why did you leave Ann Arbor so suddenly?"

"Curt's death scared the shit out of me. I was literally eating breakfast, getting ready to go to class, and there was his face on the news." Marc's voice cracked, and he swallowed hard. "Somebody was making threatening phone calls to me, and then Curt was murdered on a street not far from where I lived. It couldn't be a coincidence. I knew I had to leave. I was afraid I'd be next."

The room fell silent for several seconds.

"Thank you, Marc," Jake said. "I know this hasn't been easy for you. We're going to make sure Curt's killer goes away for a long time. But I will likely need to contact you again, and you need to answer your phone when I call."

"I will. I promise."

Jake had expected his call with Isley to provide more details about Intact. He had not expected to learn that the killer knew a great deal about Curt's investigation, including the identity and phone number of his primary source. The person who killed Curt had likely been watching both of them.

This information led Jake to a stunning but disheartening conclusion, Curt's death was premeditated, and they most likely had the wrong man in custody.

By the time three o'clock arrived, Jake had suffered enough for one day. His *routine* appearance in court was anything but, with a lying defendant who accused him of all kinds of misconduct, despite that, all of their interactions were on video. And now he had an angry voicemail from Pauline. Reluctantly, he dialed her number.

"How the hell does Sohni Silver know about your investigation!" she yelled.

"I have no idea. I've been discreet."

"Like hell you have. It took her one whole day to find out. You've ruined my case, you know."

"Pauline, calm down. From what I've learned, I no longer believe Henry Martinez killed Curt Redmond. You brought charges too soon. We missed important details."

Silence on the other end.

"What details?" she said, finally, with a voice so icy Jake could feel the cold through his phone.

"Curt was an amateur investigative reporter. But he wrote some powerful articles. He was in the process of an investigation that would have revealed a defect in a new automotive component that would have devastated the manufacturer."

"You're kidding me. That's all you've got? That's the same story Sohni and Helen pitched to me, trying to convince me their client was innocent."

It was Jake's turn to fall silent.

"What did you say?" he finally said.

"Sohni and Helen called me a while back with the same story, that Curt Redmond was writing an article that may have gotten him killed. I can't believe you fell for that."

"Let me get this straight. You were made aware of evidence suggesting that the man you are prosecuting for murder may not have committed the crime, and you ignored it?"

"Detective Clarke, I suggest you tread very carefully."

Jake took a breath.

"The victim's source, Marc Isley, the only person who knew about the defect, started receiving disturbing phone calls. When he saw that Curt had been killed, he ran, literally. He quit school and moved back home. Wouldn't take anyone's phone calls. He was terrified because he thought he'd be next. We never had Curt's phone records analyzed, but Sohni did. I reviewed his phone log, and he had been receiving short calls from some of the same phone numbers as Marc Isley, all burner phones. I think both of them were receiving threatening calls that were intended to intimidate them into dropping the story."

"Jake, a few phone calls is still a far cry from murder."

"I'm not done. Did you know Sohni has also been receiving the same type of calls? From the same numbers. Somebody also slashed her tires and threw a rock through the window of her house."

Pauline didn't respond.

"You did know, didn't you? She's being threatened just like Curt and Marc. Another detective has been investigating those matters, but hasn't been able to come up with any good leads. Sohni has been insisting that the person making the threats is the same person who killed Curt Redmond, but of course no one here will take the idea seriously because they trust we have his killer in custody."

"Even if everything you're saying is true," Pauline said, "how do you explain the bloody knife and wallet in Martinez's bag? You can't just ignore that evidence."

"I think it was planted. Martinez was sleeping only yards away from where Curt was murdered. His bag was there, too. The killer walked back up Hill Street, took less than a minute to place the wallet and knife in Martinez's bag, and fled. Remember, not one item from Curt's wallet had been used. Why take a wallet full of money and credit cards, especially one that can incriminate you in a murder, and then never bother to use them? Martinez's prints weren't on either item, which also doesn't make any sense."

"Is that everything?"

"No. There's one more thing. The company that manufactures the defective component—the one that stands to lose everything—is co-owned by Robert Bender and the Detroit Mafia."

Jake let Pauline process the information. Her benefactor was now directly implicated. Jake was sure she was reconsidering Bender's efforts to control the investigation from a new perspective.

"I'm meeting with Bender tonight," he said, "and I'm not treating him with kid gloves. I don't care how much damn money he gives to you. He had easy access to Curt Redmond and all the information he collected. He had motive, and he had the Mafia at his disposal. He needs to explain some things."

In a defeated tone that was uncharacteristic for Pauline, she agreed.

"But keep me informed of every step, Jake. Everything you learn."

"I will."

"Oh, and I refused Sohni's request for a delay of the trial, but I know she's going to request one from the court. So, let's get this done as quickly as possible so we don't need to adjourn."

Jake held back a sigh and shook his head. Delaying the trial was precisely the right thing to do so he could complete his investigation, and Pauline could confirm she was prosecuting the right man. But Pauline was all about appearance.

"I'll do what I can," he said.

After his call, Jake returned to the question of how Sohni knew about his investigation. Dalmakis had to be her source. When he met with the reporter, he had insisted he would only take the information to Martinez's attorney if the police did not properly investigate the new leads. He'd either lied, or thought the police were taking too long.

Jake was aware that the reporter planned to publish the results of his investigation into the Intact product, but what if the reporter had also decided to publicly identify the new suspects in the murder. Jake could see the headline now, *Police Miss Crucial Evidence, Arrest Wrong Man for Murder of College Student.* An acquittal of Henry Martinez would be the least of his worries.

Even more troubling to Jake was that he deserved whatever dressing down he received. So far, his renewed investigation had confirmed everything Dalmakis had told him. It was easy to blame Pauline—and mind you, she was not blameless—but ultimately the investigation was his responsibility. He had never before allowed himself to be bullied by a prosecutor, even one as strong headed as Pauline.

But while Pauline expected the arrest of Henry Martinez to be an easy solution, it had instead created new problems for the city. Tensions still ran high. Pro- and anti-homeless factions engaged in verbal warfare on the street and in the press. Jake's home had changed for the worse, and he was partly to blame.

Jake accepted his own complicity in the false solution. He could have insisted on a more thorough investigation, pointing out the holes in the evidence. But he had remained silent, and in his silence bore guilt as surely as anyone else.

As painful as the consequences might be, Jake had to get at the truth. He now believed that the wrong man was on trial for murder, and that was a travesty his conscience could not live with. Even if it cost him his job and his reputation, he would not rest until he knew who really killed Curtis Redmond.

And it was time to throw subtlety out the window. Sohni already knew of his secret investigation, and the whole world would know soon enough. There was nothing left to lose.

# CHAPTER 23

WITH A MIX OF EXCITEMENT AND EXHAUSTION, DANIEL clicked the send button. He closed his eyes, leaned his head back against his laced fingers, and in the blackness pictured the data pulsing through the cables on its way to his editor's email box, leaving behind it a trail of sparks and dancing colored lights. Dramatic. But a moment like this required more than a dimly lit second-hand desk in an empty office building. He should be toasting the completion of his article with expensive champagne on the balcony of a penthouse surrounded by beautiful women. But alas, Daniel didn't own a penthouse, couldn't afford expensive champagne, and was invisible to beautiful women. Instead, he raised his bottle of Sam Adams in a solo toast, then tipped it to his lips, where he drained the last drop. A day like this warranted a little drinking on the job. Besides, it was three o'clock in the morning. No one was around to care.

The first article was finished. His sources had been checked, twice, his quotes gathered, his experts consulted, and fifty-five hundred words written. It was now in the hands of Della, who would undoubtedly snip, move, condense, and otherwise mold his writing to meet her high standards. Della was seriously gifted with the power of language, and she pulled artful prose from any article she graced with the privilege of her attention.

In light of the potential impact of Daniel's latest piece, Della chose to personally shepherd the article through the editing process. That was fine with Daniel. This was his chance to garner national attention, and he'd take all the help he could get.

After burying his empty bottle beneath some pop cans in the recycling bin, on his way out, he strolled to the elevator. His footfalls thundered in the silent stillness of the elevator alcove. In all his years working for the *Michigan Courier*, he had never seen the building so empty. Publishing a paper was a twenty-four-hour job, so you could usually find someone else busy at work. Obviously, those someone's were performing their jobs on another floor tonight.

When the bell signaled the elevator's arrival at the third floor, Daniel started.

"Damn, has that bell always been so loud?"

As the doors parted, he rushed inside, but the elevator was not empty. Daniel narrowly avoided a head-on collision with Jacob, the night security officer, who was making his rounds. Jacob had been around the *Courier* longer than him, and like Daniel, was starting to show his age. Jacob's formerly pitch-black crew cut had turned half gray, and the creases on his tanned, weathered face had deepened. Daniel figured he had to be at least seventy. But his eyes sparkled like those of a mischievous child, and he wore a permanent grin. The officer had a grandfatherly air about him, and was well-liked. He treated employees like his family, offering an endless supply of corny jokes and after-dinner mints he pilfered from a local diner.

An unwelcome guest bent on making trouble would likely find little to be intimidated by with Jacob, a grandpa with a pocketful of candy. What said troublemaker wouldn't know was that Jacob had served in the US Marine Corps for decades, seeing combat in several skirmishes, subsequently serving in intelligence, and eventually retiring as a colonel. Underneath his jovial exterior, Jacob was as tough as nails. He still attended martial arts training five times a week, and ran six miles a day. Frankly, he put Daniel to shame.

Daniel once again lamented his poor physical state. There was a time when he ran 5k races. Now Daniel could barely walk a flight of stairs without being winded. This seventy-year-old security guard could easily kick his ass.

"Hey there, Mr. Dalmakis!" Jacob boomed. "Whatcha doin' here so late?"

"Just finished a big story." He leaned toward Jacob, and whispered, "It's gonna make some waves."

Smiling broadly, the guard threw his head back and emitted a belly laugh like only he could. Daniel couldn't help but laugh along.

"I can't wait!" Jacob's eyes twinkled even more than usual.

He winked and held the elevator door for Daniel.

"Would you like me to walk you to your car?" he said, suddenly serious.

"Nah, I'm a big boy. Besides, who would keep everyone safe here?" Daniel gestured to the empty office space he had just left.

Jacob shot Daniel a mock angry look as the door closed.

"I know where you work, newspaper man," he shouted, as the elevator began its descent.

Daniel appreciated how Jacob could always bring a smile to his face, even at three in the morning. He felt the elevator slow and finally settle at the parking garage level. As he stepped out, he noticed that a few vehicles still remained at this late hour, but not surprising, there wasn't a soul about.

Daniel fumbled in his coat pocket for his keys, rummaging through gum wrappers, a flash drive, and several quarters. He could hear the hum of overhead lights, and enjoyed the sound of his footsteps ricocheting off the cement floor and walls. Despite walking the same path hundreds of times before, on this night he picked up on sounds, sights, and even smells that he didn't notice during regular working hours. Something about the emptiness of 3:00 a.m. heightened his senses and brought to his attention things that had, until now, escaped his attention.

Perhaps it was this heightened sensitivity that drew his gaze to a black Cadillac parked behind him, on the other side of the elevator. Nothing seemed particularly out of the ordinary about the car, and at first, he couldn't place what had attracted his attention. Then he noticed, despite the tinted windows, a figure moved inside. Slowly, the passenger door opened and a man emerged. He removed a lit cigarette from his mouth, flicked it to the cement garage floor, and crushed it out with his heel. The man had not yet made eye contact, but Daniel harbored no doubt that he was there for him.

His heart began thumping so loud he swore he could hear it reverberating through the confines of the parking garage. His breath caught in his throat. More than anything, he wanted to run to his car, lock the doors, and hit the expressway as fast as his classic Mustang would carry him. But at the same time, he did not dare take his gaze off the man in the black Cadillac, who was now walking toward him. The manner in which the man walked unnerved him. His pace was forceful, yet still seemed leisurely. He exuded strength and confidence, and for reasons Daniel couldn't put his finger on, the man scared the shit out of him.

He debated his options. He could run to his car and hope to get out of the garage before the man could corner him. He could confront the man. Or he could run back to the elevator and seek out Jacob, like a little boy running to his father to protect him from the neighborhood bully.

Not only did his manliness suffer most in the third scenario, but it also wasn't feasible because the man now stood between Daniel and the elevator. The first option was unlikely to work, as the man could easily catch up to him while he fumbled with his old-fashioned keys with no remote unlock or starter.

That left only one choice.

"What do you want?" he shouted toward the man, with as much bravado as he could muster.

The man's expression suggested he was amused by Daniel's attempt at confrontation.

"I just want to talk, Mr. Dalmakis."

"OK, I'll talk. But how about you tell me who you are, since you apparently already know me."

The man's thin lips stretched in a humorless smile that sent a shiver through Daniel.

"You can call me Tony. But my name's not important. What's important is that Mr. Mancuso sent me to have a word with you."

Daniel's composure almost broke. The bile rose in his throat, and he barely avoided vomiting. He noticed his hands shaking, so he shoved them in his pockets. He was face to face with one of Salvatore Mancuso's henchmen, in an empty parking garage at 3:00 a.m.

He took a deep breath and forced himself to speak.

"OK. What would you like to talk about?"

Tony eyed Daniel up and down, and considering his expression of distaste, apparently was not impressed by what he saw.

"I hear you paid a visit to my colleague, Mr. Bender. He wasn't very happy about your questions. And neither is Mr. Mancuso."

Daniel remained frozen to the spot, and silent, as Tony continued his leisurely approach. The mobster didn't care what he had to say. He was only there to send a message.

"Whatever information you think you have," Tony said, "you've been misled. DAE has done nothing wrong. There is no story. I'm sure you wouldn't want to print false information. Falsehoods like that could get, you, in *trouble*."

Tony's inflection on the word *trouble* left no doubt as to his meaning. In case Daniel was deaf and stupid, a second man emerged from the Cadillac. If ever the word *goon* applied to anyone, it applied to him. He stood at least six-foot-five, and likely weighed over three hundred pounds. He was shaved bald, and his face appeared flattened in places, like a boxer's. He wore khakis and a polo shirt, but appeared ready to burst out of both at any moment. Worst of all, a handgun rested in a holster at the man's hip, and on that rested the man's hand.

Sal Mancuso was apparently not one for subtlety. The Detroit Mafia had probably already killed one reporter. What was one more?

Daniel shifted his gaze back to Tony, who appeared to be waiting for his response. He knew what was expected of him. He was to forget what he knew about Intact, erase every word he'd written, and go back to writing about the latest UAW collective bargaining agreement. Of course, he wouldn't do that, not even for Sal Mancuso. In fact, this little show of power only reinforced his conviction to bring down DAE and those who own it. He hated bullies, and that was all Sal Mancuso was.

He felt a drop of sweat trickle down the back of his neck. His armpits were drenched. As he faced the two lethal men, he struggled for the right words, the ones that would allow him to leave with his life. The men had to believe they had the upper hand. That they had scared him into doing whatever they wanted.

"You're right," Daniel finally said. "My information was faulty. I have no intention of publishing any of it."

Tony, who now stood about eight feet away from Daniel, simply stared, trying to determine whether the reporter was just telling him what he wanted to hear. But before the mobster could make up his mind, the elevator bell chime echoed through the structure, causing all three men to jerk their heads toward the parting doors. Whistling loudly, Jacob emerged from the elevator, then stopped as he took in the tense scene before him.

Assuming a more defensive stance, Jacob glanced first at Tony, then at Daniel. By that time, the third man had slipped back in the Cadillac as stealthily as he had appeared. It worried Daniel that Jacob was unaware of the armed man only a couple of yards behind him.

"Is everything OK, Mr. Dalmakis?" Jacob looked every bit the old marine.

Daniel had a split second to decide how to respond. Should he send Jacob away so as not to put him in any danger? Or should he embrace this opportunity to escape, perhaps go back inside the building with Jacob. Certainly, telling Jacob the truth was not an option. At least, not at the moment.

"I think I left my keys inside," he blurted, deciding that he had to at least try to get out of the parking garage. "I was just coming back to look for them. Can you let me back in the office?"

Jacob's demeanor showed that he knew trouble was afoot, and that Daniel was lying, but that he also knew that their removal from the situation was the wisest move. So, he went along with Daniel's story.

"Of course. Come with me."

Jacob pushed the button to summon the elevator, and the doors opened immediately. He held one door back with his arm and waved Daniel inside, all the while maintaining eye contact with Tony, who hadn't moved or spoken since Jacob's entrance.

Daniel walked quickly toward the elevator on rubbery legs, allowing a wide berth as he passed by Tony, whose focus was still on Jacob. Daniel found that he was holding his breath, praying that he and Jacob made it safely inside the elevator, all the time remembering the gun behind the tinted windows.

He finally exhaled when the doors closed and the elevator began to rise. Then his legs gave out, and he found himself on his knees, nothing more than a trembling soggy puddle on the elevator floor. Jacob got down on one knee so that he was eye to eye with Daniel.

"Are you OK?"

"Yeah. Just shaken up."

Jacob rose again and said nothing more until they arrived in the building's lobby, where he escorted Daniel to the security office, which was little more than a glorified walk-in closet. Jacob locked the door behind them and offered Daniel a seat on a small sofa, which Daniel accepted. Jacob poured old coffee into a plastic cup and handed it to Daniel, he gulped it down.

Both men stared at the bank of monitors that displayed video footage from several security cameras positioned around the building. The camera mounted across from the elevator door in the parking garage was the focus of their attention. The men sat in silence until they saw the black Cadillac pass by the elevator on its way out of the structure. Their attention then shifted to another monitor that showed vehicles entering and exiting the parking structure. About eight seconds after the first viewing of the Caddy, it came into view again, this time as it pulled out of the garage and turned onto the empty downtown street.

Daniel sighed.

"Do you want to tell me what was going on down there?" Jacob said.

"Disgruntled customer. Didn't get his paper on time."

Jacob cracked a smile and shook his head. "At least your sense of humor is still intact."

"Thank goodness. How else would I charm the ladies?"

Jacob accepted that a truthful answer would not be forthcoming, and let the issue drop. Daniel was thankful for that. He didn't want to get Jacob involved. The less he knew the better.

Daniel set down his cup of coffee and looked at the gray-haired man who was old enough to be his father. He was struck by overwhelming gratitude. That man may have saved his life.

"Thank you."

Jacob only nodded and squeezed Daniel's shoulder. In typical male fashion, nothing more was said, but much was communicated.

Jacob rose from his chair. "I'd better get back to making the rounds. But I want you to stay locked inside my office for a little while. When I get back, I'll walk you to your car. And no arguments this time."

"Don't worry. You won't get any."

Jacob stepped into the lobby, looking in every direction. Satisfied that no danger lurked outside his door, he exited and closed the door behind him. Daniel heard the deadbolt turn into place. Jacob even shook the door from the outside for good measure, to ensure no one was getting in. The staccato of Jacob's hard-soled shoes faded down the hallway.

Daniel took the last gulp of his coffee, but found himself overcome by exhaustion. The security office was tiny and had no exterior walls, so it stayed toasty all winter long. The comforting warmth, combined with the hypnotic ticking of the wall clock, made it impossible for Daniel to keep his eyes open. He sank onto the couch, removed his coat to roll it under his head for a makeshift pillow, and closed his eyes. Tomorrow he would have to deal with what had happened tonight. He should pass on the information to Della, and also Detective Jake Clarke. He would also need to be more alert and do a better job of looking over his shoulder. But for now, he was warm, safe, and tired.

More importantly, unlike Curt Redmond, he was alive.

# CHAPTER 24

"I thought they were going to kill me!" Daniel told Jake. "I don't know what would've happened if our security guard hadn't shown up."

Jake hadn't planned to meet with the reporter on Friday morning, but there he was, at the station for the second time that week. The Curtis Redmond investigation became more intriguing by the minute. Daniel's early morning encounter with Salvatore Mancuso's men seemed to confirm that he, and now Jake, was on the right track. Robert Bender and the mobsters were both jumpy, worried about what the reporter would print about them. The question, though, was whether they were just concerned about the reporter's revelation about the Intact product, or if they feared the implication that they were connected to Curt's murder.

"It wasn't clear," Daniel replied. "He said that DAE hadn't done anything wrong, and that I'd been misled by false information. It really could be either, or both."

The new information suggested that his meeting with Robert Bender had become more important than ever, and he was thrilled to have Mancuso's threats as additional fodder for his ambush of Bender. He could pay a visit to Mancuso as well, to question him about the visit and threats to Dalmakis, but it would be a waste of time. Mancuso wasn't scared of a local cop. Bender, on the other hand, might be a tough and confident businessman, but he was not accustomed to dealing with law enforcement. Until now, Bender had always maintained a spotless reputation. Being on the other end of an interrogation would be a new experience for him, one that he—Jake guessed—would not handle well.

Daniel also dropped on Jake a second piece of unexpected information. Though Jake came on strong, Daniel adamantly denied sharing his information with Sohni.

"I have never spoken to Sohni Silver in my life. I don't even know who she is, other than that she represents Henry Martinez."

Sure, he could have been lying, but Jake was usually a good judge of a person's truthfulness—he had to be in his line of work—and his instincts convinced him of the reporter's honesty. That left him perplexed as to Sohni's source.

The mystery deepened after he spoke with Tracy Zorn. At one point during their conversation, the woman mentioned that she had already spoken with Sohni. When Jake asked when her conversation with Sohni took place, Zorn admitted that it was a couple of months ago.

Months ago! Jake was floored. Sohni appeared to be two steps ahead of him. She obviously had learned that Curt wrote for The Truth Zone, and suspected that his death was connected with one of his stories. But how did she know he was writing about the Intact product? But more importantly, how in the world did she learn about the renewed police investigation?

Jake struggled with that question, and considered all the possibilities, but time and again he came to the same conclusion, the only one that seemed to make sense was, Frank Redmond. On the surface it seemed impossible that the victim's father would partner with the attorney defending the man accused of killing his son. But Jake recalled Frank's statement that he never believed Martinez had killed Curt. If Frank believed that Curt's killer was still at large, then, as opposed to being at odds, he and Sohni had a common interest, finding the real killer. And Frank could do what the gag order prevented Sohni from doing herself.

Jake had worked with Sohni for quite a few years, and not for a minute would he have believed her capable of orchestrating such a plan. She didn't have the guile. But here he was, confronted by the reality that Sohni had information that very few people possessed. Frank probably called Sohni as soon as Jake left his house. The timing of her call to Pauline was right, and that would explain how she knew so quickly.

And while Sohni was fighting tooth and nail to prove her client's innocence, Jake had been sitting on his hands, content to let the prosecutor's office run roughshod over him. He needed to right the wrong, not just for himself, but for Frank and Cathy Redmond, and Henry Martinez, and the entire city of Ann Arbor. He owed it to all of them.

To that end, he had spent the previous afternoon reconstructing the evidence, scouring every word, every picture, every detail. The first investigation happened so fast, and the police had made the evidence fit the suspect instead of the other way around. Now Jake followed the evidence.

He concluded that the murderer was likely a man, standing at least five-foot-ten. The murder was premeditated, as the perpetrator apparently followed Curt and arrived at the scene with the murder weapon. That implied a motive other than robbery. The primary suspected motive was, of course, that Curt was killed because of his investigation into Intact, in which case the person who murdered Curt had to be someone who knew about Redmond's investigation, and had something to lose if Curt lived to write his story. That last criterion narrowed the field of suspects significantly. The stakeholders of DAE had to be the primary ones. It was unlikely, though, that Bender or the Mafia dons did the deed themselves. Thus, the men's colleagues and associates were also people of interest.

Although the ME's report also suggested that the victim had been in a physical altercation shortly before he was killed, a second conversation with Zach Bender had provided a name, and not surprisingly, a check of the MSU student's alibi had ruled him out. Zach had also confirmed the alibi of a jealous ex-boyfriend mentioned by Curt's girlfriend. But Jake's instincts told him that this murder was something more nefarious than a fight between two college students.

After speaking with Jake that morning, Daniel had looked through photo books of known associates of the Detroit Mafia, which Jake had obtained from the FBI, until he had located pictures of Mancuso's men from the parking garage. Jake intended to send officers to recanvass the residents and businesses along Hill Street and the surrounding area, armed with those photos, but it was going to take a few days to get the job done. It was a long shot. The killer could have been any number of people, and a professional would've been careful to avoid being noticed. Plus, several months had passed since the murder, and memories would have faded. But it was all they had.

Jake cursed his failure to search Curt's room, and especially his computer. During Jake's recent conversation with Zach, he had asked him if he would consent to a search of the computer that Curt used, but he refused, telling Jake he'd have to come back with a warrant. Embarrassingly, the best evidence he had was the forensic examination of Curt's cell phone—from Sohni's efforts—the flash drives brought to his attention by a reporter, and the evidence collected from the attacks on Sohni, which he hadn't even known about until this week, but he believed were connected to the Curt Redmond case. Everything else they'd collected during the short investigation was useless. Except, perhaps one item.

Jake examined photos of the murder weapon. He had used the knife's serial number to trace its purchase from a local store, but that's where the trail ended. Records reflected that it was paid for with cash, providing no way to trace the buyer. Plus, because it was bought years ago, the employees working at the time of purchase were long gone, as was any security camera footage. But the knife told its own tale. It was a beautiful piece of work that cost over a hundred dollars. Not a knife used by gangs or hoodlums. They preferred switchblades, which are easier to conceal. It was also in pristine condition, except for the victim's blood, despite that it had been purchased several years ago, suggesting that it was a collector's item, or bought for a special hunting trip that had never manifested.

Jake couldn't shake the feeling that the knife was the key to solving this mystery. He placed the photos into a protective cover, completed the appropriate paperwork to take temporary custody of them, and placed them in his briefcase with his notepad.

When his cell rang, he rushed to push the answer icon. But in his hurry, Jake neglected to check the caller's name, and cringed when he heard Pauline's voice. There was no yelling, though. No criticism or blame. Pauline was subdued, and sounded resigned to a not-so-happy fate.

"We have a problem," she said.

"What happened?"

"Sohni Silver happened."

"What now?"

"I just got out of court. Judge Watkins is pissed, Jake. She ordered us to turn over everything—and I do mean everything—that pertains to our renewed investigation. All the information Dalmakis gave you, the names of everyone you've interviewed and what they said. Plus, every step we take going forward. If you take a piss, you'd better call Sohni and let her know."

"Wow."

"Yeah, wow is right. We might as well just hand reasonable doubt right over to her. Sohni made it sound like we were railroading Martinez. Like we had loads of exculpatory evidence that we were consciously hiding. How ridiculous!"

Jake didn't think Sohni's portrayal was that far from the truth, but he held his tongue.

"After all," Pauline said, "you only just started exploring a potential new lead. We don't even know if there is any merit to it. But apparently, everything we do now is an open book."

He had no desire to commiserate with Pauline. In fact, the sooner she was off the phone, the better.

"I was just heading back to my desk," he said. "I'll put everything together for you."

"Thanks."

He started to end the call—

"You know what I don't understand, though?" she said.

"What?"

"How did Sohni know so damn much about your investigation? At first, I figured she had gotten a whiff that you were asking questions, and was grasping at straws. But once we got in court, it was obvious she knew almost as much as we do. She knew about the article Curt was writing, about Marc Isley and the U of M professor, and she even knew about Dalmakis's investigation. Where the hell did she get all that information?"

Despite Pauline's sour demeanor, Jake couldn't help but smile. Sohni had truly outdone herself this time. She had even left the cunning prosecutor scratching her head.

"I have no idea," he replied.

He wasn't going to share his conclusion with Pauline. Let her figure it out for herself.

"Perhaps we've all underestimated her," he said.

"Yeah, whatever. She just got lucky this time."

Jake's smile widened. Pauline was a sore loser.

"Anyway," she said, "I'll send someone by the station in an hour to pick up whatever you've got. And God help us if you miss anything. The judge will have us all in jail before sundown."

Jake sipped from his now cold coffee, with a secret thrill at Sohni's annihilation of Pauline, who had made a name for herself as a hard-driving prosecutor. But she was known for her questionable tactics which often rubbed judges up the wrong way. It was only a matter of time until she pushed it too far. Judge Watkins was historically less tolerant of her games, and it was Pauline's sheer bad luck that the Martinez case had been assigned to Watkins's docket.

Jake had never before rooted for the defense attorney. It felt odd and uncomfortable. But he had given up any illusions that Henry Martinez had killed Curtis Redmond.

Jake and Sohni were on the same side now, and a victory for Sohni brought them both closer to the truth.

# CHAPTER 25

SOHNI WAS AMAZED. SHE HAD REALLY DONE IT. HER PLAN—
if you could even call it that—had worked. In fact, it had
succeeded beyond her wildest expectations. On that day when
she reluctantly asked Frank to take her findings to the press,
she had no idea what, if anything, would transpire. Now, here
she was, with a court order in her hand that gave her everything she could have wanted, all the information that Daniel
Dalmakis had uncovered, as well as every piece of evidence
and every statement the police obtained as a result, and an
extra month to process it all before trial. A runner from the
prosecutor's office had just dropped off a treasure trove of evidence consisting of new witness statements, including Marc
Isley's, and incredibly, a police report detailing threats made
by the Detroit Mafia against the reporter about to expose the
very same dirty secret Curt was poised to reveal. Didn't get
much better than that.

Sohni realized she had lost track of time while reveling in her victory. It was already six twenty. She and Matt had six thirty reservations at the Gandy Dancer. It was, after all, Friday night, and she had plenty to celebrate.

She shoved all the new evidence into her briefcase so she could review it more closely over the weekend. After shutting down her computer and grabbing her coat, she hurried out of her office and down to the lobby. She contemplated whether to call her security escort. He'd walked her to her car each night after work, and there'd been no trouble. But if she called him now and waited for him to arrive, she'd definitely be late for their reservation.

Sohni peeked out at the sky, which was painted in beautiful shades of pink and orange. The sun hadn't fully set, so there was still enough light to stay aware of her surroundings in the couple of minutes it would take her to get to the parking structure. Plus, it was Friday night in downtown Ann Arbor. There were people everywhere.

She made up her mind and exited onto the street to begin the two-block walk. Just as she left the building, her phone dinged with a new text message. *Matt, of course, wondering where I am.* But she didn't recognize the number.

She pulled up the message: *Where's your friend tonight?*

Her breath caught in her throat, and she scanned her surroundings, looking for someone observing her, but saw nothing out of the ordinary. She picked up her pace. Her phone dinged again.

*I like your new coat. It's Burberry, isn't it? You've got great taste.*

Sohni clutched at the Burberry gabardine coat she was wearing. She'd just purchased it last weekend at a discount outlet, thrilled to find it for 50 percent off.

Her heart was racing. Was he watching her right now? She had been wearing the coat all week. He could just be guessing.

She picked up her pace to a jog as she turned to enter the parking structure, but the heel of her shoe got stuck in a crack in the pavement, nearly sending her tumbling to the ground.

Another ding: *Be careful. You'll twist an ankle.*

"Fuck you," Sohni said, between clenched teeth.

All pretense of calm now gone, Sohni sprinted into the garage and made a beeline for the administrative office. She banged on the door to get the attention of the attendant inside. When the door opened, Sohni plunged inside.

"Someone is following me!" She panted. "I need someone to help me get to my car safely."

The attendant, a middle-aged woman, looked her up and down. Satisfied that she didn't pose a threat, the woman used her walkie-talkie to call another attendant, who was cruising the garage in the security patrol vehicle.

"He'll be right down," the woman said. "Are you OK? Do you need the police?"

"Not right now. I just need to get out of here, and to my husband. I'll call the police once I'm safe."

The woman looked uncertain, but said nothing more. When the security vehicle arrived, Sohni climbed in and pointed the driver the way to her car. The driver stood by until she was inside, and followed her vehicle until she exited the garage.

By this time, Sohni was already late for the reservation, and Matt had texted her twice, doing a poor job of camouflaging his concern. She called him, and he picked up right away.

"There was an incident leaving work tonight," she said, verging on tears. "I'll tell you about it when I get there, but right now I just need you to stay on the line with me."

"Are you OK?"

"Yeah. I'm only a couple of minutes away."

"I'll meet you at the valet stand. I'll just hang on the line with you until then."

With Matt still on the line, Sohni pulled up to the front of the Gandy Dancer, where Matt and a valet awaited her arrival. She handed over her key fob and squeezed her husband in an embrace, feeling the fear melt away. They stood like that until the valet starting casting annoyed glances in their direction.

"Let's go inside before we lose our reservation," Sohni said.

"You sure? We can just go home."

"I'm sure. If there's one thing I could use right now, it's a drink."

For the first time, she noticed how wonderful Matt looked. He wore a royal blue sweater she had bought him for his last birthday, and black slacks that emphasized his toned legs. He smelled good, too.

She clutched his hand in hers. The hostess seated them right away at a table for two in a dimly lit corner of the restaurant.

Sohni was pretty sure Matt had something to do with securing that prime, romantic location.

Sohni had always loved the Gandy Dancer not only for the fabulous food, but for its setting in a historic Ann Arbor building. The stone structure had served as the Michigan Central Depot, an elegant piece of architecture built in 1886. With stained glass windows, arched doorways, and ivy-covered walls, the depot had been a hub of railway travel. It survived until 1970, when well-known restaurateur, Chuck Muer, purchased it, and preserving many of its original features, turned it into a beautiful and highly regarded restaurant. The restaurant's name, a term used to refer to early railroad workers who manually laid and maintained the track, paid homage to the structure's railroad heritage.

Matt remained amazingly restrained until the couple had completed their drinks order.

"So, are you going to tell me what happened?"

"Well, up until I left the office, it was a really good day."

Sohni filled Matt in on the day's events, from being in court and what she'd learned. When she got to the story of the mobster's appearance in Dalmakis' parking garage, Matt's smile faded.

"Holy shit!"

"I know," Sohni said. "That poor man must have been terrified. But bad for him is good for me. That was exactly what I needed to establish reasonable doubt."

Still, Matt remained silent, chewing on his lower lip in a tell-tale fashion.

"So, it really might be the mob who's been threatening you? I knew it was possible, but it seemed so crazy."

"I really don't know. The methods seem different. The way the guy confronted the reporter was in his face, fearless. My guy hasn't shown himself. It doesn't seem like a Mafia-like approach."

"That is true. But if you think the Mob killed Curt, then who else would it be?"

"I wish I knew. And I haven't even gotten to the events of tonight."

"Oh, geez! I was so absorbed in your story I forgot about that. What the heck is wrong with me? Please, tell me what happened."

She did.

"Why in the world would you skip your escort? What were you thinking?" Matt raised his voice, and his face turned red.

Customers at the next table cast glances at them.

"I got complacent, Matt. I am so sorry." She reached across the table to grasp his hand. "Believe me, I regret it, and I will never do it again."

Matt held his tongue and took a long swig of his drink.

"We're calling the detective first thing tomorrow," he said. "This has got to stop. I can't keep worrying about you twenty-four hours a day. What I really want to do is take you somewhere remote and hide away with you until this is over. It's killing me that I can't."

"Like where?" she said.

"What?"

"Where? Where would you take me?"

"Northern Canada, maybe?"

"Too cold."

"Mexico, then."

"Too hot."

Matt smiled. "I love you. You know that?"

"I know. I love you, too."

# CHAPTER 26

J AKE ARRIVED AT ROBERT BENDER'S HOME AT SEVEN O'CLOCK
sharp. The house was lit up inside and out, its enormity
on full display. He pushed the doorbell button and heard the
muted litany of chimes in response. With envy, he reflected
that his own doorbell only made a ding-dong sound.

Soon after, Robert Bender pulled open one of the two intri-
cately carved mahogany front doors, and Jake was struck by
the beauty behind them. Despite himself, he was eager to see
inside.

"Good evening, Detective Clarke."

"Good evening, Mr. Bender. I trust your flight was good."

"Ah, overcrowded, but at least on time."

Jake stepped through the front door and into a large foyer
that reminded him of cathedrals he'd visited while in Europe.
Thick Italian tiles lay under his feet, and a domed ceiling high
over his head, with ornate plaster beams, stretched in a hub-
and-spoke pattern from a crystal chandelier dangling from

the center. The look was completed by an enormous, curved staircase leading to the second level of the house. Bender's residence was more than he had ever imagined. Not a single design detail was overlooked. And it was immaculate. In fact, it was hard to believe anyone lived there. If not for the ear-splitting rap music emanating from somewhere upstairs, Jake would have insisted he had mistakenly stepped into a museum, not a family home.

As though reading Jake's mind, Bender frowned and glared upstairs as though his sheer will would silence the sound pollution. When his dirty look didn't get the job done, the man started up the stairs.

"My son, Zach, is home from college for the weekend. He probably doesn't know I've returned. Please give me a moment."

Jake nodded, watching Robert Bender wind the staircase. A few moments later, the music ceased, and Bender returned down the staircase.

"There. That's better. May I take your coat?" Bender extended his hand.

Jake's first chance to throw Bender off his game.

"No thanks. I'm good."

Bender paused for only a second, then began down one of the long hallways that extended from the entryway, and gestured for Jake to follow him. As the men advanced down the hall, Jake peeked into each room they passed, observing whatever he could.

One room made him stop.

"Oh, my God!" he said.

The other man turned to look at Jake, surprised at his outburst.

"Are those real?" Jake pointed into the dimly lit room he stood in front of.

A proud smile spread across Bender's face.

"Of course. Would you like to see them?"

"If you don't mind."

"Not at all."

Bender entered the room and flicked on the lights. The scene was equally stunning and terrifying. In the center of the large room stood a grizzly bear standing at least seven feet tall, on its hind legs. It had thick shiny fur and an open mouth full of razor-sharp teeth. The once-alive animal was now a piece of décor in a rich man's house.

While the bear was the centerpiece, many other equally fascinating specimens were displayed around the room. Jake walked by each, taking them in one at a time. He observed a full-sized tiger, a leopard, a mounted head of a rhinoceros, and those of moose and deer, all with impressive racks. There were others, but Jake didn't have time to study them all.

"Did you kill all of these?"

"I did. Hunting trips are my way to unwind."

"I love nature, too. But I'm more interested in watching the animals than shooting them."

"Oh, I do plenty of that, too. They are quite majestic."

Jake abhorred hunting, especially big game hunting. But he decided to keep that to himself for the time being. The man was obviously proud of his trophies, and the subject caused him to let his guard down and talk freely.

Jake swiveled and continued his perusal of the room, which was filled with hunting paraphernalia, including a glass-fronted case housing several hunting rifles, framed photos of Bender with his quarries, and a shelf containing books with titles such as Elmer Keith's *Big Game Hunting*, *Big Game Hunting in Central Africa*, and *African Experience: A Guide to Modern Safaris.*

"Would you like a drink?" Bender said. "I could really use a scotch, myself."

"No thanks. I'm still on duty." A not-so-subtle reminder, lest his host forget.

The man left the room to retrieve a glass of what was surely the best and most expensive scotch available. Jake was certain he wouldn't be able to tell the difference. It would only be wasted on him.

To kill time, Jake continued to wander around the safari room, amazed, and disgusted, by Bender's glorification of what Jake viewed as unjustified killing. His obvious obsession with the big kill was not altogether surprising, though. Everything about Bender was big and showy, from his house and his business, to his clothing and cars. Big game hunting was exactly the kind of hobby that Jake would expect from a man who felt accomplishment was everything and money was no object.

Jake heard him exchanging words with another male, probably his son. But their voices were low, so he couldn't hear what was being said. While the men finished their conversation, Jake turned to yet another case, this one displaying a beautiful set of hunting knives in their leather sheaths. Unlike the rifles, though, these weapons were displayed in a showy manner, as if they were intended more for decoration than actual use.

Jake was about to move on to the next gaudy display, when something caught his eye. The third leather knife sheath was empty. Jake searched the case, but couldn't find the knife that was meant to occupy that sheath. It seemed odd to Jake that a man as meticulous as Bender would allow this glaring omission to blemish his otherwise pristine man cave.

Then Jake noticed something else. He put his face as close as he could to the glass lid of the case. What he could see of the handles protruding from the sheaths looked familiar. He didn't dare open the case and take one out for fear of violating proper police procedure, but he was pretty sure the knives in the display case were Buck brand knives with cocobolo handles. Jake couldn't see the end of the blades, which were out of sight inside the cases, but he could certainly see the end of the handles, which had polished brass butts.

Jake reached into his briefcase, which still hung from his shoulder, and retrieved the photos of the murder weapon. He laid them on top of the glass to view the knife side by side with knives in Bender's case. From the portion of the knives he could see, they appeared to be a perfect match with the murder weapon. And the case that once held the missing knife appeared to be approximately the right size to house a six-inch blade.

As he heard Robert's footsteps approaching, he shoved the photos back into his briefcase. Jake's heart was racing now, his adrenalin pumping. He turned to Bender and attempted his best casual smile.

"These are beautiful knives," he said. "Are they Buck?"

Surprised, and seemingly impressed by Jake's unexpected knowledge, Bender raised his eyebrows.

"Yes, they are. I thought you didn't hunt?"

"Oh, I don't. But a police detective does get to know his weapons, too, you know."

"Ah, very true."

Jake pointed at the leather case intended to hold the missing knife.

"What happened to that one?"

Bender bent over the glass to take a closer look.

"I don't know. Maybe the cleaning lady mislaid it. I'm sure it's around here somewhere."

"What size would that knife have been?"

"Well, I have a three-, a four-, a six-, an eight-, and a nine-inch. They should be in order, so that case would presumably belong to the six-inch knife."

Jake's skin tingled. "Are these straight-edged blades, or serrated?"

"They're straight edged," Bender replied, his suspicion starting to show.

That was all Jake needed to hear. He reached into his briefcase and pulled out the knife photos.

"Does your missing knife look anything like this Mr. Bender?"

Bender looked startled. "Where did those photos come from?"

"The evidence room. This is the knife used to kill Curtis Redmond. I'd say it's a pretty damn close match to your missing knife."

A flash of wild panic shone in Bender's eyes, but then his unflappable businessman façade returned. He said nothing for a moment, his sharp mind working.

"This meeting is over. I'm calling my attorney."

"That's a good idea, because you're under arrest." Jake recited the Miranda warning while the other man stared in disbelief. "Your attorney will have to meet you at the station."

Bender glared at the detective. "You really don't want to do this, Detective," he growled, between clenched teeth.

"You will cooperate and accompany me to my car, or I will lead you out there in handcuffs, in front of all your hoity-toity neighbors. Which will it be Mr. Bender? I'm game for either."

Jake saw pure hatred in the man's eyes, but he was powerless. He reminded Jake of a caged animal.

"May I at least tell my son where I'm going?"

Jake nodded.

As the men moved down the hallway toward the kitchen, Jake kept his hand clamped on Bender's arm, and the man's face stretched with barely controlled rage. Zach turned to look at them from his position in front of the open refrigerator, with a jug of Gatorade lifted halfway to his mouth. The young man had obviously been working out. He was wearing nylon shorts and no shirt, and his torso and face glistening with sweat. He made quite a picture with his tall, toned body and handsome features. It flitted through Jake's mind that a bystander could mistake Zach for an actor in a sports drink commercial. Except for his face. Though a full-grown adult, Zach looked like a scared little boy, his eyes registering a level of terror more appropriate for a young child unable to understand what was happening.

His father's voice pulled him out of his stupor.

"Call Sam Henderson. His number is in my phone. Tell him to meet me at the Ann Arbor Police Station immediately."

Zach responded with a barely perceptible nod.

"Zach! Do you hear me?"

The young man finally awoke from his stupor.

"Yes, Dad. I'll call him. Can I go with you?"

"No!"

Zach flinched at his father's outburst, but the man didn't seem to notice.

"Actually, Zach, that's not a bad idea," Jake said. "I'm sure we'll have some questions for you as well. You can follow in your own vehicle if you want."

Jake gave his charge a nudge toward the front door, where he allowed him to slip on some loafers and a coat, it was December, after all. Zach followed from a distance, looking pathetic and helpless.

"Call Henderson!" Bender bellowed.

His son ran back to the kitchen to find his father's phone. Jake frisked Bender, ensuring he possessed nothing that could be used as a weapon, then helped him into the backseat of the unmarked police car. Once on the road, the detective called Pauline to update her on the evening's strange turn of events, and asked her to get someone started on a request for a warrant to search the Bender house.

Then he called his wife. It was going to be a long night.

# CHAPTER 27

SOHNI'S CELL PHONE RANG AT 8:15 P.M. AS SHE AND MATT waited in the restaurant's valet line. She pulled it from her coat pocket, surprised to find Pauline's name on the screen.

"Well, that's odd," Sohni said.

"Who is it?" Matt replied.

"It's Pauline. What could she want at this hour?"

She accepted the call. "This is Sohni."

"Sohni, it's Pauline." The prosecutor sounded pained, which made Sohni all the more intrigued.

"Hi. What's going on?"

"There's been a development in the Redmond murder investigation, and in light of the court's order today, I thought I should make you aware of it."

"What kind of development?"

"Jake believes he's found where the murder weapon came from."

Sohni was disappointed by the news. She was hoping for a new murder suspect. Or even better, a confession. Instead, Jake had probably tracked down a stolen-weapon report, which was not helpful to her.

"And where did it come from?" she said.

"Robert Bender's house."

Sohni froze.

"We're trying to get an expedited search warrant for his house," the prosecutor said, "and Jake is on his way back to the station with Bender now. He should be here any minute. The judge said you should be privy to any formal interviews, so I, uh, guess you're entitled to join us if you want." She spat out the final sentence, as though it tasted bad in her mouth.

Sohni knew this unconventional arrangement was extremely difficult for Pauline, but she had no sympathy for her. It was her own damn fault.

"Thanks for letting me know. I'll be there shortly."

Sohni hung up and looked at Matt with sheepish eyes.

"Where will you be shortly?" he said.

"The police station. You're not going to believe what just happened. They think the murder weapon found in Henry's bag came from Robert Bender's house."

Matt's eyebrows shot up. "Wow!"

"They're bringing Bender in now. I need to get over there before they start interviewing him."

"I don't want you driving there alone. Not after what happened tonight."

"Well, my car is here. What am I supposed to do?"

Matt thought for a moment. "Tell you what, I'll drop you off at the door of the police station and make sure you get inside safely. Then I will find someone, either Darnell or another friend, to ride with me back here, and I'll drive your car back, and the other person can drive mine."

"Oh, honey, that's too much—"

"This is not negotiable. I don't even like the idea of you being out of my sight tonight. But since this is work-related and you'll be at the police station, I'll deal with it. But you are not driving there or home alone."

"OK."

Once Matt stopped outside the police station, she leaned over and kissed him, then slid out of the car. He didn't pull away from the curb until she was face to face with the officer at the security screening area.

She took the elevator to the second floor and informed the officer at the front desk who she was, and why she was there. The officer made a brief phone call, and Sohni was directed to wait in one of the uncomfortable chairs in the front desk area.

"Miss Fitzpatrick will let you know when they're ready for you."

Sohni was used to waiting. At police stations, at courthouses, at jails. From her briefcase, she pulled out a pen and a half-completed crossword puzzle which she kept for exactly this purpose.

After ten minutes passed, an imposing gentleman wearing an expensive-looking three-quarter-length black wool dress coat, and carrying a new leather Coach briefcase, stormed through the door and approached the front desk with an air of authority. Though Sohni's pen remained poised over the crossword, her gaze was focused on the new arrival. She couldn't hear the words exchanged between the man and the front desk officer, but she didn't need to, everything about him shouted lawyer. Actually, everything about him shouted ultra-expensive lawyer. And she was pretty sure he was there for Robert Bender.

Like Sohni, the man was relegated to a wobbly plastic chair in the waiting area. She was glad to see Pauline treated all defense attorneys equally poor. Unlike Sohni, though, who sat with her legs curled under her bottom, and her face hidden behind a newspaper, her male counterpart sat ramrod straight, his knees spread apart wide, his gaze constantly roving, keeping tabs on activity in the vicinity. While Sohni was all about being inconspicuous, he strove to be noticed. She didn't recognize him, but she knew the type.

Lost in her thoughts, she didn't notice Pauline emerge from behind the front desk.

"Mr. Henderson, Miss Silver, you can come on in now. Everybody's here."

Upon hearing her name, Sam Henderson turned to look at Sohni with a bewildered expression, as though he had not previously noticed her sitting merely six feet from him. Or perhaps because she didn't choose to carry herself in his arrogant fashion, he hadn't regarded her as worthy of notice. Regardless, once her presence was brought to his attention, he made no effort to avert his gaze. Bender's attorney paused under the guise of allowing Sohni to proceed ahead of him, but took that opportunity to scan her from head to toe in a wolf-like fashion that made her cringe. She collected her coat and bag, but stood her ground and gestured for Henderson to go ahead.

"You should go," she said. "I'm sure Mr. Bender is eager to speak with you."

The man's smile faded, and he narrowed his eyes as he tried to determine who the hell she was, as well as her relationship to this investigation. He did what she suggested, and took the lead. She followed, wearing a smirk that even Pauline returned.

When they arrived at the interrogation room area, the prosecutor escorted Bender's attorney into a private room, where his client was already waiting. She closed the door, giving the pair an opportunity to consult in private, and led Sohni to another room, where she would eventually be able to observe Bender's interrogation.

On her way, a familiar face caught Sohni's eye. Being escorted in the other direction was Zach Bender, looking terrified, and repeatedly asking to see his father. His requests were met with silence, which frustrated the young man even more.

The observation room contained a window the full length of one wall, from which one could see into the adjoining interrogation room. Sohni had never been on that side of the window before, and found it surreal. Jake was already there, downing a coffee, which by the look on his face, he found distasteful.

When Sohni entered, he stood to clasp her hand in both of his, and flashed a large, sincere smile. While she appreciated the hospitality, she was puzzled by his warm welcome. Years of serving as defense counsel had made her accustomed to playing the role of the enemy.

An officer appeared in the doorway and informed the detective that the men were ready to speak to him. Jake disappeared briefly, then returned, this time to the adjoining interrogation room with Bender and his attorney. The two men made quite a pair, dressed to the nines, well-groomed, and emitting supreme cockiness. Sohni was surprised there was enough space in that small room for both of their egos. They sat comfortably, legs crossed, backs leaned against their chairs.

"Before we get started," Henderson said, "I want to make clear that my client is going to voluntarily answer some of your questions so that he can help you clear up this misunderstanding. But he'll only be responding to questions that are directly related to the evidence you claim to have against him. If we find this is nothing more than a fishing expedition, the interview will end."

"I understand," Jake replied.

"Good. I also want to let you know that my client has a solid alibi for the night Curt Redmond was killed. He was in Phoenix, on business. He has his flight and hotel records, as well as a variety of other receipts. We will provide those to you as soon as someone can get into his office to retrieve them."

"Great. I look forward to seeing them."

"It seems to me that Mr. Bender's alibi should clear up this matter. Obviously, he couldn't have killed Curt if he was in Arizona."

"I didn't say that Mr. Bender personally killed Curt Redmond."

"Now you're just playing games, Detective. What is that supposed to mean?"

"I believe Mr. Bender knows." He cast a glance at Henderson's client. "I'll get to that shortly."

The attorney sighed. "I'll wait with bated breath."

"Mr. Bender, when I was in your house, I observed a series of Buck brand knives with leather cases. How long have you had those knives?"

Sohni observed that Bender came off as inordinately bored.

"A couple years."

"Where did you get them?

"I purchased them at some outdoor recreation store. I don't remember which one."

"What do you use those knives for?"

"Actually, I don't. I thought I might use them for hunting one day, but the appropriate occasion never arrived, so now they're more collector pieces."

"But you're missing one, aren't you?"

"Well, I don't know if it's missing. You are correct that it was not in its usual place, but you gave me no opportunity to search the house to determine if it was simply misplaced. I suspect the cleaning lady may have moved it."

"Why would the cleaning lady move one knife from its usual spot, but leave the others?"

"I wouldn't know, Detective. You'd have to ask her."

Jake slid a piece of paper and pen toward the man.

"Write down her name and contact information."

As Bender wrote, the detective set in front of him the murder weapon, still bagged and labeled.

"Mr. Bender, this knife looks just like your knives, doesn't it?"

Bender studied it, before sliding it back to Jake.

"It certainly looks like mine. But I have no way of knowing if it is. I'm sure there are thousands of those knives. Maybe tens of thousands."

Jake leaned close to him and placed his finger on some tiny print on the knife handle.

"But only one with this serial number."

Sohni knew that the police's search for information using the knife's serial number had been fruitless, but Bender didn't know that.

"Curt Redmond was your son's roommate at U of M, wasn't he?"

"Yes."

"So, you knew him?"

"Of course."

"I find it suspicious that he was murdered with your knife. Don't you?"

"We've already established that you don't know if that knife belongs to Mr. Bender," Henderson said.

"But we've also established that Mr. Bender has no idea where his identical knife is. Tell me about Intact."

Bender's eyes became guarded.

"Did I not make myself clear, Detective?" Henderson said. "My client is not answering questions unless they directly relate to the purported evidence against him. His business dealings have nothing to do with his arrest."

"Ah, but they do. Right, Mr. Bender?"

"How, exactly?"

"They relate directly to his motive."

"What motive?"

Jake looked at Bender. "Curt Redmond was about to ruin you, wasn't he?"

Henderson's previously bored eyes came alive. He glanced at his client.

"I have no idea what you're talking about," Bender said.

"So Intact isn't highly flammable?"

"Of course not!"

The attorney put his hand on Bender's arm and whispered in his ear.

Sohni scooted to the edge of her seat.

"That's not what the U of M lab says," Jake continued. "That's not what Macomb Comprehensive Testing says. So, all those labs are wrong?"

"Apparently."

"You knew about Curt's article, didn't you? It was easy enough to find out, he and your son shared a computer. Maybe you overheard something. Or maybe he started asking around, and his questions got back to you. You couldn't have that, some young Woodward wannabe making his name at the expense of your life's work."

"This again? The reporter came at me with the same nonsense. Curt was just a college kid who hung out with my son."

"You had him killed, didn't you? Your son's best friend. It didn't matter. He was a threat to you and everything you are. How dare he?"

"Ah, so now that you know Mr. Bender was out of town," Henderson said, "you change your story to say he *had* him killed. What, did he put out a hit on a college kid?" The attorney scoffed.

Sohni smiled. She knew what was coming next.

Jake stared at Bender. "Your attorney's closer than he knows, isn't he? You and I know that you have plenty of *friends* to take care of the dirty business, don't we?"

Bender's smile faded, and he clenched his jaw.

Sohni's smile widened. She glanced at Pauline, who clearly found no amusement in any of this. Sohni figured she probably wouldn't either if she was witnessing the end of her career.

"By the way, did you know that your friend Sal Mancuso had an associate pay a visit to Daniel Dalmakis the other night? A 3:00 a.m. visit in an empty parking garage, to be exact. He brought a friend, too. An armed friend."

Both men stared at Jake. Bender surveyed Jake's face to see if he was bluffing. Henderson did his best to not look surprised.

Sohni exhaled after realizing she been holding her breath.

"Fortunately for Dalmakis, a security guard interrupted their visit. Or he may have ended up just like Curt Redmond."

"What the hell does the mobster Sal Mancuso have to do with this?" Henderson said. "This interview gets crazier and crazier by the minute."

Jake smirked. "Do you want to tell him, Mr. Bender? Or should I?"

The man shot virtual daggers at the detective.

Jake shrugged. "OK. I will. You see, Mr. Bender here is not the only owner of DAE. A certain ... family, shall we say, is also part-owner."

Henderson stared at his client. "I'd like a minute with my client, please."

Sohni muttered, "He didn't know."

Pauline cast her a dirty look.

"They took matters into their own hands, didn't they?" Jake said. "They did it once, with Curt, and were going to do it again with Dalmakis. Maybe you didn't even know about it. Or maybe you only found out about it afterwards. But it looks like they set you up to take the fall, Mr. Bender. They used your knife. Lifted it right from under your nose. "

"Detective, I said I need to consult with my client!"

"If the police didn't buy that the homeless man did it, they'd eventually find their way to you. And you'd have no explanation for where that knife went, would you?"

Henderson lurched up, causing the table to jump.

"Detective, this interview is over!"

Sohni gasped, startled by the bang of the table leg as it dropped back on the floor.

"You're going to lose everything, Bender," Jake said. "All because of your ego. I did my research. Bender Industries lost a whole lot of money during the recession, and then again during the COVID-19 pandemic. Sure, it had assets, but they weren't liquid. You would've had to have taken a loan to manufacture the Intact product. That wouldn't have looked good to your investors, your customers. What a blow to the company's image. But the mob? What the hell were you thinking?"

"That is enough!" Henderson stepped in front of his client and put his face inches from Jake's.

Sohni was riveted to the scene behind the window, her eyes wide, and her breathing was shallow. All five of them turned to face the hallway, where behind the closed doors a ruckus ensued. Men's voices, shouting, carried into the rooms, along with the sound of running footsteps. The door to the interrogation room flew open and Zach Bender lurched in, with the officer Sohni had seen escorting him close on his heels.

"Dad!" Zach shouted. "They wouldn't let me see you."

The wild-eyed young man was dripping sweat and appeared disheveled.

"I'm sorry, Jake," said the rookie officer, whose name plate bore the name Tate. "He just took off."

Tate wrapped a meaty hand around Zack's upper arm and began tugging the young man out of the door, but Jake stopped him.

"Hold on a minute. Let him see his dad."

Officer Tate obliged, and Zach scrambled to the other side of the room, where his father still sat. Despite his son's obviously troubled mental state, Bender looked more annoyed than concerned. The father rose to face his son, and Sohni noticed that the older man stood only about an inch taller. But it might as well have been two feet, in light of the power dynamic between them.

"Zach, what are you doing here? Go back outside and wait for me. As you can see, I'm just fine."

"But you didn't kill Curt! They're wrong. You would never do that."

"Of course I didn't, Zach. We're just talking here. You need to leave!"

Sohni was struck by Bender's utter lack of compassion for his son, who was obviously in the midst of a mental breakdown. Her heart broke for the young man. Even she, who had no children of her own, felt the maternal instinct to wrap her arms around the young man and comfort him.

Zach then turned his manic attention to Jake at the other side of the table.

"He didn't kill anybody. You need to stop this. Let him go home!"

Before the detective could respond, Robert Bender grabbed his son by the shoulders and shook him.

"Zach, snap out of it. Get out of here!"

The voices of father and son began to overlap, one pleading manically, the other instructing with force, neither hearing the other. Jake and Officer Tate tried to interject by separating them, hoping to bring one or both back to his senses, but the cacophony only escalated, and finally reached an emotional crescendo as Bender lost his composure.

"Zach, stop being so worthless, and act like a man for once!"

Silence fell across both rooms as the man's statement hovered in the air. Bender's words hit his son like a slap in the face. The young man stood rooted to the ground, his mouth gaping, a bead of sweat dangling from the tip of his nose. Sohni knew she would never forget the look in his eyes at that moment, the look of betrayal, of a hurt beyond words.

With an eerie calmness, Zach said, "I did it for you, Dad."

"I don't need your help. Now you need to leave."

"He was going to ruin you, Dad. After everything you did for him. I couldn't let him do that. I did it for you."

A collective gasp rose from those assembled. Shock registered on the faces of all but one. As usual, Bender heard nothing his son had said. He continued urging the young man to leave, oblivious to the new tension in the room. Henderson rose from his seat and strode toward Bender's son. He grasped him by his shoulders and looked him in the face.

"Zach, don't say another word!"

Bender cast a puzzled look at Henderson, clearly mystified by the attorney's actions. Zach appeared to have lost all touch with reality. He just stared into space.

Officer Tate grabbed him by the arm and led him into the hallway. His fight spent, he put up no resistance. Pauline and Sohni bounded out of the observation room and watched in shock as Tate took him away. Zach turned around one last time, as though hoping to catch a glimpse of his father, but instead saw Sohni. As he stared at her, his face changed to an expression of pure violence. She took a step back.

"You! You did this!" He pulled against Tate with strength that the officer obviously didn't expect, lunging toward her with such force that he broke free from the officer's grasp.

Before anyone could react, Zach head butted Tate, who fell to his knees, then grabbed the man's gun from his holster. He spanned the short distance to Sohni in two steps. She felt the hard, cold steel against her forehead before she saw the gun. The unhinged young man stood only inches in front of her, his eyes bloodshot and vacant.

"You stupid bitch! You should've left it alone. I warned you, over and over, but you wouldn't stop. You did this to my dad, just like Curt tried to."

She stood firm on wobbly legs as she watched Jake and Tate, and three other officers who had arrived at the scene, quietly surround Zach from behind, guns raised. The young man was focused so completely on his target, he neither noticed nor cared about anyone else. He pressed and twisted the gun barrel into Sohni's forehead. It took everything for her not to cry out in pain.

"Zach, please don't do this," his father begged, a newly found sympathy in his voice. "You did good, Zach. You took care of me. Let me take care of you now."

His words had no impact on his son. He was too late.

"Zach, this is Detective Clarke. You are surrounded by police officers with guns aimed at you. You have to put the gun down. You don't want to die, Zach. Not like this. And we don't want to hurt you, but we won't let you harm Miss Silver. Just put the gun down, and you'll be OK."

Zach said nothing, but Sohni noticed a shift in his eyes.

"Zach, please don't do this." His father sobbed. "When I lost your mom, I'd never known pain like it. I couldn't handle it. I didn't know how. I shut down, stopped feeling. But it wasn't fair to you. You needed me, and I should've been there for you and your sister. I'm so sorry, Zach. I can't lose you, too."

Sohni could tell that Bender's words had affected his son. His armed hand began to shake, and his face lost its contorted expression. He resembled, once again, a sad little boy. He stood like that for several seconds, obviously conflicted. Then with a quick move of his arm, he pulled the gun away from Sohni and pressed it against his own head.

The officers made their move. Jake and two others tackled Zach to the ground and wrestled the gun from his him, while Tate wrapped Sohni in a bear hug, and they tumbled to the floor. When the action ended, and she was able to lift her head from the floor, Zach was already in handcuffs and being escorted out by Jake and two other officers. She heard the detective reading him his Miranda rights. Pauline followed, as did Sam Henderson, the latter yelling at Zach not to say another word.

Only Sohni and Robert Bender remained in the hall. She sat against the wall, trying to calm her racing heart and regain the use of her shaking limbs. The man stood in place with his head down, shoulders slumped, arms dangling at his side. With mussed hair, a splotchy face, and an untucked shirt, his image of perfection was gone. And with it, his confident air.

He turned to Sohni, pain in his eyes. He was a shell of the man he'd been only minutes before.

"I'm so sorry," he said.

"So am I."

Despite everything, her heart still hurt for Zach.

# CHAPTER 28

THE NIGHTSTAND CLOCK READ 10:30 A.M. BUT SOHNI STILL couldn't find the energy to drag herself out of bed. Her forehead throbbed from the purple, gun-barrel-shaped bruise. And the rest of her body ached from exhaustion and post-traumatic stress.

Matt peeked in the doorway. "Good morning," he whispered. "How are you feeling?"

"Like I got hit by a truck."

He sat on the edge of the bed and brushed away her hair to examine her forehead.

"Does it hurt?"

"Yeah. I think I need more Excedrin."

He returned minutes later with toast, orange juice, and two tablets. She popped the pills in her mouth and washed them down with almost the entire glass of juice, then nibbled at the toast in her mouse-like way.

"Thank you. You take such good care of me."

"I almost lost you, Sohni. I can't even think about what you went through last night. I would've never left you there if I thought there was any chance you could be harmed. But it was the police station, for God's sake. Who would've—"

"Matt, stop it. You had no way of knowing. No one did. It happened right in the midst of several cops, on their own turf. You are the last person bearing any responsibility for what happened."

"Is it really over?"

"Seems that way. Pauline has been sending me updates throughout the night. Zach admitted he was the one who had been making the threats, including slashing my tires and throwing the rock through the window. He was also the one calling Curt and Marc Isley. He so desperately wanted to stop the investigation out of a twisted sense of loyalty to his dad, a man incapable of ever returning the same level of devotion."

Sohni omitted that Zach had denied sending her the texts the previous night on the way to her car. His denial was corroborated by Jake, who confirmed that Zach was at his father's house when he arrived at seven. Zach would've had to drive at extremely high speeds and catch every light, to make it from downtown Ann Arbor to Bloomfield Hills in a half-hour. Plus, Zach admitted every other threat he'd made. Why would he deny that one?

Sohni didn't want to think about that implication right now, and she certainly didn't want Matt to dwell on it either.

"I think it's time for me to join the land of the living," she said. "Does the land of the living happen to have coffee?"

"Of course. What kind of uncivilized place would it be without coffee?"

"Awesome! Let me put on some clothes and wash up a bit. I'll be out in a couple minutes."

Matt kissed her cheek and left her alone. On unsteady legs, she tugged on some clothes, then held a cold washcloth to her face. She ran her fingers through her hair before heading to the kitchen. As she took her first sip of coffee, her cell phone rang. It was Frank.

"Hi, Frank."

"Hey, Sohni. Uh … how are you?"

Pauline had already mentioned that they'd told the Redmonds about the incident.

"I'm still rattled, but I'll live. Last night was sure an unexpected turn of events, huh?"

"You could say that. All this time, it was Zach who killed Curt. I still can't wrap my head around it. He and Curt were like brothers."

"Though Zach hasn't had a mental exam yet, those working with him already believe he has some kind of undiagnosed mental illness, and probably has had it for years."

"You know, I think Curt knew that."

"Really?"

"Yeah, I do. He probably couldn't put a name to it, but we all saw signs. At times, Zach would come off as charming and confident, even cocky, telling jokes and flirting with girls. Other times, he'd fall into a state of sadness, moping around and barely talking."

"Now that you mention it, I remember that other members of the fraternity said sometimes the two of them would hole up in their room for days at a time. You're right. That isn't normal behavior for college students."

"Exactly. And during those times, Curt took care of him. He would make excuses why the boys would stay home instead of going out as planned. He'd order dinner in so Zach would be sure to eat. When Curt was a child, he wanted to feed and rescue every homeless or wounded animal he came across. He used to sneak food from the house to feed neighborhood strays. He thought we didn't know, but of course we did. We let him do it because it brought him such joy. He wasn't any different when it came to people. He wanted to save them, too. But saving people is a lot more difficult than feeding a starving animal."

"Zach had some kind of break last night, Frank. He had lost touch with reality."

"I know I should hate him for what he did. But as angry as I am, that kid was a victim too. He was neglected. Someone should have noticed his symptoms years ago, but no one paid enough attention. My anger is really directed at Zach's dad. That smug SOB is the one responsible for Curt's death. As horrible as it is to say, I take a little pleasure in knowing that Dalmakis's articles are going to destroy him."

"Frank, you didn't see him last night. He's lost his son, either to mental illness, or prison. The man's already destroyed."

"Hmm. You're probably right. I know what that feels like."

"Frank, can I ask you a question?"

"Sure."

"Do you think Curt knew Robert Bender owned DAE?"

"I keep wondering the same thing. Part of me wants to say, of course not, he'd never do that to Zach. But then I've seen some changes in him over the last couple of years."

"What do you mean?"

"The older he got, the more self-righteous he became. He began to see corporations and excessive wealth as the root of all evil. He used to carry on about the evils of money and capitalism. He wanted to be a kind of Robin Hood reporter who could help bring down the rich to help the poor. So, I guess I'm not sure what he'd do when faced with that knowledge."

A few moments of silence passed between them.

"Anyway," Frank said, "I just wanted to make sure you were OK. And I also wanted to thank you. You were the only person who was fighting for the truth. Without you, I don't think this ever would have been solved. And through it all, you were being threatened and harassed, but you still didn't stop. Cathy and I will be forever grateful to you."

"That's kind of you. Thank you."

"Oh, what's going to happen with your client, by the way? Has he been released?"

"Not yet. But he will be soon. Paperwork and all that. I haven't had the chance to give him the good news yet."

"Well I hope he appreciates what a good lawyer he has."

"I have a feeling he will when he walks out of that jail."

"I'll let you go, Sohni. I'm sure you have plenty of things to do. Glad you're OK."

"Thanks for calling, Frank."

Sohni turned to Matt. "I completely forgot about Henry. I doubt he even knows yet."

"Can you call him?"

"I could contact the jail and set up a call, but I feel like this is something I should do in person."

"Come on, give yourself a couple of days. A call will do for now. You can go see him next week when you have more information."

"Don't worry, Matt. It's a building filled with police. What could possibly happen to me?" She shot Matt a lopsided grin.

"That is not funny, missy."

"Too soon, huh?"

Matt just shook his head and sighed.

Sohni settled for a call.

"If you're calling me on a Saturday, something's up," Henry said. "What's going on?"

"You're not going to believe what happened yesterday. Another man confessed to the murder of Curt Redmond."

Henry was silent.

"Are you serious?" he finally said.

"Absolutely. It's a long story, and I'll fill you in on Monday when I come by. But Curt was killed by someone he knew. The assailant admitted to planting the knife and wallet in your bag while you slept. As soon as the police and prosecutor complete their searches and confirm everything, he told them, I'm sure they'll be dismissing the charges against you. If they don't move fast enough, I'll kick 'em in the butt. They don't want any more bad publicity than they're already going to get, so I don't think that will be a problem."

"Wow! I'm shocked. I can't believe this nightmare is over. You are one hell of an attorney, Sohni Silver. You believed me when I said I was innocent. I didn't expect that. I don't know what to say. Thank you."

"You're welcome, Henry. I don't like seeing innocent men going to prison."

Just as she hung up, the doorbell rang.

"Can't a poor woman rest around here?" Matt said, on his way to the front door.

Before he could fully open it, Manju burst through and ran straight to Sohni. She threw her arms around Sohni and squeezed tight.

"Careful, Manju. She's already beat up enough."

The woman turned and stuck out her tongue at him. Sohni buried her head in her sister's shoulder.

Matt sighed and walked away. "Sisters."

# CHAPTER 29

"I wish there was some way I could thank you, Sohni."

Henry and Sohni waited at the bus station for the 10:20 a.m. to Toledo, where Henry's sister would be meeting him.

"You've been given a second chance, Henry. Take it and run with it. That's the best thank you, you could give me."

"That's exactly what I plan to do. I'll be back in my sister's guest room for now. But this time, I'll do it right. I'll get a job, go to meetings, whatever it takes to get back on my feet. I'm done living like this."

"Sounds like a good plan. You already look the part."

"Yeah, I do, don't I?" Henry struck a pose, making them both laugh.

She had paid for a proper haircut, a shave, and a new outfit. He now sported crisp blue jeans and brown Timberland knock-offs, with a brown and white checkered button-up shirt, as well as a brand-new winter coat. The look was ruined, though, by Henry's tattered yellow duffel bag, which hung from his wrist.

Sohni reached over and tugged the handle of the bag out of Henry's hand.

"Hey, what're you doing?" He tugged back.

"It's time to lose the old duffel bag, Henry."

"What am I gonna carry my stuff in?"

"This." Sohni pulled a brand-new Columbia backpack from her department store bag.

Henry grinned and took the bag. "This is great! Thanks so much."

"You're welcome."

He hadn't discovered the bag's contents. Sohni had loaded it with additional clothes, toiletries, some snacks, and even a prepaid cell phone.

"You have been so good to me. You are an angel God sent down to help me."

"I don't know about an angel. I just believe in helping people when I can."

"Well, the world needs more people like you, then."

"Maybe one day you can pass it on. Please stay in touch."

"I definitely will."

"Are you sure you won't reconsider filing a lawsuit against the city?" she said, once again. "You've got a great case, Henry. Even now, the city is investigating what went wrong. The police department's role is being examined, and Prosecutor Fitzgerald has been suspended from her duties, pending a determination of whether she engaged in prosecutorial misconduct. There's no question they botched the investigation, and that you were wrongfully prosecuted and imprisoned. I bet the city would settle for a lot of money, money you could really use right now."

He smiled but shook his head. "Thank you for looking out for me, Sohni. But I want all this to be behind me. I'm starting over. Clean slate, remember?"

"I remember."

The crowd around them came alive as the bus they had been waiting for pulled into the bay.

"Would it be OK if I hugged you?" Henry said.

"I'd be insulted if you didn't."

They shared a quick, but meaningful, embrace. Then he joined the crowd shuffling toward the bus's boarding door, disappearing from view.

He reappeared and made a beeline for Sohni, his breath manifesting as little white clouds around his head. He extended his hand to her.

"I almost forgot to give this to you."

Sohni held out her palm, and Henry dropped into it a tiny gold pendant the shape of a cross.

"It's beautiful, Henry. You sure you want me to have this?"

"Absolutely. It was my mother's. Now it's yours." He closed her hand over the pendant, gave it a pat, then jogged off to catch the bus.

There was a new bounce in his step, a fresh light in his eyes. A transformation had taken place in the man since she had first met him, and she knew his new outlook on life was largely because of her efforts on his behalf.

Sohni watched until he disappeared inside the coach. She turned and headed back towards her car. Once inside, she examined the gold cross more closely, for such a small item, it contained intricate detail. She removed the delicate gold necklace around her neck, slid the pendant on the chain, and reclasped it. She checked the new addition in the visor mirror and smiled.

She was unsure what her Jewish husband and Hindu parents would think of her new bling, but it didn't matter. She knew what it meant to her.

# EPILOGUE

THE BOOKSTORE, BETWEEN THE LINES, WAS A NEW ADDITION to downtown Ann Arbor, and was already a favorite of the Silvers. The pursuit of the next great novel hadn't brought them to the store that day, though. They came to celebrate with a friend.

Upon entering the beautifully renovated space, Sohni spotted Daniel seated behind a table piled high with hardcover books. Intent on charming the three women currently seeking to have their books signed, he didn't notice her right away. Sohni and Matt leaned against the bookshelves lining the wall, waiting for their turn with the man of the hour.

Between The Lines wasn't the typical choice for a book signing of this sort. It was far smaller than the chain bookstores located in the heart of downtown Ann Arbor, but it represented the mom and pop bookstore of yesterday, where the owners knew the names of their regular customers. Daniel felt the bookstore was the antithesis of the corporate greed that formed the backdrop for his new book, and therefore was a perfect fit. The store was certainly busy, whether because of Daniel, or despite of him, she couldn't say.

The reporter finally caught sight of Sohni and waved her over. As she approached, he enveloped her in a bear hug, nearly breaking a rib or two, and lifted her feet right off the ground.

"I'm so glad you could make it!"

Sohni introduced Matt to Daniel, who pumped her husband's arm.

"You've got a great woman here."

Matt beamed. "Don't I know it." He put his arm around Sohni's shoulders.

"You look great, Daniel!" she said. "You must have lost at least twenty pounds since I last saw you."

"Thanks. Yeah, thirty-five in all. I started running again. Forgot how much I enjoyed it."

"Let me see the finished product." Sohni selected a book from the stack and flipped through it. *The Fall of the Bender Empire: How a Student, a Reporter, and a Grieving Father Brought Down a Giant.* "What an awesome title."

Sohni had met with Daniel several times during his writing process. She had answered his questions honestly but made him promise that he would omit her role in the investigation. She wanted Frank, Curt, and Daniel to get full credit.

Sohni noticed a familiar face hidden behind Daniel. She walked behind the table and smiled at Frank, who sat quietly against the wall. She had not seen him face to face since their meeting at Como's. Curt's death and everything that had come afterwards had taken a toll on him. She was saddened to notice that he no longer wore his wedding ring. He had lost even more weight, and his face looked gaunt and tired. But his eyes sparkled when he saw her.

"Hi, Frank."

Frank rose to greet Sohni. His smile was genuine, but unlike Daniel, he settled for a warm handshake.

"I didn't know you'd be here," she said.

"I wasn't sure myself. I'm not much for being the center of attention, but Daniel felt someone should be here to represent Curt's part of the story—to speak for Curt—so I agreed."

"How are you?" She looked him in the eye.

"I'm OK today." He gave a dry laugh. "But you might want to ask me again tomorrow."

Sohni nodded. "Let me introduce you to my husband."

She turned around and waved over Matt, who had moved over to a nearby wall, where he bemusedly watched Daniel interact with his readers. Matt came over and placed his hand on the small of her back in an affectionate gesture that warmed her to the toes.

"Matt, I want you to meet Frank Redmond."

"It's a pleasure, Matt."

"Oh, the pleasure is all mine. I've heard so much about you."

They were interrupted by Daniel, who grasped Sohni's hand and virtually dragged her to the table, where he had left an elderly couple awaiting his return. With a flourish, he presented Sohni to the couple.

"This is Sohni Silver," he said, in dramatic fashion. "She is the public defender who represented Henry Martinez, the homeless man wrongly accused of the murder."

The elderly couple ooh-ed and ahh-ed, and seemed impressed, recalling the headlines of a year ago.

"She didn't want to be featured in my book—too modest, if you ask me—but her fight to prove her client's innocence played a large role in unearthing this scandal, and ultimately finding the real killer."

Sohni wanted to giggle at his melodrama and the equally melodramatic reactions of the couple, but instead responded graciously. They even asked her to sign their copies of the book, which she did.

"You really should hang out for a while, Sohni," Daniel said. "People would love to meet you."

"I appreciate the invitation, Daniel, but today is your day. Enjoy it."

Another trio of women standing at the table, flipping through a copy of Daniel's book caught his attention, so he excused himself. Sohni had experienced enough excitement for one day, so she reached for Matt's hand and led him from the store, and stopped to say goodbye to Frank on the way.

Sohni and Matt walked the three blocks in comfortable silence, enjoying the unseasonably warm, fall day. In the car, Sohni pulled from her bag the signed copy of Daniel's book, and began to peruse. Daniel was an excellent writer, and she found herself drawn in by his dramatic retelling of the events of last year. She was proud to know she was part of them.

She took Matt's hand in hers, closed her eyes, and basked in the weak sun falling on her face through the car window. She was determined to enjoy her Sunday, because on Monday there would be more clients who needed her. Sadly, there always would be.

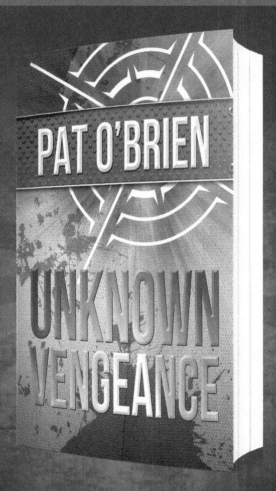

9 781952 404474